Colleagues Praise
Mike Resnick

"Mike Resnick delivers pure entertainment and a rollicking good time."
—Alan Dean Foster,
bestselling author of
Quozl and *Cat*A*Lyst*

"His name on a book guarantees a solid story . . . Most important of all, it guarantees entertainment."
—Raymond E. Feist

"Resnick may well be on his way to becoming the Stephen King or John D. MacDonald of science fiction."
—Edward Bryant

"Mike Resnick spins a great yarn!"
—Jerry Pournelle

D1011761

Ace Books by Mike Resnick

SOOTHSAYER
ORACLE

ORACLE

MIKE RESNICK

ACE BOOKS, NEW YORK

If you purchased this book without a cover, you should be aware that this book is stolen property. It was reported as "unsold and destroyed" to the publisher, and neither the author nor the publisher has received any payment for this "stripped book."

This book is an Ace original edition, and has never been previously published.

ORACLE

An Ace Book / published by arrangement with
the author

PRINTING HISTORY
Ace edition / October 1992

All rights reserved.
Copyright © 1992 by Mike Resnick.
Cover art by Keith Birdsong.
This book may not be reproduced in whole or
in part, by mimeograph or any other means, without
permission. For information address:
The Berkley Publishing Group,
200 Madison Avenue, New York, New York 10016.

ISBN: 0-441-58694-5

Ace Books are published by The Berkley Publishing Group,
200 Madison Avenue, New York, New York 10016.
The name "ACE" and the "A" logo are trademarks
belonging to Charter Communications, Inc.

PRINTED IN THE UNITED STATES OF AMERICA

10 9 8 7 6 5 4 3 2 1

To Carol, as always,

And to Mark and Lynne Aronson,
close friends for half a lifetime

Contents

Prologue

It was a time of giants.

There was no room for them to breathe and flex their muscles in mankind's sprawling Democracy, so they gravitated to the distant, barren worlds of the Inner Frontier, drawn ever closer to the bright Galactic Core like moths to a flame.

Oh, they fit into human frames, most of them, but they were giants nonetheless. No one knew what had brought them forth in such quantity at this particular moment in human history. Perhaps there was a need for them in a galaxy filled to overflowing with little people possessed of even smaller dreams. Possibly it was the savage splendor of Inner Frontier itself, for it was certainly not a place for ordinary men and women. Or maybe it was simply time for a race that had been notably short of giants in recent eons to begin producing them once again.

But whatever the reason, they swarmed out beyond the farthest reaches of the explored galaxy, spreading the seed of Man to hundreds of new worlds, and in the process creating a cycle of legends that would never die as long as men could tell tales of heroic deeds.

There was Faraway Jones, who set foot on more than five hundred new worlds, never quite certain what he was looking for, always sure that he hadn't yet found it.

There was a shadowy figure known only as the Whistler, who had killed more than one hundred Men and aliens.

There was Friday Nellie, who turned her whorehouse into a hospital during the war against the Setts, and finally saw it declared a shrine by the very men who once tried to close it down.

There was Jamal, who left no fingerprints or footprints, but had plundered palaces that to this day do not know they were plundered.

There was Bet-a-World Murphy, who at various times owned nine different gold-mining worlds and lost every one of them at the gaming tables.

There was Backbreaker Ben Ami, who wrestled aliens for money and killed Men for pleasure. There was the Marquis of Queensbury, who fought by no rules at all, and the White Knight, albino killer of fifty men, and Sally the Blade, and the Forever Kid, who reached the age of nineteen and just stopped growing for the next two centuries, and Catastrophe Baker, who made whole planets shake beneath his feet, and the exotic Pearl of Maracaibo, and the Scarlet Queen, whose sins were condemned by every race in the galaxy, and Father Christmas, and the One-Armed Bandit with his deadly prosthetic arm, and the Earth Mother, and Lizard Malloy, and the deceptively mild-mannered Cemetery Smith.

Giants all.

Yet there was one giant who was destined to tower over all of the others, to juggle the lives of Men and worlds as if they were so many toys, to rewrite the history of the Inner Frontier, and the Outer Frontier, and the Spiral Arm, and even the all-powerful Democracy itself. At various times in her short, turbulent life she was known as the Soothsayer, and the Oracle, and the Prophet. By the time she had passed from the galactic scene, only a handful of survivors knew her true name, or her planet of origin, or even her early history, for such is the way with giants and legends.

But she had an origin, and a history, and a name.

This is her story.

PART 1

The
Whistler's
Book

1

His real name was Carlos Mendoza, but it had been so many years since he used it that it seemed almost alien to him.

Here on the Inner Frontier, among the sparsely populated worlds between Man's sprawling Democracy and the Galactic Core, men changed names with the ease, and occasionally the frequency, that their brothers in the Democracy changed clothes. Mendoza had had many occupations in his sixty-five years, some of which he wished to forget and some that he wished his enemies would forget, and he had had almost as many names, but the one that had stuck was the Iceman.

There were people who said he was the Iceman because he had once been the ruler of a planet totally covered by a mile-thick glacier. Others said no, that he got the name because he was a cold-blooded killer. A few suggested that he possessed a rare disease that threatened to kill him by lowering his body temperature, and that's why he had finally settled on the hot, desert world of Last Chance.

The Iceman didn't care what people thought about the genesis of his name. In fact, there wasn't much that he did care about. Money, of course; and the power he exercised as the owner of the End of the Line, the only tavern on Last Chance—but over the years he had lost interest in most other things.

Except gossip.

Miners, traders, explorers, adventurers, and bounty hunters would stop on Last Chance to refuel their ships, or lay in their supplies, or register their claims, or occasionally to wait for their mail or their rewards to catch up with them, and they would come to the End of the Line, and they would talk. The Iceman never asked any questions, never volunteered any information, but he listened intently, and once in a long while he would hear some tidbit that momentarily brought a touch of animation to his impassive face. When that happened he would disappear for a week or a month, after which he would return to Last Chance as suddenly as he had left. Then he would sit in the bar and listen to more gossip, more tales of adventure and derring-do, of fortunes made and fortunes lost, of battles won and empires fallen, his face expressionless.

Those who cared about him—and they were few and far between—occasionally asked him precisely what he was hoping to hear, what it was that he went off to find on his rare excursions. He would politely sidestep their questions, for despite his reputation he was a courteous man, and shortly thereafter they would see him sitting at another table, listening to another traveler's tale.

He was not a physically impressive man. He was an inch or two below normal height, and he carried about thirty pounds of excess weight, and his hair was thinning on the top and white on the sides. He walked with a decided limp; most people assumed that he had a prosthetic leg, but no one ever asked him and he never volunteered any information about it. His voice was neither deep nor rich, though when he spoke on Last Chance it carried a ring of absolute authority that very few men challenged (and none ever challenged it twice).

He was known throughout the Inner Frontier, but nobody knew quite what he had done to acquire his notoriety. He had killed some men, of course, but that was hardly sufficient to establish a reputation on the lawless frontier worlds. It was rumored that he had once worked for the Democracy in some covert capacity, but by its very nature nothing was known about his job. Once, fourteen years ago, he had disappeared from Last Chance for a number of months, and word had it that he had been responsible for the deaths of quite a few bounty hunters, but no one could verify it and the details were so vague that very few people put much credence in the story.

There was one woman who had heard the story and believed it, and after many false starts she finally tracked him down in his refuge on Last Chance, half a galaxy away from the affluent, populous worlds of the Democracy. She was middle-aged, with blue eyes and nondescript, sand-colored hair. Her nose had a small lump at the bridge, as if it had been broken many years ago, and her teeth were too white and too even to be her own.

The End of the Line was filled with the usual crowd of adventurers and misfits, humans and aliens, when she entered it. The aliens—seven Canphorites, a pair of Lodinites, two Domarians, and one each from a trio of races she had never seen before—were clustered together at a number of small tables. Most of them couldn't metabolize the bar's offerings, and were obviously waiting for the large casino, which consisted of some two dozen tables and an equal number of exotic games of chance, to open its doors. A small sign, written in various human and alien languages, announced that that happy moment would occur at sunset.

The heads of a quartet of alien carnivores, each snarling in mute defiance, were positioned above the long hardwood bar, and in a glass case just next to the changemaker was a tattered copy of a poem written by Black Orpheus, the Bard of the Inner Frontier, which he had created and autographed when he had stopped on Last Chance for an evening some two centuries ago.

Twenty humans, some dressed in colorful and expensive garments, others wearing the dull browns and grays of miners and prospectors, stood at the bar or sat at tables. None of them paid her any attention as she entered the tavern, looked around for a moment, and finally approached the bartender.

"I'm looking for a man known as the Iceman," she said. "Is he here?"

The bartender nodded his head. "Right over there, sitting by the window."

"Will he speak to me?" she asked.

The bartender chuckled. "That depends on his mood. But he'll listen to you."

She thanked him and walked over to the Iceman's table, giving the aliens a wide berth as she did so.

"May I join you?" she asked.

"Pull up a chair, Mrs. Bailey," he said.

She looked surprised. "You know who I am?"

"No," he answered. "But I know your name."

"How?"

"You had to identify yourself when you requested landing coordinates," said the Iceman. "Nobody lands on Last Chance without my approval."

"I see," she said, sitting down. She stared across the table. "I can't believe that I've finally found you!"

"I wasn't lost, Mrs. Bailey," he said expressionlessly.

"Perhaps not, but I've been looking for you for more than four years."

"And what's so important that you would spend four years of your life trying to find me?"

"My name is Bettina Bailey," she began.

"I know."

"Does it mean anything to you?"

"Should it?"

"If the name Bailey doesn't, then I've wasted an enormous amount of time."

"I've never heard of anyone called Bettina Bailey," he replied noncommittally.

"I've heard stories—rumors, really, to be honest—that you may have known my daughter."

"Go on," said the Iceman.

"Her name is Penelope."

The Iceman pulled out a small cigar. "What did you hear?"

"I heard that you knew her." Bettina Bailey paused, studying the Iceman's face. "I've even heard that she spent some time on Last Chance."

"That was fourteen years ago, Mrs. Bailey," said the Iceman, lighting his cigar. "I haven't seen her since." He shrugged. "For all I know, she's dead now."

Bettina Bailey stared unblinking at him. "If we're talking about the same girl, you know that's impossible."

The Iceman returned her stare for a long moment, as if considering his answer. Finally he took another puff of his cigar and nodded. "We're talking about the same girl."

"She would be twenty-two years old now."

"That would be about right," agreed the Iceman.

Bettina Bailey paused again. "I've heard other rumors, too," she said at last.

"Such as?"

"That she's living with aliens."

"*An* alien," the Iceman corrected her.

"Then you know where she is?"

He shook his head. "No. I just know who she was with the last time I saw her."

"I've also heard that you've spent a lot of time looking for her," continued Bettina Bailey.

He stared impassively at her and made no answer.

"And that you know more about her than any other man alive," she continued.

"It's possible," he agreed.

"It's more than *possible*. It's a fact."

"All right, it's a fact. Now what?"

"I want my daughter back."

"Pardon my pointing it out, Mrs. Bailey, but it took you long enough to come to that decision."

"I have been looking for her for sixteen years." She paused. "She was taken from me in the Democracy. The Democracy encompasses more than ten thousand worlds; it took me more than a decade, and most of my late husband's money, to discover that she was no longer there, but was on the Inner Frontier."

"She was on the Inner Frontier fourteen years ago, Mrs. Bailey," said the Iceman. "She could be anywhere now—the Inner Frontier, the Rim, the Spiral Arm, the Outer Frontier, even back in the Democracy. It wouldn't be difficult for someone with her abilities to hide from anyone who was looking for her."

"She's on the Inner Frontier," repeated Bettina Bailey adamantly.

He stared at her, unable to totally conceal his interest. "How do you know?"

"When you are willing to be open and frank with me, I will respond in kind," she replied. "For the moment, you will have to take my word that I know where she is."

He paused for a long moment. "All right," he said at last. "You know where she is."

She nodded. "And I want her back."

"And you want her back," he repeated. "Why have you come to *me*? Why don't you just go to wherever she is and take her home?"

"It's not that simple," she said. "She may not recognize me— and even if she does, she's been with aliens for most of her life. She may not want to come back with me."

"She's an adult by now," said the Iceman. "That's her choice to make."

"I'm willing to let her make it," said Bettina Bailey. "But away from the influence of the aliens."

"There's only one alien that I know about."

She shook her head. "She's on an alien planet."

"Which one?"

"I'll tell you when we have an agreement."

"What kind of agreement?" asked the Iceman.

"I want you to bring her back to me."

"If you don't think she'll go with *you*, why do you think she'll come with me?"

"I told you—I've studied you. You've had experience dealing with aliens and operating on the Inner Frontier. If you need help, you'll know what kind to get and where to get it."

The Iceman stared at her thoughtfully. "It could be very expensive, Mrs. Bailey."

"*How* expensive?"

"A million Maria Theresa dollars now, another million when the job is done."

"Maria Theresa dollars?" she repeated, frowning. "I thought they were only in use in the Corvus system. What's wrong with credits?"

"We don't have much faith in the longevity of the Democracy out here, Mrs. Bailey," answered the Iceman. "We have even less faith in its currency. Credits are unacceptable. If you can't get the Maria Theresa dollars, I'll take double the amount in New Stalin rubles."

"I'll get the dollars," she replied.

"How soon?"

"I can have them transferred here in three days' time."

"Then I'll set the wheels in motion three days from now," said the Iceman.

"What do you mean: set the wheels in motion?"

"I'll select who I want to find your daughter."

"But I thought *you* would be going."

He shook his head. "She knows me, Mrs. Bailey—and I don't think she'd be too happy to see me again."

"But I chose you precisely because she *does* know you!"

"That's not necessarily an advantage with your daughter," he said dryly. "Now, where is she?"

Bettina Bailey was silent for a moment. Then she shrugged. "She's on Alpha Crepello III."

"Never heard of it."

"It's in the Quinellus Cluster."

"And what makes you so sure she's there?"

She leaned forward intently. "We both know that my daughter has a rare talent."

"Go on."

"Word has gotten back to Deluros VIII that there is a human female on Alpha Crepello III. The public isn't supposed to know about her, but I've bribed sources within the government. No one seems to know if this female is in the employ of the aliens who inhabit Alpha Crepello III, or if she is their prisoner, but she is known as the Oracle." She paused. "If I were to choose a name for Penelope, I couldn't choose a more accurate one than that."

"And that's the sum total of your knowledge?" asked the Iceman. "No description? No communication with her or anyone who's dealt with her?"

"Just that," answered Bettina Bailey. "The Alpha Crepello system isn't part of the Democracy and has almost no commerce with it. It took me two years to ascertain that the Oracle was a human, and another two to determine that she was a female."

The Iceman stared at her. "Do you know the odds against this being your daughter, Mrs. Bailey?"

"I've spent sixteen years piecing together these bits of information," she replied. "I could die of old age before I came up with concrete proof." She paused. "Do we have a deal?"

For just an instant the interest he had tried so hard to conceal flashed across his face. Then, just as quickly, the impassive mask was back in place.

"We have a deal," said the Iceman.

2

The star charts called it Boyson III. Locally it was known as The Frenchman's World.

In the beginning it had been a wild, untamed jungle planet, covered with dense vegetation and a plethora of exotic animals. Then Man had moved in, had killed most of the animals and plowed under the jungle, and had turned it into an agricultural world, supplying food for all the nearby mining planets. But within twenty years alien viruses destroyed the imported meat animals, the imported corn and wheat, and even the hybrid animals and crops. After that the colonists all went elsewhere, and Boyson III slowly reverted back into a jungle world over the next six centuries.

Then the Frenchman had arrived. They said that he'd spent his whole life collecting alien animals for zoos back in the Democracy, and that he had retired to Boyson III to spend his remaining years hunting for sport. He had erected a sprawling white house on the banks of a wide river, had invited some friends to join him, and eventually word of the hunting leaked out and a small safari industry developed.

All that had been more than two hundred years ago. The Frenchman's World hadn't changed much in the interim, except that its wildlife had been pretty thoroughly decimated, and only a handful of guides remained, the rest having migrated to newly opened worlds where their clients could fill their trophy rooms with less effort.

It was estimated that the permanent human population of The Frenchman's World was now less than two hundred. One of them, who was said to be the last man to have been born on the planet, had moved into the Frenchman's old house and created his own private landing strip by the river.

His name was Joshua Jeremiah Chandler. He had been a very successful hunter in his youth, but no one had seen him on the safari trail in almost a decade. He was known, initially on the Frenchman's World and finally all across the Inner Frontier, as the Whistler, from a trick he had of whistling to get an animal's attention just before he shot it. He was a very private, even secretive, man, who kept his business and his thoughts to himself. He was gone from the planet for long periods of time, and he did almost all his banking on other worlds. No mail or radio messages ever came for him, though from time to time a small ship landed at his strip by the river.

The Iceman's ship was the most recent to touch down, and as he walked up the long, winding path to the house, he found himself sweating profusely in the heat and the humidity, and wondering why anyone would choose to live in such surroundings. He slapped a purple-and-gold flying insect that had landed on the side of his neck, barely avoided stepping on a nasty-looking horned reptile that hissed at him and scuttled off into the thick undergrowth, and mopped his face with a handkerchief.

When he emerged from the bush, he climbed a stone staircase and found himself standing on a large deck that extended far out over the river. The water was teeming with life: huge aquatic marsupials, delicate water snakes, long ugly reptiles, all swam among a plethora of colorful fish that dwelt near the surface. The forest that lined the water had been cleared from the far bank, so that observers on the deck could watch herbivores coming down to the river to drink. Right now there were clouds of butterflies flying low over the water, and a score of avians walked methodically across the clearing, pecking at the ground, while a handful of water birds waded in the shallows, searching for small fish.

The Iceman heard a glass door slide into a wall, and a moment later a tall, lean, auburn-haired man in his late thirties walked out onto the deck. He was dressed in a nondescript brown outfit that seemed to have pockets everywhere. A large-brimmed hat shaded his eyes from the glare of the sun.

"I see you made it," said Chandler by way of greeting.

"You're a hard man to find, Whistler," replied the Iceman.

"You managed." Chandler paused. "Care for a drink?"

The Iceman nodded. "Please."

"I really ought to charge you," said Chandler with an amused smile as he led the Iceman into the interior of the house. "I don't recall you ever giving me a free drink back on Last Chance."

"And you never will," said the Iceman, returning Chandler's smile. The room in which he found himself was quite large, and the cool stone floor, whitewashed walls, and widespread eaves helped to dissipate the heat. There were a few stuffed chairs, covered with the pelts of native animals, a rug made of the head and fur of a large carnivore, a small book and tape case, a subspace radio set, and a clock made of some strange translucent substance that seemed to be forever shimmering and changing colors. The walls were lined with framed Wanted posters, each depicting an outlaw that Chandler had killed or captured.

"Interesting trophies," commented the Iceman, gesturing to the posters.

"People make the best hunting," answered Chandler. He walked behind a hardwood bar and opened a small refrigerator. "What'll it be?"

"Anything cold."

Chandler mixed two identical drinks and handed one to the Iceman. "This should do it."

The Iceman took a long swallow. "Thanks."

"Anything for a client," said Chandler. He looked intently at the Iceman. "You *are* a client, aren't you?"

"Potentially." The Iceman looked out across the river. "Do you mind if we go back out on the deck? It may be a pain in the ass to get here, but it's really lovely once you arrive."

"Why not?" assented Chandler, leading him back out to the deck.

"It must be very convenient, to be able to stand right here and shoot dinner," continued the Iceman.

Chandler shrugged. "I wouldn't know."

"Oh?"

"I never hunt within five miles of here. I don't want to frighten the game away." He paused. "Some animals are for eating, some are for sport, and some are for looking at. *These* are for looking at."

"You know," said the Iceman, "now that I think of it, I haven't seen any weapons around here."

"Oh, there are weapons," Chandler assured him. "But not for the game."

A delicate white avian landed atop one of the aquatic marsupials and began picking insects off its head.

"I miss this place whenever I'm away from it," said Chandler, standing at the edge of the deck and looking across the river. "If I take this assignment, how long will I be gone?"

"I won't lie to you," said the Iceman. "This job doesn't figure to be easy *or* fast."

"What does it entail?" asked Chandler, sipping his drink and staring out at the river.

"I'm not sure yet."

Chandler arched an eyebrow, but made no comment.

"Have you ever heard of Penelope Bailey?" continued the Iceman after a pause.

"I think *everyone* must have heard of her, back about ten or fifteen years ago," answered Chandler. "They were offering one hell of a reward for her."

"That's the one."

"As I recall, everybody wanted her: the Democracy, a couple of alien worlds, even some pirates. I never did hear what happened to her, just that one day a bunch of bounty hunters turned up dead, and after that nobody seemed all that interested in trying to collect the reward." He turned to the Iceman. "There was a story making the rounds that *you* were involved in some way."

"I was."

"What was all the fuss about?" asked Chandler. "Hundreds of people were after her, but no one ever said what made a little girl worth five or six million credits."

"She wasn't exactly your normal, run-of-the-mill little girl," said the Iceman wryly.

Chandler picked a few pieces of stale bread out of one of his pockets and laid them out on the railing, then watched as a trio of colorful avians descended, picked them up, and flew off with them. "If you want me to find her and bring her back, you're going to have to tell me what made her worth all that money," he said at last.

"I will," said the Iceman, taking a sip of his drink. "And you won't have to find her."

"You know where she is?"

"Perhaps."

"Either you do or you don't."

"I know the location of the person I'm sending you after," replied the Iceman. "I don't know if she's Penelope Bailey."

"Would you know Penelope Bailey if you saw her?" asked Chandler.

"It's been a long time, and she's a grown woman now," answered the Iceman. "I honestly don't know if I'd recognize her."

"Then how will you know if I bring you the right woman?"

"There are other ways of telling." The Iceman paused. "Also, if she *is* Penelope Bailey, there's every likelihood that you won't be able to bring her back."

Chandler looked up at the sky, which had suddenly clouded over. "It rains every afternoon about this time," he said. "Let's go inside and make ourselves comfortable, and you can lay it out for me."

He led the Iceman back inside the house, ordered the glass portals to slide shut, and walked over to a pair of chairs that had been carved out of the native hardwood of the surrounding forest and covered with the pelts of some blue-skinned animals.

"All right," he said when both men had seated themselves. "I'm listening."

"Penelope Bailey was eight years old when I met her," said the Iceman. "The Democracy had taken her away from her parents when she was five or six, and an alien had stolen her from the Democracy. By the time I ran across her, she was in the company of a woman who used to work for me."

"Why did the Democracy seize her in the first place?" asked Chandler.

"She has a gift—a talent, if you will—that they wanted."

"What was it?"

"She's prescient."

"You mean she can predict the future?"

The Iceman shook his head. "It's not that simple. She can see an almost infinite number of possible futures, and she can manipulate events so that the one most favorable to her comes to pass."

Chandler stared at him for a long moment. "I don't believe it," he said at last.

"It's the truth. I've seen it in action."

"Then why isn't she Queen of the whole damned universe?"

"When I first met her, she could only see those futures in which she faced imminent danger. By the time we parted, she could see the outcome of everything from poker hands to gunfights, and could manipulate things so they'd come out the way she wanted them to—but she could only see a few hours into the future." He paused. "If her power never extended beyond that, she could make herself a very rich, very powerful woman, but in the larger scheme of things she'd be no more than a nuisance."

"But you think her talent has continued to mature," said Chandler. It was not a question.

"I don't know why it shouldn't have," replied the Iceman. "It grew more powerful almost daily when I knew her."

"I'm surprised you didn't try to kill her."

"I did." He patted his prosthetic leg. "This is what I got for my trouble."

Chandler nodded, but said nothing.

"The last time I saw her she was with an alien called the Mock Turtle—I'll swear that's what it looked like—and to the best of my knowledge, no human has seen her since."

"Why an alien?"

"It practically worshipped her, and it seemed convinced that once she developed her powers, she could keep the Democracy from assimilating its world."

"Is the girl on its world?" asked Chandler.

The Iceman shook his head. "No. I've been there twice, and there's no sign of them."

"So *that's* where you go when you're not on Last Chance," said Chandler, not at all surprised. "You're hunting for Penelope Bailey."

"It hasn't done any good." The Iceman grimaced and finished his drink. "If there's someone better equipped to stay hidden than a woman who can see all possible futures, I can't imagine who it is."

"Then how did you find her?" asked Chandler.

"I didn't," answered the Iceman. "But a week ago I was approached by a woman who represented herself as Penelope's mother. She thinks she knows where the girl is, and she hired me to bring her back."

"Represented herself?" repeated Chandler. "That's a curious choice of words."

"She lied from start to finish."

"What makes you think so?"

"She knew things she had no business knowing."

"Such as?"

"She knew that Penelope escaped with an alien—but only about ten people on a little planet called Killhaven know that. She knew that I've been searching for her—but I've never told that to anyone." He paused. "She knew that she was looking for the Iceman, and not for Carlos Mendoza."

"She works for the Democracy, of course."

The Iceman nodded in agreement. "Nobody else has the resources to spy on me for fourteen years."

"They've been after her for fourteen years . . ." began Chandler.

"Sixteen," interjected the Iceman.

"All right, sixteen. Why have they approached you now?"

"Because they think they've found her."

"That's not good enough," said Chandler. "Why did they lie to you? Or, better still, if they've found her, why don't they just go in after her themselves?"

"I'm sure they've sent their best people in after her and failed, or else they would never have approached me." The Iceman suddenly noticed his drink and finished it with a single swallow. "As for why they sent someone who pretended to be Penelope's mother, it's simple enough: the Inner Frontier doesn't owe any allegiance to the Democracy, and they don't know if I'd be willing to help them. Also," he added, "I killed some of their bounty hunters fourteen years ago."

"Why did you want to save her from a bunch of bounty hunters?"

"She was never in any danger from them," answered the Iceman. "I was trying to save another member of her party." He paused. "It didn't help."

"You make Penelope Bailey sound very formidable," commented Chandler.

"She is," the Iceman assured him seriously. "Make no mistake about it."

"Where do they think she is?"

"A planet called Alpha Crepello III, out in the Quinellus Cluster."

"And they're sure it's her?"

The Iceman shook his head. "They think it is; they don't know for sure."

"What makes them think so?"

"There's supposed to be a young human woman there, living among the aliens, who's known as the Oracle."

"And that's it?"

"Probably not," said the Iceman. "Almost certainly not. But that's all I've been told."

"That's not much to go on," said Chandler. "What do you think they've kept back?"

"Probably something about how many men they've sent in and never heard from again. That's the kind of thing that would convince them they're right, and it's also guaranteed to discourage a potential recruit."

Chandler was silent for a long moment. Then he looked across at the Iceman. "I've got a question for you."

"What is it?"

"This little girl cost you a leg, and I gather she killed a friend of yours."

"Indirectly."

"Then why aren't you going after her yourself?"

"I'm a sixty-five-year-old man with a potbelly and an artificial leg," answered the Iceman. "If it really *is* Penelope Bailey, I'd be dead before I could get close to her. Maybe I could have done it twenty years ago, but not now." He looked directly at Chandler. "That's why I've come to you, Whistler—of all the men in this business, you're just about the best. You've infiltrated half a dozen worlds, and you're a better killer than I ever was."

"*Can* she be killed?"

The Iceman shrugged. "I don't know."

"What kind of money are we talking about here?"

"Half a million up front, another half million when the job is completed."

"Credits?" asked Chandler with a frown.

"Maria Theresa dollars."

Chandler nodded. "Time limit?"

"If you haven't gotten to her in six months' time, you're never going to reach her."

"What if I come back empty-handed?"

"If you accept the assignment, the front money's yours no matter what happens," said the Iceman.

"Will your client agree to that?"

"Considering that she's not really Bettina Bailey, I don't see that she has any choice."

"What about expenses?" asked Chandler.

The Iceman chuckled. "Not with a half million up front."

"I may need to hire some help along the way."

"I'd advise against it," said the Iceman.

"Why?"

"The less attention you attract to yourself, the more likely you are to come out of this alive."

"I may want to hire some men to draw attention *away* from me."

"That's your privilege." The Iceman stared at him thoughtfully. "If you're successful and you can prove to me that you needed them, you'll be reimbursed."

Chandler eyed him thoughtfully. "What do *you* get out of this?"

"Money, satisfaction, revenge—take your choice."

Chandler smiled. "All of the above." He paused. "Do they speak any Terran on this planet?"

"I don't know . . . but according to my star charts, it's got three terraformed moons that are inhabited by humans. They're your logical starting point."

"Why not just approach her directly?"

"If direct approaches worked, the Democracy wouldn't have sought me out," answered the Iceman. "Will you take the job?"

Chandler considered the proposition for a moment, then nodded. "Yeah, I'll take it."

"Good," said the Iceman. "If it turns out that the Oracle isn't Penelope Bailey, bring her out."

"And if she *is* Penelope Bailey?"

"Once you know it's her, find a way to get word back to me. There's no way you're going to bring her out if she doesn't want to come, so kill her if you can. If I don't hear from you in six months, I'll know you're dead."

"You mean you'll *assume* I'm dead."

"I meant what I said," replied the Iceman seriously.

3

The radio beeped to life.

"You are now within the Alpha Crepello system," said a mechanical voice. "Please identify yourself."

"This is the *Gamestalker*, registration number 237H8J99, eight Galactic Standard days out of The Frenchman's World, Joshua Jeremiah Chandler commanding."

"We have no record of The Frenchman's World, *Gamestalker*."

"It's the third planet in the Boyson system on the Inner Frontier," responded Chandler.

There was a brief silence.

"What is your purpose for visiting the Alpha Crepello system, *Gamestalker*?"

"Business."

"State the nature of your business, please."

"I'm a salesman."

"What do you sell?"

"Rare stamps and coins."

"Have you a confirmed appointment with any inhabitant of the Alpha Crepello system?"

"Yes."

"With whom is your appointment?"

"Carlos Mendoza," replied Chandler, using the first name that came to mind. "I believe he resides on Alpha Crepello III."

Another silence.

"We have no record of any Carlos Mendoza living on Alpha Crepello III. Is Carlos Mendoza a human?"

"Yes."

"He does not reside on Alpha Crepello III," said the voice with finality.

"Then perhaps he is merely a visitor," said Chandler. "All I know is that I was supposed to meet him there."

"The Alpha Crepello system is not a member of the Democracy," said the voice. "We have no reciprocal trade agreements with the Democracy, we have no military treaties with the Democracy, and we do not recognize Democracy passports. No one may land on Alpha Crepello III without special permission of the government, and this permission is rarely given to members of your race." There was a brief pause. "You may land on any of Alpha Crepello III's terraformed moons, but if you attempt to land on Alpha Crepello III itself, you will be detained and your ship will be subject to confiscation."

"Thank you," said Chandler. "*Gamestalker* over and out."

The Iceman had told him that he wouldn't be allowed to land on the planet itself, so he was neither surprised nor disappointed that permission had been denied him. He sighed, stretched, and stared at his viewscreen.

"Computer," he said, "bring up holograms, charts, and readouts on Alpha Crepello III's terraformed moons."

"Working . . . done," replied his ship's computer.

There were three of them—Port Maracaibo, Port Samarkand, and Port Marrakech. Each had once been rich in fissionable materials and had been terraformed by the long-defunct Republic almost two millennia ago. The inhabitants of Alpha Crepello III had objected, and the Navy had subdued them in a brief but furious battle. Then, when the Democracy had succeeded the Republic, Alpha Crepello III—which had been dubbed Hades by its human ambassador because of its reddish soil and incredibly hot climate—had declined to remain an active member of the galactic community and had cut all ties with its neighboring worlds as well as with Deluros VIII, the huge, distant world that had become the capital of the race of Man. Since the moons were virtually mined out by that time and Man had more immediate conquests and problems to deal with, Hades had been allowed to go its own way.

The three moons were of little or no use to the residents of Hades, and as the miners left, other Men moved in, men who were seeking worlds that had no official ties with the Democracy. Hades had originally objected, but the prospect of another war convinced them to practice a form of benign neglect toward the moons and their new inhabitants, and over the centuries the moons gradually became a clearinghouse for black market goods, a sanctuary for human outlaws, a gathering place for mercenaries, and a conduit between the free worlds of the Quinellus Cluster and the regulated worlds of mankind's vast Democracy.

"Computer," said Chandler, "how many humans reside on each of the terraformed moons?"

"126,214 on Port Maracaibo, 18,755 on Port Samarkand, and 187,440 on Port Marrakech," replied the computer. "These figures are accurate as of the last census, taken seven years ago."

"What form of currency is in use on each of the moons?"

"They accept all forms of human currency that are traded within the Democracy and on the Inner Frontier, plus the currencies of Hades, Canphor VI, Canphor VII, and Lodin XI. The value of each is pegged to the daily exchange rate of the Democracy credit as determined on Deluros VIII."

"Please give me their climactic and gravitational readouts."

"All three moons were terraformed by the same Republic Pioneer team, and are identical in climate and gravity," responded the computer. "Gravity is .98 percent Earth and Deluros Standard, temperature is a constant twenty-two degrees Celsius by day and seventeen degrees Celsius by night, atmosphere is Earth and Deluros VIII normal."

"Do they all have spaceports?"

"They possess spaceports for Class H and smaller ships. Larger ships are required to dock in orbiting hangars."

"There doesn't seem much to choose among them," remarked Chandler.

It was neither a question nor a command, so the computer did not respond.

"Which one is closest to Hades?"

"Port Marrakech."

"All right," said Chandler. "Port Marrakech it is."

His landing was uneventful, and shortly thereafter he made his way through the crowded spaceport. He spotted a few faces here and there that he remembered seeing on Wanted posters, but he paid them no attention, concentrating only on making his way to the main exit. Once outside, he hailed a groundcar that took him into the heart of the nearby city—as far as he could tell the *only* city on Port Marrakech. The buildings boasted numerous exotic arches and angles, and most of them had been whitewashed. He was unaware of the genesis of the name "Marrakech," but he assumed that it was a city somewhere in the galaxy that greatly resembled the one in which he now found himself; the architecture was too much of a piece, and too different from the other worlds he had seen, not to have been carefully planned.

"Where to now?" asked the driver as they entered the heavy traffic of the city center.

"I've never been here before," replied Chandler. "Can you recommend a hotel?"

"With or without?"

"With or without what?"

The driver shrugged. "Whatever you want—women, men, drugs, gambling, you name it."

"Without, I think."

The driver grinned. "That may be a little harder. This isn't the Democracy, you know."

Chandler leaned forward and handed him a fifty-credit note. "Why don't you fill me in?" he suggested.

"You thirsty?" asked the driver.

"Should I be?"

"I can fill you in a lot better if my mouth doesn't go dry halfway through."

"I've already given you fifty credits. You can buy a drink after we're through."

"You've already made a couple of mistakes," said the driver meaningfully. "I can tell you about them while we drink, or you can learn about them the hard way."

"Suddenly I'm thirsty," said Chandler.

"I thought you might be," chuckled the driver. "By the way, my name's Gin."

"Just Gin?"

"Gin's my game, gin's my drink, Gin's my name."

"Okay, Gin," said Chandler. "Where do you think we ought to have this drink?"

"I'm already heading there," said Gin. "It's not real fancy, but they don't water the booze and people will leave us pretty much alone."

Chandler leaned back and observed the city as the vehicle sped through it. Most of the buildings were centuries old, and except for a handful of truly palatial structures in the downtown area, they looked their age. There was a definite seediness to the city, as if most of the residents were transients: small hotels and rooming houses greatly outnumbered apartments, and restaurants and bars were omnipresent, implying that almost no one ever ate or drank at home. There was an almost tangible gloom, partially due to the ambience, partially due to the fact that Hades cast its massive shadow across the moon's surface.

"Here we are," announced Gin, pulling up in front of a tavern that was indistinguishable from four others on the same block.

"Lead the way," said Chandler, getting out of the vehicle.

He fell into step behind Gin and soon entered the dimly lit interior. There were some two dozen tables and booths, half of them empty, the other half occupied by Men and aliens conversing in low voices. A very tired-looking woman was performing a very unenthusiastic striptease to recorded music in one corner; a Lodinite was observing her with clinical detachment, while none of the other customers paid her the slightest attention.

"How does this one suit you?" asked Gin, indicating a booth as far from the door as possible.

"Fine," replied Chandler.

Both men seated themselves, and Gin raised his hand and made a swift signal in the air. An overweight waiter arrived a moment later with a pair of green-tinted drinks.

"What is it?" asked Chandler, staring at his glass and frowning.

Gin shrugged. "They call it a Dustbuster on Binder X. Here it's a Number Five."

"What's in it?"

"Lots of stuff, most of it good for you," answered Gin, picking up his glass and downing it with a single swallow.

Chandler raised his own glass, stared at it for a moment, then took a sip.

"Well?" asked Gin.

"It'll do."

"Best damned drink you ever had, and that's all you've got to say?"

"You're the one with the thirst. I'm just here to talk."

"Right," said Gin, signaling for another drink. "Hope you don't mind," he said, "but talking is mighty dry work."

"I have a feeling that everything you do is mighty dry work," said Chandler sardonically.

"Now that you mention it . . ." said Gin, and laughed. "By the way, you got a name?"

"Chandler."

"Okay," said Gin with a shrug. "But if I were you, I'd change it."

"Why?"

"Why advertise that the Whistler has come to Port Marrakech?"

"There are a lot of Chandlers in the galaxy. What makes you think I'm the Whistler?"

"How many Chandlers come out of the spaceport with five guns and a knife hidden on their persons?" grinned Gin. "That was your first mistake. My groundcar's got a security system that registers on the dash."

"I know," said Chandler calmly. "I spotted it the second you opened the door for me."

"You did?"

Chandler nodded. "I figured it was for your own protection. After all, if it was against the law to bring weapons onto the planet, they'd have stopped me at Spaceport Security."

"Makes sense," admitted Gin. "Still, there are ways of landing here without being spotted. By morning, everyone will know that the Whistler is on Port Marrakech."

"Do you plan to tell them?"

Gin shook his head. "I won't have to. By now someone in Spaceport Security has checked out your ship's registration, or run your retinagram through a computer, or just out-and-out recognized you. Especially if you used Chandler as your name."

"So they know who I am," said Chandler. "So what? From what I can tell, this place is loaded with killers and worse."

"You didn't come here for your health," said Gin. "I've heard all about you: when the Whistler shows up, people start dying."

"I'm not after anyone on Port Marrakech. If I was, nobody would know I was here."

"Yeah, I believe you," said Gin. He paused. "So what are you doing here?"

"*You're* supposed to be answering questions, not me," said Chandler. "What do you think was my other mistake?"

"You asked me for a hotel." Gin smiled. "Not smart. A killer shouldn't let people know he's come to town, and he sure as hell shouldn't let people know where he's staying."

"Unless what?" asked Chandler.

Gin stared at him. "Unless you *want* people to know you're here."

"That's right."

"Then you must be after someone on Port Samarkand or Port Maracaibo." He frowned. "But that doesn't make any sense. Why would you land here?"

"Why I landed here is *my* concern," said Chandler as the waiter arrived with another drink for Gin.

"You sure you don't want to tell me who you're after, Whistler? I've got pretty good connections. Maybe I could help you find him"—he paused and grinned—"for a small consideration."

"I'm not after a who, I'm after a *what:* information, remember?"

Gin sighed. "Have it your way. I was just trying to be helpful."

"You're not trying hard enough," said Chandler. "We've been here ten minutes and you haven't told me a damned thing."

"What do you want to know?"

There was only one piece of information Chandler actually wanted, which was how to get to Hades—but he spent the next half hour asking numerous questions about Port Marrakech, at the end of which he knew more about the local trade in drugs, prostitution, and black market goods than he ever wanted to know.

"Sounds good," he said at last. "Things have been slow on the Inner Frontier. I'm considering setting up shop here."

"You'll have lots of competition in your line of work," said Gin.

"Not for long," replied Chandler.

Gin stared at him and nodded his agreement. "No, I suppose you won't—not if you're half as good as they say you are."

"Could be that I'll need a driver who knows his way around, and can tell me where all the bodies are buried," continued Chandler.

"Yeah?" said Gin, his face alive with interest.

"It's possible. Think you might know anyone who'd be interested in the job?"

Gin grinned. "You're looking at him."

"You've got a job."

"On a moon loaded with killers, I like the security of working for the best killer of all."

"Well, you're pretty good at talking, I'll give you that," said

Chandler. "How are you at keeping your mouth shut?"

"You can trust me, Whistler."

"If you come to work for me and I find that I *can't* trust you, I don't envy you your death." Chandler paused. "Do you still want the job?"

"What does it pay?"

"More than driving back and forth to the airport and taking kickbacks from bars and hotels—and you'll get it in cash."

"I still need a figure. After all, I'll have to use my own vehicle I gotta figure my expenses."

"How much are you making now?"

"Counting all the perks?" said Gin. "It comes to maybe six hundred credits a week."

"I'll double it."

Gin extended his hand across the table. "Deal!"

Chandler took the proffered hand. "Deal," he replied. "You're on my payroll, starting this minute."

"Great!" said Gin. There was a momentary silence. "Uh . . . what do we do now?"

"We finish our drinks and I find a place to sleep."

"And then what?"

"Eventually I wake up."

"I mean, what do *I* do?"

"You're on call around the clock," answered Chandler. "When I wake up in the morning, I expect to see you parked outside o wherever I spend the night. I also expect you to keep your eye and ears open. If you hear of anyone who's looking for someon in my line of work, you tell me. Even more important: if you se anyone watching me, you let me know."

"Right," said Gin. He signaled the waiter for another drink.

"And you show up sober," added Chandler.

"You got it."

"By the way, I don't plan to confine my activities just t Port Marrakech. Have you ever been to Port Samarkand or Po Maracaibo?"

"I know 'em almost as well as I know this Port Marrakech, Gin assured him.

"Good," said Chandler. "That should prove helpful." H paused. "What about Hades?"

"You don't want any part of Hades, Whistler," said Gin. "The got nothing but these blue-skinned aliens there—Blue Devils, w call 'em. Even if you got a contract to knock one of them off, you'd never be able to tell 'em apart."

"You've been there?"

"No, but I've seen my share of Blue Devils. Ugly-looking sons of bitches."

"Do any humans live on Hades?"

"Not to my knowledge," answered Gin. He shrugged. "Hell, who'd want to?"

Chandler didn't want to display too much interest in Hades, so he let the subject drop and spent another twenty minutes asking questions about the other two moons before he decided it was time to leave.

He checked into one of the better rooming houses, paid for a week in advance, and went to his room, confident that he'd made a decent start; he was in no hurry to get to Hades until he learned more about it. He'd go through the motions of setting up business on Port Marrakech, and in a day or a week or a month, Gin or someone else would tell him what he needed to know about Hades and the mysterious Oracle. In the meantime, he might even accept a contract or two, just to provide authenticity to his cover story.

He had shaved and showered, and was just about to nod off to sleep when the vidphone blinked.

"Yeah?" he said, staring at a blank screen.

"You are the Whistler, are you not?" said a voice that might or might not have been human.

"My name is Chandler."

"You are the Whistler," repeated the voice tonelessly. It paused for a moment. "A word of advice, Whistler: go home."

"Who is this?" demanded Chandler, trying without success to bring up an image on the screen.

"I will not repeat my warning, Whistler," said the voice. "I know who you are, I know why you are here, and I tell you that your mission is destined to fail. If you are still here tomorrow morning, your life is at hazard."

Then the connection went dead, and Chandler allowed himself the luxury of a satisfied smile.

4

Gin was waiting for him outside the rooming house when Chandler emerged the next morning. He had traded his company vehicle for his own somewhat battered landcar.

"Where to?" he asked as Chandler climbed into the back of the vehicle.

"Twice around the block."

Gin merely grunted and did as he was told. When he had finished, and was once again parked in front of the rooming house, he turned to Chandler.

"No one's watching us."

"No one's *following* us," Chandler corrected him. "There's a difference."

"What's up?" asked Gin.

"Nothing much," said Chandler. "I got a message last night. Someone doesn't want me here."

"That figures," said Gin reasonably. "A man with your reputation shows up, you're going to cost someone some business."

"They'll have to learn to live with the disappointment."

"I *told* you someone at the spaceport would spot you," continued Gin. He paused. "So where do I take you now?"

"Around."

"Around where?"

"Just around. I can't go into business if people don't know I'm here."

"They know," responded Gin. "Whoever tried to warn you off has probably told half the people he knows by now. I say we go get a drink and think about this."

"I'll let you know when you become an equal partner," said Chandler. "Just start driving."

Suddenly Gin grinned. "You're not advertising," he said emphatically. "You're trolling! You want whoever you spoke to last night to move against you so you can take him out!"

"Drive."

"Just a minute," said Gin, withdrawing a sonic pistol from beneath the seat. He turned it over and checked its charge.

"Do you know how to use that thing?" asked Chandler as Gin pulled out into traffic.

"Maybe not as well as you," came the answer, "but I can usually hit what I aim at."

Chandler paused. "Don't aim it at anything unless I tell you to," he said at last.

Gin nodded and tucked the pistol into his belt. "Okay, boss," he said. "Where are we going?"

"It's your city. You decide."

"Well, I can take you to where the rich folks hang out, or I can take you to where the people they hire hang out."

"First one, then the other."

Gin stared at a poorly dressed man with bulging pockets who was standing on the slidewalk, staring at them, and as he did so the landcar came up fast on another vehicle. Gin swerved just in time to avoid an accident.

"You keep your eyes on the road," said Chandler. "I'll watch for potential enemies."

"Ain't nothing potential about it," muttered Gin. "By noon you could have half a hundred of 'em out for your scalp."

"Don't let your imagination run away with you," replied Chandler as they began encountering heavier traffic.

"Don't let your confidence run away with *you*," said Gin. "The more I think about it, the more I think this isn't such a good idea."

"Thinking's not in your job description," said Chandler. "Until it is, I suggest that you leave the thinking to me."

Gin shrugged. "Whatever you say."

"*That's* what I say," answered Chandler. Suddenly he tensed. "Pull over and stop."

The landcar came to a halt.

"Did you spot someone?" asked Gin, reaching for his pistol.

"That alien," said Chandler, staring at a bald, blue-skinned humanoid who was standing across the street. "Is that a Blue Devil?"

"Yeah. So what?"

Chandler stared at it for another moment, then leaned back and relaxed. "Okay, start driving again."

"You didn't answer my question," persisted Gin. "Why do you care about Blue Devils?"

"I've never seen one before."

"You spent a long time looking at it."

"I was curious."

They drove in silence for another minute, and then Gin spoke again. "Why do you think a Blue Devil wants to kill you?"

"Did I say I thought so?"

"You didn't have to." Gin paused. "But for the life of me, I can't figure out why a Blue Devil would give a damn whether you're on Port Marrakech or not."

There was a long pause, during which Gin decided not to push the subject and Chandler totally ignored it. Finally Chandler broke the silence: "How long before we reach wherever it is you're taking me?"

"Another couple of minutes, give or take."

"Tell me about the area we're passing through."

"Do you really care?" asked Gin.

"All morning long I haven't been able to shut you up," said Chandler with an ironic smile. "Now, when I want you to talk, suddenly you aren't interested."

Gin shrugged. "You're the boss. This part of town is called Little Spica. It's inhabited mostly by descendants of miners from Spica VI and shipbuilders from Spica II. A few Canphorites live on the outskirts, but the Spicans don't think much of most other aliens." He paused. "There's a great whorehouse over on the next block, if that's to your taste."

"Not especially."

"See this storefront here?" said Gin, slowing down. "They say that Santiago himself killed two women right there on the slidewalk about two hundred years ago. And that bar there, on the left? Best source of alphanella seeds in this part of town." He paused again. "You ever chewed any seeds?" He shook his head and answered his own question. "No, I suppose not. A man in your line of work needs a clear head."

"How many other cities are there on Port Marrakech?"

"Cities?" repeated Gin. "None. There are a couple of little villages, maybe five hundred people apiece, halfway around the world, farming communities mostly. No, most of the people live right here." They drove out of Little Spica and into an even seedier area, filled with the omnipresent domed, whitewashed buildings, most of them covered with grime, many in need of repair.

"The alien quarter?" suggested Chandler.

"You got it. Mostly Blue Devils. The rest of them are a pretty mixed lot."

"Have you ever seen an alien that looked like a turtle?" asked Chandler.

"I don't even know what a turtle is," answered Gin. "Why?"

"Just curious," said Chandler.

"A man like you isn't subject to fits of idle curiosity," replied Gin. "If you'll describe it to me, maybe I can find out if there's anything here that fits the description."

"Some other time," said Chandler, dismissing the subject.

They sped through the city, Gin pointing out sites of local, historic, and criminal interest, Chandler asking an occasional question. During the next ten minutes their surroundings became progressively more elegant, and finally Gin slowed his vehicle and pulled up to a glistening hotel that looked like some ancient and exotic palace.

"Our first stop," said Gin. "This is the most expensive hotel in town."

Chandler nodded, then got out of the landcar.

"You want me to come with you?" asked Gin.

"Not necessary," answered Chandler. "I'll be back in a few minutes."

He entered the lobby, allowed the sparkling slidewalk to take him around a fountain that was engineered so that its thousands of jets of colored water met in such a manner that it formed an almost solid representation of a nude woman. As quickly as the figure lost its structural integrity, new jets of gold and red and white water would meet in midair, re-forming the figure. The slidewalk deposited him at the registration desk, where a uniformed man approached him from behind a broad, gleaming counter.

"May I help you?" he asked.

"It's possible," said Chandler. "Do you have a Carlos Mendoza registered here?"

The man asked his computer, which replied in the negative.

"That's curious," said Chandler, frowning. "I was supposed to meet him here."

"There are no reservations in the name of Mendoza," said the man.

"Well, I'm sure he'll show up sooner or later."

"We're fully booked for the next three months, sir."

"That's *his* problem," said Chandler with a shrug. "I wonder if I could leave a message for him."

"Certainly, sir."

"Good. If Mr. Mendoza should show up, please tell him that the Whistler has completed his business here."

"That's all?"

"Not quite," said Chandler. "When Mendoza gets my message, he'll probably give you an envelope with my name on it. Please deposit it in your safe until I come by for it."

"I may not be on duty when you return," said the man. "If this is a financial transaction, we'll need some form of identification before we can release the funds to you, sir."

Chandler placed his fingers on the shining counter, then pressed down on it. "Did it register?"

The clerk checked a hidden screen behind the counter. "Yes, Mr. Whistler. We now have your fingerprints in our permanent file."

"Good," said Chandler, placing a five-hundred-credit note on the counter. "I am sure I can count on your discretion."

"Absolutely, sir." He picked up the bill and placed it in a pocket. "How can we contact you if Mr. Mendoza should deliver the envelope?"

"I'll contact you," answered Chandler, turning on his heel and walking back out to the landcar.

He repeated the process at three more hotels. When he emerged from the last of them, he entered the vehicle, leaned back, and relaxed.

"All right," he said to Gin. "I think I've announced my presence sufficiently."

"I saw you slipping some money to each desk clerk," noted Gin. "Are you paying them to spread the word?"

Chandler smiled in amusement. "I gave each of them five hundred credits not to tell anyone that I was on Port Marrakech."

"Let me get this straight," said Gin. "You want to announce

your presence, so you're paying them to keep it a secret? I don't understand."

"At least a couple of them will decide that if it's worth five hundred credits to me to keep my presence here a secret, it ought to be worth a couple of thousand credits to someone else to know I'm here." He paused. "By tonight just about everyone who might want to avail themselves of my services will know I'm here."

Gin grinned. "I never thought of that!"

"You didn't have to. *I* did."

"Where to now?"

"If I weren't on Port Marrakech, and you had a sizable sum of money and wanted to have someone killed, who would you hire?"

"I'd go right to the Surgeon," replied Gin without hesitation.

"The Surgeon?"

"His real name is Vittorio something-or-other, but everyone calls him the Surgeon. He can slice you into pieces before you even know he's there."

"Where can I find him?"

Gin shrugged. "Half a dozen places. He gets around. He's got a little action here and a little action there."

"Choose the likeliest spot and drive there."

"This time of day he's probably at the Wolfman's. That's a restaurant over in the Platinum Quarter, near where we were drinking last night."

"The Platinum Quarter? I didn't see anything that opulent last night."

"It's pretty run-down," agreed Gin. "But right before Port Marrakech was mined out, someone discovered platinum, and there was one last flurry of activity before they decided that there wasn't enough to make mining it worthwhile. The Platinum Quarter is what got built over where the mine used to be. The miners left so many tunnels there that you can get from almost any building in the Quarter to any other building without ever coming up for air—*if* you know your way around." He paused. "Every now and then someone who *doesn't* know the tunnel system goes down there, and as often as not he's never seen again."

"It's not big enough to get permanently lost in," commented Chandler. "I assume these missing people don't live long enough to starve to death."

"Whistler, we got guys living down there who haven't seen the sun in ten years," answered Gin. "You pay 'em what they want for safe passage, or they take it anyway and leave your corpse for the worms." He paused again. "You've never seen anything like a Port Marrakech worm. Damned things are a couple of feet long, and they've actually got teeth. You leave a body down there and they can strip it to the bone in less than a day."

"Pleasant place."

"The men who live down there are worse than the worms. Some people say they've got the worms trained to recognize 'em and leave 'em alone; others say that they eat the worms to stay alive."

"Does the Surgeon ever go down to the tunnels?" asked Chandler.

"From time to time. Course, everyone knows who he is, so they leave him alone. Mostly, they make their money from hiding anyone who's got to disappear for a while, and they pick up a little extra from people who've got no business being there in the first place."

"Interesting," commented Chandler noncommittally.

"Interesting, hell—it's goddamned dangerous," said Gin devoutly. "If you're thinking of going down into the tunnels, you and me are gonna part company."

"I'll keep that in mind."

They drove for another few minutes, and then Gin stopped in front of a small rectangular building that seemed out of place in this city of domes and angles. There were no signs on the windows or the door, but Gin assured Chandler that advertising was unnecessary, and that everyone who had a reason to be there knew where the Wolfman's restaurant was.

"I'd better go in with you," he announced as Chandler got out of the landcar. "You go around asking for the Surgeon without anyone knowing who you are and you're liable to undergo an operation you hadn't planned on."

Chandler followed Gin into the restaurant, which seemed to be on the dismal side of normal, with cheap chairs and torn booths, scarred tables, a very small bar along the left-hand wall, and a surly-looking waiter and waitress.

Standing behind the bar was a creature out of a child's worst nightmare. It stood and walked like a man, but its head was that of a wolf, with a prolonged foreface and impressive canines. Its ears were not quite human and not quite canine, but were quite large and pointed and set high atop its head. Its face, neck, chest, and hands were covered with fur, and it wore an elegant formal outfit that covered the rest of its body.

Gin led Chandler right up to it.

"Whistler, meet the Wolfman," he said, stepping aside.

"I've heard of you," said the Wolfman, extending a hand/paw.

"I'm surprised I haven't heard of *you*," replied Chandler, reaching out his own hand. "Cosmetic surgery?"

"Yes."

"Why a wolf?" asked Chandler.

"Why not?" was the reply, as the Wolfman made a croaking sound deep in his throat that Chandler took to be a chuckle. "At least people remember me once they've seen me." He paused. "Of course, I can see where that's not necessarily an advantage in your line of work." He stared at Chandler. "Why do I think you didn't come here to sample my food?"

"I'm looking for someone."

"Oh?"

"The Surgeon."

"He's not here," answered the Wolfman.

Chandler looked questioningly at Gin, who had been studying the few occupied tables. Gin shook his head.

"You might try again tomorrow," added the Wolfman. "He's one of my best customers. He comes around four or five times a week." The Wolfman pointed toward a table near the bar, one that backed up to a wall and gave the occupant a clear view of the doorway. "That's his regular table."

"Not anymore," said Chandler.

"Oh?"

"That table is mine now," said Chandler. "You might pass the word."

"I don't know if the Surgeon is going to be real pleased with that."

"That's not my problem," said Chandler. "He's changing jobs or worlds—it's up to him."

"Does he know about it?" asked the Wolfman.

"He will," said Chandler. "If you see him first, you can tell him."

"Not me, friend," said the Wolfman. "I spent four years having this face created. The Surgeon could slash it to ribbons in three seconds."

"He won't," said Chandler. "You're under my protection, starting right now."

"I don't want any part of this," said the Wolfman nervously. He paused. "Maybe you're as good as they say you are, and maybe not. But I've *seen* the Surgeon."

"You won't see him again," said Chandler. "Remember: no one sits at that table except me."

He laid a bill on the bar, then turned and walked toward the door. Gin caught up with him just as he stepped outside.

"Boy, I hope to hell you know what you're doing!" exclaimed the driver. "I thought you just wanted to *talk* to the Surgeon."

"If he's a reasonable man, that's all I'll have to do," answered Chandler. "But I'm setting up shop here. This is the easiest way to establish my credentials and get rid of my biggest rival at the same time." He climbed into the vehicle. "Take me to the next spot on your list. I'd like to get this over with before dinner."

Gin shook his head in wonderment. "You're the first guy I've ever seen who was in a hurry to go up against the Surgeon."

"You look unhappy," noted Chandler.

"I was kind of hoping this job might last for more than half a day," said Gin ironically.

"It will."

"I don't know about that," said Gin. "You've got some Blue Devil out to kill you, and now you're going out of your way to confront the Surgeon. You're either awfully good or just out-and-out crazy."

"I guess we'll find out, won't we?" said Chandler calmly.

"I guess we will," said Gin, pulling into traffic and heading for his next destination.

Chandler leaned back on the seat and closed his eyes, totally at ease. He disliked waste, and for that reason he was sorry that he was going to have to sacrifice the Surgeon, especially since they were members of the same profession. But the Surgeon was a vital piece in the game upon which he had embarked: he had carefully mapped out his plan of attack, just as he used to plan his safaris in meticulous detail, and if he hadn't overlooked some hidden factor, this would put him one step closer to the Oracle.

If he survived.

5

"Okay, we're here," announced Gin, getting out of the vehicle and approaching the dilapidated building.

"Where's *here*?" asked Chandler.

"It's called the Dreambasin."

"A drug den?"

Gin nodded. "The Surgeon stops by here every couple of days."

"Curious."

"How so?" asked Gin.

"Professionals don't usually mess with drugs," responded Chandler. "It screws up the perceptions and destroys the reflexes."

"Oh, the Surgeon's no seed-chewer," said Gin. "But a lot of his clients are. If he's here, he's just tending to business."

They walked up to the entrance, where Gin uttered a password and smiled into an overhead camera. The door slid back a moment later, and two muscular men confronted them.

"Who do you have with you, Gin?" asked one of them.

"He's my new employer," answered the driver. "I personally vouch for him."

The man turned to Chandler. "Name?"

"Joshua Chandler."

"Where are you staying?"

"The Souk," answered Chandler. "It's a boardinghouse on the west side of—"

"I know where it is," interrupted the man. "Occupation?"

"Tourist."

The man smiled. "Well, that's original, anyway." He held out his hand. "Two hundred credits. And two hundred more for your employee."

Chandler handed over the money. "Can we go in now?"

"As soon as you check your weapons with us."

"Does the Surgeon check *his*?" asked Chandler.

"What the Surgeon does is none of your business, Mr. Chandler," was the answer. "If you don't hand over your weapons, I'll have to remove them myself." He placed a hand on the hilt of his laser pistol, as if to emphasize the point.

"That wouldn't be wise," said Chandler softly.

Something in the tone of his voice made the man hesitate.

"Either you turn them over, or you can't enter," he said lamely.

"Don't kill them," Gin said to Chandler. "They're just doing their job."

"If there's any killing done here, *we're* going to do it," said the second man, finally choosing to speak.

"You don't know who you're dealing with," said Gin with such conviction that the second man, too, seemed suddenly hesitant.

Nobody moved for a few seconds. Then Chandler removed his pistols and his knife and handed them to one of the men.

"Let's go," he said to Gin as the man stepped aside, staring at him with a mixture of anger and uncertainty.

They proceeded down a long, poorly illuminated corridor, past a number of closed doors. The sickly sweet odor of *palyp,* an alien drug that humans had appropriated for themselves and now smoked in old-fashioned water pipes, permeated the air.

They passed one open door and Chandler glanced in. Four women lay suspended above the floor on cushions of air; he couldn't tell whether they had been smoking or injecting, but three of them were near-catatonic. The fourth, her face contorted in agony, saw him and reached out a trembling, supplicating hand. Chandler stared at her for a moment with an expression of distaste, then turned away and continued walking.

Finally they came to a spacious lounge. There were no chairs or couches in it, just a number of large pillows on the floor. Some eleven men and eight women sat or lay upon them, some in clusters of two and three, some alone. Many of them looked bewildered, as if they were just coming down from a high; others looked anxious, as if they were preparing for one. A few merely looked bored. There were half a dozen Domarian actigraphs on the walls, three-dimensional creations of concentric circles and intricately weaving lines that pulsed with energy and had an almost hypnotic effect upon the viewer.

Suddenly Gin stopped and tensed.

"Where is he?" asked Chandler softly.

"See those two guys talking in the corner?" whispered Gin, indicating a bald, rotund man dressed in a blue satin outfit and a small, wiry man with a widow's peak and an aquiline nose, who wore an expensively tailored white tunic.

"Yes."

"The fat one is Omar Tripoli. He's a banker, and he owns a couple of nightclubs in the Antarrean Quarter. The little guy is the Surgeon."

"He doesn't look like much," noted Chandler.

"The graveyards are full of people who didn't think he looked like much."

Chandler stared at the Surgeon for another moment, then turned to Gin. "Wait here," he ordered the driver.

"He's probably armed," whispered Gin.

"Just do what I say," answered Chandler, walking across the room and coming to a halt next to Omar Tripoli.

"We're having a private conversation," said the Surgeon without looking up.

"I know," said Chandler.

"Then go away," said the Surgeon.

Chandler remained where he was, silent and motionless.

Finally the Surgeon looked at the man who was confronting him and got to his feet. "You don't listen very good, do you?"

"I haven't heard anything worth listening to," replied Chandler.

"You're taking a big chance, friend," said Tripoli.

"Not as big a chance as *you're* taking, Mr. Tripoli," replied Chandler.

"What do you mean?" asked Tripoli nervously.

"You mean the Surgeon hasn't told you?" said Chandler with mock surprise.

"Told me what?"

"That he's leaving Port Marrakech this evening and going into a different business. If I were you, I wouldn't pay him another credit."

"All right!" snapped the Surgeon. "Just who the hell are you?"

"Your successor," said Chandler. He paused. "I think if you hurry, you can just make the flight to Binder X."

"You've got balls, mister, I'll give you that," said the Surgeon. "I wonder how you'll feel when you see them rolling across the floor."

"Save your threats," said Chandler calmly. "Mr. Tripoli isn't impressed by them—and neither am I."

Suddenly a wicked-looking knife appeared in the Surgeon's right hand. "Are you going to tell me who you are, or am I going to have to take your ID off your body?"

"I've no objection to telling you. My name's Chandler."

"I never heard of you."

"That's just one of my names. Some people call me the Whistler."

The Surgeon's eyes widened briefly, but he didn't lower the knife or back away.

"You can still walk out of here," said Chandler. "In fact, as long as you're turning your business over to me, I'll even pay for your ticket."

"You think you can buy me off with a spaceship ticket?" said the Surgeon with a harsh laugh.

"Not really," answered Chandler. "But I thought I'd offer you the opportunity to live."

"I've got a little something to offer *you*!" grated the Surgeon. He flipped his knife back and forth between his hands a number of times, then lunged forward with his left hand extended.

Chandler grabbed his wrist, sidestepped the thrust, and then, more rapidly than Tripoli or Gin could follow, delivered three quick blows, one to the groin, one to the Adam's apple, and a final one upward against the nose, forcing the bones into the brain. The Surgeon was dead before he hit the floor. Chandler picked up the knife and tucked it into one of his many pockets. Everything had happened so quickly that most of the people in the room were too stunned to react.

Chandler turned to Tripoli. "This is neither the time nor the place to conduct our business," he said with perfect calm. "I'll be in touch with you tomorrow or the next day; you'll find that my prices are quite reasonable for the services I provide. In the meantime, you might tell your friends that the Whistler has come to town."

He stepped over the Surgeon's body and walked across the

lounge, paying no attention to any of the men and women who stared in awe at him.

"Let's go," he said to Gin.

They walked back down the long corridor to the Dreambasin's entrance, picked up Chandler's weapons, and were in the landcar and driving away before anyone reported the killing.

"That was some show you put on, Whistler!" said Gin with the enthusiasm of a small boy for one of his sports heroes. "You were awesome!"

"Well, I've established my credentials, anyway," said Chandler. He paused. "It was a necessary if wasteful object lesson."

"Wasteful?" asked Gin, puzzled. "How?"

"I had to kill a man who had never met me, who presented no threat to me, and who was not my enemy. Wouldn't *you* call that wasteful?"

"Not at all."

"Then it's a fortunate thing that you don't have my ability to kill," said Chandler.

"We're growing a strange crop of assassins this season," remarked Gin, amused.

"This was not an assassination," said Chandler. "It was an execution."

"Well, whatever you call it, he's dead," replied Gin, dismissing the subject with a shrug. "Where to now, Whistler?"

"Take me back to the Souk," replied Chandler. "I think I've accomplished quite enough for one morning. I'm going to read for a while and then take a nap."

"Just like that?"

"I'm sorry his death was necessary," said Chandler irritably. "I have no intention of joining the mourners."

"I'd be surprised if there are any," said Gin. He paused. "By the way, I think you can expect the authorities to come calling on you. As long as we confine our killing to each other, they won't give you too much trouble, but they'll have to at least talk to you, just for show."

"It was self-defense," answered Chandler. "I've got more than a dozen witnesses."

"True," agreed Gin. He paused again. "You want me on call outside the Souk?"

"Not for a few hours," answered Chandler. "Right now I want you to make the rounds and tell everyone what happened." He handed a pair of bills to Gin. "And since talking is such dry work, you can use this to lubricate yourself."

"With pleasure," said Gin, taking the bills and stuffing them into a pocket. "I never liked that mean-spirited little slasher, anyway."

"He was just a man doing a job," said Chandler. "From now on *I'll* be doing it."

"Well, you're the man of the hour, as they say," enthused the driver. "By tomorrow the whole damned city will know you're here to stay."

"How soon will word of this reach the other moons?" asked Chandler.

"Before nightfall," Gin assured him.

He wanted to ask if Hades would hear of it, too, but decided not to. The one person for whom he was putting on this performance already knew who he was, and he would be surprised if she didn't also know of the Surgeon's death by the time he reached his rooming house. It was a perfectly logical step for a man in his business to have taken: you could work your way up through the ranks, or if you were good enough and strong enough, you could take on the top dog and assimilate his territory. He had evinced no interest in Hades, had made no inquiries about the Oracle, nor would he. He had come to Port Marrakech for business, and he now had a ready-made clientele to service. It was as simple and clear-cut as that.

The only question, he mused wryly as the landcar pulled up to the Souk, was whether or not she'd buy it.

6

The police woke Chandler from his nap and took him to the local station to record his statement concerning the Surgeon's killing. He got the distinct impression that they were just going through the motions, that the death of an assassin, regardless of the circumstances, didn't bother them in the least. When his deposition matched the various eyewitness accounts, they released him with the bored instructions to keep within the law during his stay on Port Marrakech.

Gin was waiting for him when the police dropped him off at the Souk.

"I see you had company," he noted as the police vehicle sped away.

"They weren't any problem."

"They'd probably have pinned a medal on you if they could have gotten away with it," said Gin. "The Surgeon wasn't exactly the most popular guy in town."

"Neither will I be, when I take over his client list."

"Yeah. Well, in his case, it was a matter of preferring the devil they don't know to the devil they knew."

"I get the distinct impression that they'll leave me alone as long as I don't kill the wrong person."

"That's about right."

"So," continued Chandler, "I think until I know my way around a little better, I might be well advised to confine my activities to the other moons and Hades."

"I can help you out," said Gin. "I know who to lay off of."

"Thanks for the offer, but I don't really want to stake my life on your expertise."

"Okay," said Gin with a shrug. "Have it your way. But you might as well forget about Hades. There can't be a thousand Men on the planet."

"That implies they're pretty important men," said Chandler. "Someone might want one of them dead."

"Forget it," said Gin with conviction. "Ever since the Oracle set up shop there, the place is a goddamned fortress."

"Who is the Oracle?" asked Chandler. "One of the Blue Devils?"

Gin shook his head. "They say she's a human woman. I don't know if it's true or not: almost nobody ever gets to see her."

"Why would a human woman want to live on Hades?" asked Chandler.

"Beats me."

"More to the point, if the Blue Devils hate us, why would they *let* her live there?"

"Who knows?" replied Gin. "I don't pay much attention to politics."

"Politics?"

"Well, maybe it's not politics. But whatever it is, it doesn't concern the three Ports, and if they leave us alone, that's good enough for me."

"It's interesting, though," said Chandler, "a woman living down there. Why do they call her the Oracle? Has she got a real name?"

"You got me," said Gin.

"Could you find out?"

"I dunno. I never thought much about it." Gin paused. "It wouldn't do you much good, though."

"Why not?"

"First, because you aren't allowed to land on Hades. Second, the Oracle and the Blue Devils leave us alone. And third, because every now and then someone shows up on one of the Ports and starts asking too many questions about her, and then one day he just isn't around anymore. So, since you like being alive and I like being employed, let's concentrate on the Surgeon's client list."

"Find out what you can, anyway."

"Why are you so interested in her?" asked Gin.

"I never met an Oracle before. Maybe she could tell me what numbers to bet on next time I play roulette."

"You can make a lot more money just doing what you do best, and you don't have to risk your life trying to meet her."

"Are you telling me that the Oracle kills people?"

"Whistler, I don't know anything for sure about the Oracle," said Gin in exasperation. "But I know the Blue Devils will kill you if you try to land on Hades without their permission."

"Sounds like the Democracy ought to move in," suggested Chandler.

"We keep waiting for them to, but so far they haven't shown any interest in it." He paused. "Now, can we let the subject drop?"

"You look nervous."

"People who talk about the Oracle have this habit of disappearing," answered Gin. "Me, I like it here."

Chandler shrugged. "What the hell, I was just curious. It's time to consider more important things."

"Such as?"

"Such as dinner. Give me a chance to change, and then I want you to take me to the best restaurant in town. We'll add it to Mr. Tripoli's bill."

"Have you heard from him?"

"I will," replied Chandler confidently. "He has work to be done, and I've already proven to him that I'm better at it than the Surgeon." He walked to the airlift. "I'll be back down in about twenty minutes."

He went to his room, took a quick Dryshower, shaved, and dressed in a semiformal dark gray outfit that had been specially tailored to hide the bulk of three handguns—one sonic, one laser, and one projectile. Then, feeling somewhat refreshed and quite hungry, he left his room, strode to the airlift, and floated gently down to the lobby.

"Well?" he said, walking up to Gin. "Where are we going?"

"*You're* going to the Green Diamond," said Gin. "I'm taking my budget and my wardrobe to a place that's more to my taste." He paused. "I can supply you with a companion, if you'd like."

"Some other time."

Gin shrugged and led the way to the landcar and drove through the early evening traffic.

"This looks familiar," remarked Chandler as they began entering a seedy-looking area. "Isn't this the Platinum Quarter?"

"Not bad for a guy who's only been here once," answered Gin.

"Are you sure we're going to the best restaurant in the city?" continued Chandler dubiously.

"It's a private club," said Gin. "Don't pay any attention to the exterior; they don't want people wandering in off the street."

"How am I going to get in if it's private?"

Gin smiled. "Word about this morning has gotten out. You won't have any trouble."

"You'd better be right," said Chandler. "I don't like making a fool of myself."

"Trust me," said Gin, pulling up to a dilapidated building. The windows were boarded up, the walls badly needed a coat of whitewash, and the door was one of the few on the block that didn't boast intricate carvings. "Well, here you are."

"You're kidding, right?" said Chandler.

"This is the Green Diamond, Whistler. Just walk up to the door."

"No password, no secret knock?"

"Look, if you don't want to eat here, just say so and I'll take you somewhere else."

"No," said Chandler. "We're here and I'm hungry."

He got out of the vehicle and walked up to the door, then turned to Gin. "Be back in two hours."

"Right," said Gin. "If you finish early, I'll be at the Wolfman's. It's about two blocks north of here."

The landcar pulled away, and Chandler turned back to the door. Now that he was closer he could see that there was a very intricate computer lock on it, and he spotted a pair of holo cameras concealed in the shadows.

He waited for almost thirty seconds, then was about to knock on the door when the lock clicked and the door slid silently into a wall. A short, dapper man, clad in green, was standing a few feet from him in a diamond-shaped foyer.

"Good evening, Mr. Chandler," he said smoothly. "Are you here for dinner or entertainment?"

"First one, then the other," replied Chandler, entering the building as the door slid shut behind him.

"Your table is ready for you," said the man, turning and walking toward a large, crowded room.

"Just a minute," said Chandler.

"Yes?" said the man, stopping instantly.

"How did you know I'd be here tonight?"

"I didn't."

"Then why is there a table for me?"

"Every diner has his own private table," explained the man. "This one belonged to your . . . ah . . ."—he searched awkwardly for the word—"*predecessor*. No one else may use it."

"I see," said Chandler. "And your name is . . . ?"

"Charles."

"All right, Charles. Lead the way."

"Thank you, sir," said Charles, starting off once again.

He led Chandler into a large room with a shining green floor and a prismatic ceiling that separated an artificial light from an unseen source into a variety of muted hues. The ceiling was twenty feet high, and domed at the top, but the room was divided into some forty diamond-shaped alcoves, each with walls ten feet in height. There were artificial green diamonds everywhere—on the walls, sunken into the floor, on the waiters' and waitresses' elegant uniforms—and in the center of the room was a large diamond-shaped fountain.

Charles led Chandler to an alcove, and suddenly the impression was one of intimacy rather than vastness. Chandler settled back on an expensively upholstered booth, and a moment later a waiter approached him and rattled off the evening's menu.

Chandler ordered a salad composed of vegetables grown on Port Samarkand and a mutated shellfish in a cream sauce.

"Very good, sir," said the waiter. "Would you care to start with a fine Alphard brandy? We just received a new shipment this morning."

"Later."

"As you wish, sir."

"By the way, is Mr. Tripoli here?"

"No, sir."

"If he should come in, please tell him I'm here."

"Yes, sir."

"And if anyone else is looking for me, let me know."

The waiter nodded and scurried off, leaving Chandler to admire that portion of the room he could see from his alcove. A string quartet, which had been on their break, came out, stood beside the fountain, and began playing soothing if not brilliant music, and a blonde waitress stopped by his table carrying an hors d'oeuvre tray. He looked at the various selections, chose one, and a moment later his salad arrived.

He stared idly at the plate for a moment, trying to identify the various alien vegetables—and then he saw it. Maybe it was the light, maybe it was the texture of the vegetables, maybe it was simply the angle, but suddenly he saw the artificial light reflecting off something bright.

He picked up a fork and dabbed at it gingerly, then lifted it very slowly and brought it closer to his eye.

It was a tiny fragment of glass.

He moved a greenish leaf with his fork, then found another piece, and yet another.

He sat perfectly still, staring at the plate while he tried to sort things out in his mind.

Somebody had known he would be in the Green Diamond on this precise evening. Even Gin hadn't known where they were going until he had come back from the police station. Of course, the driver had had time to tell someone while Chandler was showering and dressing, but he doubted it; if he survived, Gin had to know that he was going to have to answer some difficult questions, and he'd already seen Chandler in action.

That meant someone else knew—someone who didn't have to be told where he would be dining, who simply *knew*.

And that meant that the Oracle was indeed Penelope Bailey.

The next question was more difficult: why did his would-be murderer use ground glass, when a poison would never have been spotted? If the Oracle had foreseen that he would be here, then she must have foreseen that he would spot the fragments of glass. Was this just a warning—or was there some limit to her abilities? The Iceman had said that even as a little girl, with her powers not fully developed, she could foresee potential threats to herself; surely he was more of a threat alive than dead. So was he being manipulated, or had she simply proven to be fallible?

He didn't have enough information to answer the question, so he let it pass and moved on to the next one: somebody within the Green Diamond had tried to kill him. Who?

He stared at Charles, who was escorting an elderly couple to their table about forty feet away. It was a possibility. He looked for his waiter, but couldn't spot him. Another possibility. But somehow he didn't believe it: ground glass wouldn't kill him instantly, and his reputation had preceded him here. They would have to know he'd live long enough to take them both out before the glass ripped his insides enough to totally disable him.

Then who? He thought about it for another moment, then signaled to Charles.

"Yes, Mr. Chandler?" said Charles, approaching his table.

"I'd like to see your kitchen," he said.

"Certainly, Mr. Chandler. We're quite proud of our operation. If you'll come back tomorrow morning, I shall be happy to give you a tour."

"I'd like to see it right now."

"I'm afraid that's out of the question, Mr. Chandler," answered Charles. "This is our busiest time of the day."

"That wasn't a request, Charles," said Chandler.

Charles blinked at Chandler as his hand went meaningfully into a pocket.

"You're quite certain, Mr. Chandler?" he said, flustered.

"Quite."

"Might I ask why?"

"You might," answered Chandler. "But it wouldn't do you any good." He got to his feet. "Let's go."

"Please make no sudden or threatening movements," said Charles. "We don't wish to alarm our members."

"Follow your own advice and we won't have any problems," said Chandler.

Charles turned and headed off toward a short but broad corridor that led to the kitchen, then stopped before a door.

"Do you wish me to enter with you, Mr. Chandler?"

"No, that won't be necessary."

Charles turned and began walking away.

"And Charles?" Chandler called after him.

"Yes, Mr. Chandler?"

"Would I be correct in assuming that you plan to immediately summon either the police or a bouncer?"

"Absolutely not, Mr. Chandler."

"You're a lousy liar, Charles," said Chandler. "But there are two things you should know."

"Sir?"

"If you send a bouncer after me, I'll kill him. And if you call the police, I'll charge the Green Diamond with attempted murder."

"I beg your pardon?" said Charles, genuinely surprised.

"Someone put a little something extra in my salad, Charles," said Chandler. "If you don't want to call attention to yourself, just leave my plate where it is."

Charles stared at him for a long moment, then turned and walked back into the dining room.

As Chandler approached the door, it instantly slid back, revealing the interior of the kitchen to him. There were numerous stoves, grills, ranges, freezers, and refrigerators, and some six men and women and two Lodinites, all dressed in light green, were carefully tending the food, arranging it artistically on dishes or setting it carefully onto trays for the waiters who kept brushing past him. None of them paid him the least attention.

Then he saw what he expected to see.

A man and a Blue Devil entered from an alcove, each bearing half a dozen salads. The man noticed Chandler, stared curiously at him for an instant, then shrugged and continued walking toward a large counter.

The Blue Devil took one look at Chandler, dropped its tray to the floor, and ran back into the alcove.

Chandler raced across the kitchen, ignoring the yells and protests from the staff, and entered the alcove. The alien wasn't there, but a door was just snapping shut, and as Chandler headed toward it, it slid open again.

He found himself in a dank, dimly lit alley behind the building, and the Blue Devil was just disappearing around a corner. He immediately gave chase, and within a block had narrowed the gap between them from eighty yards to no more than forty.

Then the Blue Devil ducked around another corner. Chandler followed it, and suddenly found himself in a dead end, facing the wall of a large building with the Blue Devil nowhere in sight.

He came to a stop, withdrew his sonic pistol, and surveyed his surroundings. The alley led to a solid wall some twenty yards away, and there were no doors on any of the buildings. He looked up; there were no windows within reach. He walked along each wall; there were no alcoves where anything the size of a man or a Blue Devil could hide.

He walked back along the buildings that led to the dead end and stood there, trying to figure out where the Blue Devil could have hidden in the five seconds it had before he had turned the corner.

And then, as Port Samarkand moved overhead and cast its light down into the alley, he saw a manhole cover about ten feet away.

The Blue Devil couldn't have pulled it up and entered the

manhole in five seconds . . . but if he had been prepared for this eventuality, if he had left the manhole uncovered and programmed it to close as soon as he plunged into it, he would have just enough time to vanish before Chandler came into view.

Chandler frowned. What was it Gin had told him? Something about tunnels beneath the Platinum Quarter. He considered going to the Wolfman's and getting Gin to act as a guide, but there was no telling where the Blue Devil would be by then, or even that he would still be in the tunnels, and Chandler wanted answers more than he wanted a guide.

His decision made, Chandler removed the manhole cover and, pistol in hand, entered the winding, twisting world that lay beneath the Platinum Quarter.

7

Chandler found himself in a small circular chamber, with tunnels going off in three directions.

Now he ceased being the assassin and once again became the hunter of The Frenchman's World. The floor was damp, and he instantly saw that the water in a small puddle just in front of the left-hand tunnel was moving slightly, as if someone had walked through it within the last minute or so. Crouching slightly, ready to flatten himself against the wall in an instant, he carefully entered the tunnel.

Here and there he was able to detect signs in the millennia-old tunnels that showed him he was still on the right track, tiny disturbances that only the trained eye of a hunter could spot. He wanted to increase his pace so that the Blue Devil didn't get too far ahead of him, but the trail was difficult to follow, and there was no sense racing ahead if his prey had turned down one of the many branches.

After ten minutes he came to a larger chamber, and here he lost the Blue Devil's trail, for a number of men had passed through it even more recently, no more than two or three minutes ago, and had obliterated all sign of his quarry.

The chamber branched into four more tunnels, and as he was trying to determine which one to follow, he heard a slight shuffling sound off to his right. He backed into the tunnel from which he had entered the chamber, crouched down, and waited.

A moment later a small man, a laser rifle tucked under his arm, entered the chamber, looked around, and uttered a shrill whistle.

The whistle was answered from the depths of another corridor.

He whistled again, and again he was answered, this time from a new direction.

"I know you're here somewhere," he said.

Chandler remained still and silent.

"Come on," said the man. "The more we have to look for you, the harder it'll be on you when we find you."

A second man emerged from a tunnel.

"Any sign of him?" he asked.

"No," said the small man. "But he's close. I can feel it in my bones."

Two more trilling whistles reverberated through the tunnels, and in another moment four men, all armed, stood within the chamber.

"Come out now," called the small man, "and all it'll cost you is your money. You make us hunt for you, and it'll cost you a lot more."

Chandler heard yet another man coming down his corridor and quickly stepped into the chamber, moving a step to his left and keeping his back to a wall.

"Drop the pistol, pal," said the small man as all four of them became aware of his presence and turned to face him.

"When you do," answered Chandler.

The small man smiled. "There are four of us. What chance do you think you have?"

"There are five of you," Chandler corrected him. "I don't want to kill you. I just want some information."

"*He* doesn't want to kill *us*!" laughed one of the men.

"That's right," said Chandler. The footsteps stopped. "Come on in and join the party," he said.

"I think I'll wait here until it begins," answered an amused voice from the tunnel he had just left.

"I'm looking for a Blue Devil who entered the tunnels about ten minutes ago," said Chandler, his gun still trained on the small man. "Have you seen him?"

"*We* ask the questions down here, friend," said the small man. "This is our domain, and there's a fee for trespassing. How much money have you got with you?"

"I don't pay tributes," said Chandler. "But I *do* pay for information. I'll pay five thousand credits to whichever one of you will lead me to the Blue Devil."

"Five thousand credits," said the small man, his face lighting up. "That's a lot of money to be carrying around with you, friend."

"Too much," said one of his companions.

" 'Way too much," agreed another. "A man carries that much money, he's just begging to be robbed." He paused and leered. "I think we're going to have to teach you a little object lesson about carrying so much money around with you."

"You're making a mistake," said Chandler ominously.

The small man trained his laser rifle on Chandler. "We've talked enough, friend. Drop your pistol or I cook you right now."

The four men fanned out, and Chandler, with a shrug, dropped his sonic pistol to the floor, where it landed with a noisy clatter.

"Glad to see you've decided to use your brain, friend," said the small man. "Now, it just so happens that the toll for walking to the next exit is exactly five thousand credits—unless you happen to be carrying a lot more."

"And if I am?"

"Then we'd be very insulted that you thought you could buy us so cheaply."

"And when we get insulted, we get greedy," said one of the other men.

The small man grinned and nodded his head. "And nasty."

"So I hope you only have five thousand credits," said a third man, approaching him. "You wouldn't like us when we're nasty."

"I don't like you much right now," said Chandler.

"That's going to cost you another thousand, friend," said the small man. "Or if you haven't got it, we'll take it out in trade."

"Now just hold still," said the third man, stopping in front of Chandler and reaching for his tunic pocket. "Or this is going to hurt you a lot more than it hurts me."

"I doubt it," said Chandler. He flexed his wrist and the concealed projectile weapon slid into his hand. He fired point-blank into the man's chest, then used him as a shield while he sprayed the chamber with bullets.

Two seconds later he was the only man standing. Three of his antagonists lay absolutely still, and the small man was writhing in agony, clutching his belly in a futile effort to staunch the flow of blood.

"You in the tunnel," said Chandler. "Come out with your hands up."

He heard footsteps running away from him, quickly stepped to the entrance to the tunnel, and fired twice. The sounds of the explosion were deafening, but as they faded he was able to hear the weak, rasping moans of the man he had shot.

He quickly walked to the small man and appropriated his laser rifle.

"Help me!" hissed the man.

"The way you helped me?" asked Chandler caustically.

"I'm dying, damn it!"

"You're probably good for another hour or so," said Chandler. "Tell me where I can find the Blue Devil and I'll send help for you."

"You go to hell!"

"Warm up a seat for me," said Chandler, straightening up and heading off into the left-hand tunnel.

"Wait!" cried the small man weakly.

Chandler turned but did not approach him. "Is there something you want to tell me?"

"A Blue Devil entered the tunnels about five minutes ahead of you."

"Where can I find him?"

"Help me first!"

Chandler shook his head. "By the time I get you to a doctor, he'll be long gone. Tell me where he is, and if I get done with my business in time, I'll contact the nearest medics and tell them where to find you."

"They won't come down here."

"That's *your* problem. Mine is finding the Blue Devil."

"You'll never find him without me."

"I'll never find him if I waste any more time with you," said Chandler.

"I'll make a deal!" gasped the man. "Get me to a doctor and I'll help you find him."

"He'll be back on Hades before you can get to a hospital." Chandler turned toward the tunnel once more.

"You can't leave me here!"

"That's precisely what you were going to do to me," replied Chandler. "You might consider it poetic justice."

"Who *are* you?" demanded the man.

"I'm the man who killed you," answered Chandler, heading off into the tunnel. The man's protests and curses grew weaker and weaker, and finally vanished as Chandler turned a corner.

The tunnels were illuminated by a dim Eternalight every ten yards, and he soon saw a pattern to them: most of the lights were purple, but an orange one preceded a fork and a green one a chamber where two or more tunnels joined.

He continued going from one tunnel to another, borrowed laser rifle at the ready. From time to time he could hear the shuffling of feet in distant corridors, but by the time he approached them they were gone.

He realized that if the Blue Devil knew its way around the tunnels he was never going to catch up with it, and indeed it had probably already surfaced through some other manhole or exit. But Gin had never mentioned Blue Devils when describing the tunnels, and the man he had just killed hadn't referred to the Blue Devil by name, so there was a better-than-even chance that the Blue Devil he was chasing had no more business being in the tunnels than he himself did, and that in turn meant there was at least a possibility that it was even now undergoing the same treatment that he had been threatened with in that first chamber.

A green light told him he was approaching another chamber, and he slowed his pace, listening intently. When he was within ten feet of the entrance he could hear two people—a man and a woman—conversing in muffled tones.

He made his way to the chamber in utter silence. They both had their backs to him and were still speaking softly.

"They say it was the Whistler," the man was saying. "He killed the Surgeon earlier today."

"Why would he want to take over the tunnels?" asked the woman. "We're small change to a high roller like him."

"When you want to be a kingpin, you don't worry about large or small," answered the man knowingly. "You grab for it all."

"Well, if he comes down here, he's going to wish he'd stayed up top."

"He's *already* down here," said the man. "Who else could have killed Boris and the others? It's got to be the Whistler."

"Whistler or not, if he shows his face, I'll slice him."

"Freeze!" said Chandler softly, stepping into the chamber. "Not a word, not a movement."

Both of them tensed, but neither moved.

"Nobody's slicing anyone," continued Chandler, approaching them. "Turn around."

They turned to face him.

"You're the Whistler?" asked the man.

"Some people call me that," answered Chandler.

"You're not taking over the tunnels!" snarled the woman. "I don't care how good you are, you can't kill all of us!"

"I don't want to kill any of you," said Chandler. "I just want some information."

"Then why did you kill Boris and his men?" she demanded.

"They wouldn't give it to me."

"We don't turn on our own, Whistler," said the man defiantly. "You might as well shoot us right now."

"I don't want one of your own," replied Chandler. "I'm after a Blue Devil."

"We got no Blue Devils down here," said the woman. "Just Men."

"He doesn't work for you, at least I don't think so. He entered the tunnels a couple of minutes ahead of me." He paused. "I want him."

"What for?"

"That's none of your business, but it has nothing to do with the tunnels. I want no part of them."

"Why should we believe you?" she persisted.

"Because the only other reason I could have for being here is to kill you, and you're still alive," said Chandler.

The man and woman exchanged looks.

"If we take you to the Blue Devil, that's all you want?" said the man. "You'll take him up top and leave the tunnels to us?"

Chandler nodded. "That's all I want."

"And you won't ever come back down here again?"

"I can't promise that. But I won't come back down without a reason."

The man stared at him for a long moment, then nodded his head. "All right, you've got a deal."

"Lead the way," said Chandler.

"I've got to find out where your Blue Devil is first."

"Can you do it without leaving my sight?" asked Chandler.

"Yes."

As the two men conversed, the woman's hand had moved down to her belt and closed over the handle of a knife.

"Pull it out and you're going to spend the rest of your life with one arm," said Chandler ominously.

"Don't be stupid," snapped the man. "This is the Whistler you're facing!"

She glared at him for a moment, then relaxed and dropped her hand to her side.

The man looked around the chamber, picked up two small stones, then walked to one of the corridors and clicked them against a wall in an irregular pattern. The sounds were still echoing in the dank air as he walked to a second corridor and clicked them again. He then repeated the procedure at the entrance to the corridor from which Chandler had emerged.

"It's our own code," said the man, returning to the center of the chamber. "If your Blue Devil is anywhere in the tunnels, we'll know it in a minute or two."

"If you've called for help," said Chandler, "I want you to know that I have no intention of dying alone."

"If we all keep calm, nobody has to die at all," said the man. "You just make sure you take your Blue Devil up top and don't come back."

They fell silent again, waiting for a reply to the message. About ninety seconds later they heard a faint tapping, followed by a shrill whistle.

"All right," said the man, turning to Chandler. "We've got the Blue Devil."

"Let's go."

"It's not going to be that easy. They've figured out that you're the one who wants him." He paused. "They're willing to sell him to you."

"How much?" asked Chandler.

"It's negotiable."

"You're sure this is the one who entered just ahead of me?"

"It's the only Blue Devil that's entered the tunnels all night. They know what's likely to happen to them down here." He paused. "So are you willing to bid for him?"

"I'm willing to pay a reasonable price," said Chandler.

"And if we don't agree to your price?" asked the woman, still staring sullenly at him.

"Why don't we worry about that when the time comes?" suggested Chandler. He turned to the man. "Lead the way."

The man headed off into the right-hand corridor, and the woman stepped aside to let Chandler follow him.

"You go next," he said.

She glared at him, but fell into step behind her companion, and Chandler brought up the rear.

They went almost fifty yards, then took a hard left, bore left at another fork, and then began a gradual descent. When they were almost a quarter mile beneath the surface of the moon, they came to the largest chamber Chandler had yet seen.

The Blue Devil was tied to a post, and it was obvious that it had been badly beaten. Four men and two women stood near it, and another man, quite burly, with a neatly trimmed beard and clad in colorful satins, sat on a crudely constructed stone chair behind a makeshift granite desk at the far end of the chamber.

"Ah, Mr. Chandler!" said the seated man. "How nice of you to pay us a visit."

"He's not Chandler," said the man who had guided him there. "This is the Whistler."

"That is merely his professional name," replied the man at the desk. "He is Joshua Jeremiah Chandler and"—he smiled—"he has had a busy day."

Chandler stared at him, but made no reply.

"But where are my manners?" said the man, rising to his feet. "Allow me to introduce myself, Mr. Chandler. My name is Lord Lucifer."

"Interesting," said Chandler noncommittally.

"Accurate," was the reply. "Lucifer's domain is the Underworld of Earth, and mine is the underworld of Port Marrakech." He paused. "Would you prefer that I call you Chandler or Whistler?"

Chandler shrugged. "Whatever makes you happy."

"Excellent!" said Lord Lucifer with a smile. "I can tell that our negotiations are going to be cordial."

"How did you know who I was?"

"I asked Charles to point you out to me."

"Charles?"

"The headwaiter at the Green Diamond," answered Lord Lucifer. "When I heard that you had killed the Surgeon, I knew it was only a matter of time before you showed up at the Green Diamond; sooner or later, anyone who *is* anyone shows up there. And since I myself am a member, I merely tipped Charles to tell me when you had arrived." He paused. "When I saw you enter the kitchen, I became curious. And when you didn't return, I found out that you had left in pursuit of a Blue Devil. Had the two of you stayed on the surface, there was no way I could enter the equation—but on the chance that the Blue Devil had escaped to the tunnels, I passed the word to my people to capture but not kill it, on the assumption that it might be of considerable value to you if it was still alive." He smiled again. "And here you are."

Chandler looked at the Blue Devil. "Does it speak Terran?"

"If it was working on Port Marrakech, it would have to," answered Lord Lucifer.

"All right," said Chandler, turning back to Lord Lucifer. "How much?"

"Well, we must take into consideration that you murdered five of my operatives this evening," said Lord Lucifer. "And then there's the effort we went through to capture the Blue Devil, and there's my own time and overhead. And of course, both you and the Blue Devil can now identify me, so I shall have to take that into account, too."

"The price," said Chandler in bored tones.

"On the other hand, I like you, Mr. Chandler, I truly do. How many men would actually place themselves in my power and continue to look so calm and collected? Make me an offer, my friend."

"Five thousand credits."

Lord Lucifer shook his head sadly. "I couldn't possibly place such a small price on my fallen comrades. I really couldn't consider less than thirty thousand."

Chandler reached into a pocket and pulled out a wad of bills, then peeled five of them off and put the rest back. He then walked across the chamber and placed the bills on the desk.

"Five thousand credits," he repeated.

"You are either a very brave or very foolish man, Mr. Chandler," said Lord Lucifer.

"I'm on a budget."

Lord Lucifer threw back his head and laughed. "Excellent!" he said at last. "I think you and I are going to become great friends, Mr. Chandler." The smile vanished from his face. "You have the Blue Devil for five thousand credits, on one condition."

"What is it?"

"You asked if the Blue Devil could speak Terran," answered Lord Lucifer. "That implies that you wish to question it before killing it or giving it its freedom." He stared at Chandler. "My condition is simply this: I want to be present when you question it."

"Why?"

"You have done no harm to any Blue Devil since landing here, and I know that you haven't been to Hades. No Blue Devil on Port Marrakech is in our particular line of business, Mr. Chandler, so I would like to know why this one wants you dead."

"Still why?"

"Don't be obtuse, Mr. Chandler," said Lord Lucifer. "Murder is one of my organization's most lucrative enterprises. If the Blue Devils are thinking of going into competition with me on Port Marrakech, I want to know about it."

"I can assure you that they aren't," said Chandler.

"Doubtless you can," answered Lord Lucifer. "But I would prefer to hear for myself."

Chandler shook his head. "What it has to say doesn't concern you."

"Let me be perfectly clear, Mr. Chandler: my business interests start and end on Port Marrakech. If the Blue Devil had any other reason for attempting to kill you, it is of absolutely no interest to me. If you are afraid that I will act on such information as I may hear, let me assure you that I will not." He met Chandler's gaze. "I will order my people to leave the chamber, so that only you and I are here when you question the Blue Devil—but this is the only way I will accept five thousand credits as payment."

Chandler considered Lord Lucifer's statement for a moment, then nodded his assent.

"You heard us," Lord Lucifer said to the others. "Leave us alone until I send for you." He turned to Chandler. "If you should kill me, please believe me when I tell you, you will never live to see the surface again."

The five men and three women filed out of the chamber, and Chandler and Lord Lucifer walked over to the post where the Blue Devil was bound.

"Have you got a name?" asked Chandler.

The Blue Devil stared at him and did not answer.

"Its name is Boma," said Lord Lucifer.

"How do you know?"

"I wasn't in quite as much of a hurry as you were," replied Lord Lucifer with a smile. "I asked while I was in the kitchen." He paused. "It's been working at the Green Diamond for about two weeks."

"And I talked to the Iceman about two weeks ago," said Chandler. "She's good, I'll give her that."

"Who is the Iceman?" asked Lord Lucifer. "And what 'she' are you referring to?"

Chandler ignored his questions and faced the Blue Devil.

"When did she tell you to kill me, Boma—two weeks ago or today?"

Boma made no answer.

"Can you contact her from Port Marrakech?"

The Blue Devil remained silent.

"How do I get in touch with her, Boma?"

No answer.

"Just tell me how and you can walk out of here in one piece," said Chandler.

No answer.

"You're sure it speaks Terran?" Chandler asked Lord Lucifer.

"Absolutely."

"It understands what I'm asking it?"

"Yes."

"All right, Boma," said Chandler, withdrawing his laser pistol. "She can't help you now. Only *you* can. If I have to burn off one finger and one toe at a time, I can. Then we'll go to work on the joints. Sooner or later you're going to talk to me."

Boma looked into Chandler's eyes.

"Never," it said.

"See? You *can* speak when you want to," said Chandler. "Now, just tell me how to contact her and you can save yourself a lot of pain."

Boma stared at him and made no reply.

"Last chance, Boma," said Chandler, deactivating the safety mechanism and holding the muzzle of the laser pistol next to one of the Blue Devil's digits.

"You cannot win, Whistler," said Boma.

"You think not?"

"She is the Oracle."

The Blue Devil clenched its jaws together, hard, and instantly slumped over, held upright only by its bonds.

"Shit!" muttered Chandler, forcing the creature's mouth open. "One of its fangs is broken off. It probably had an old-fashioned suicide capsule in there." He straightened up, frowning.

"I should have guessed!" said Lord Lucifer, his face alive with dawning comprehension. "I *knew* Port Marrakech was too insignificant for you. You've come for *her*!"

"You know about her?"

"I know enough not to envy you, my friend."

Chandler stared at the corpse of the Blue Devil for a long moment, then looked up.

"What kind of hold does she have over a member of an alien race, that it would rather kill itself than tell me how to contact her?"

"That should tell you precisely what kind of hold she has, Mr. Chandler," said Lord Lucifer. "It preferred facing you in the flesh to displeasing her from a distance of some 300,000 miles. And it preferred death to relinquishing any information, no matter how trivial, that might aid you." He shrugged. "Well, nobody ever said Blue Devils were smart."

"I don't quite follow you."

"It could have told you anything you wanted to know," explained Lord Lucifer.

"Why?"

"I should have thought the answer would be obvious, Mr. Chandler," replied Lord Lucifer. "She can't be killed."

8

They were sitting in a small chamber whose leather furnishings and woven rugs were in total contrast to its stone walls and floor. Lord Lucifer held a large Sirian cigar between his fingers and was sipping a century-old Alphard brandy, while Chandler took a long swallow of his beer and then set his glass down on an exquisite table of Domarian hardwood.

"Understand, Mr. Chandler," said Lord Lucifer, "I'd help you if I could. I would very much enjoy working with a man of your abilities." He sighed. "I have no love for any human who has sold out to an alien race, and I would certainly like the opportunity to expand my operations to Hades itself, but there is simply no way you can succeed."

"You've never seen her," replied Chandler. "As far as I can tell, nobody on this world except me even knows what her abilities are. So why are you so afraid of her?"

"I know the power she wields," answered Lord Lucifer. "It is not necessary for me to know *how* she wields it."

"All right. Tell me about her power."

"The Democracy has never been stronger than it is right now, Mr. Chandler," said Lord Lucifer. "It is expanding in all directions, gobbling up worlds right and left. It was all set to assimilate Hades about fourteen years ago."

"Just a minute," interrupted Chandler. "I thought the Democracy had no interest in the Alpha Crepello system once the Ports were mined out."

"That's the official story. In point of fact, the Seventeenth Fleet was positioned to, shall we say, *pacify* the inhabitants of Hades. Then *she* showed up. I don't know what she did, but suddenly the Fleet retreated and Hades was an independent world again. I also know that the Democracy has sent in five or six of their top operatives, and none of them has ever been heard from again." He took another sip of his brandy. "I don't *have* to know what her abilities are, Mr. Chandler. I know that she can hold the Democracy at bay, and that's good enough for me. In fact, I'm surprised they were able to convince you to come here."

"They didn't," answered Chandler. "I'm working for a private party."

"This Iceman you mentioned?"

Chandler nodded.

"Well, whatever he's paying you, it isn't enough." He took a puff of his cigar. "What have you actually accomplished tonight? You were fortunate enough not to die at dinner, and you've killed one of her operatives. And my answer to that is: so what? There are two hundred million more Blue Devils where Boma came from."

"But only one Oracle," said Chandler. "I wonder if it's possible to lure her away from Hades?"

"How?"

"I don't know yet. Perhaps by killing more of her operatives?"

Lord Lucifer shook his head. "I'm sure they're all expendable. Why don't you just find some way to obliterate the whole damned planet and be done with it?"

"First, because contrary to what you may think, I'm not a genocidal maniac. And second, because my instructions are to kill her only if I can't bring her out."

"Bring her out?"

Chandler nodded. "She's a very valuable commodity. Nobody wants her dead—unless it looks like they can't have her any other way." He paused. "That's the real reason the Fleet backed off when she arrived. They didn't want to risk harming her."

"You've piqued my curiosity more in fourteen minutes than *she* has in fourteen years," said Lord Lucifer. "What is it about her that everyone wants? What powers does she have?"

"Just one: precognition."

"She sees the future?"

"As I understand it, she sees a number of futures, and by her actions she's able to bring about the one she wants."

"That's some talent!" said Lord Lucifer admiringly. "How do you approach someone who knows what you're going to do long before you yourself know?"

Chandler shrugged. "I suppose I've got to put her in a position where there are *no* viable futures."

"I don't see how you can do it from Port Marrakech."

"I know. They wouldn't give me permission to land on Hades, so I thought I might at least establish a valid reason for being here while I probed for weaknesses."

"So that's why you killed the Surgeon."

Chandler nodded. "If a killer comes to town, he'd better kill someone quick or people will wonder what he's doing here." He grimaced. "Obviously it didn't work." He paused, frowning. "At least, I don't think it did."

"You seem puzzled," noted Lord Lucifer.

"I am. If I fooled her, why did she try to kill me? And if she tried to kill me, why did she fail?"

"Ah!" said Lord Lucifer, his expression brightening. "So she *does* have her limitations! Obviously proximity has something to do with it. She could foresee that you eventually planned to kidnap or kill her, because that would involve your being in her presence—but she couldn't see what could happen here, some 300,000 miles away from Hades." He stared at Chandler. "You look unconvinced, Mr. Chandler. Why? It makes perfect sense to me."

"If she can't see what will happen on Port Marrakech, how did she even know I was here?"

"Perhaps in one of those futures in which you confront her, you tell her so, and she worked backward to try to kill you."

Chandler shook his head. "Boma was in place at the Green Diamond the day after I accepted the commission—and that took place a hell of a lot more than 300,000 miles from Hades."

"An interesting point," agreed Lord Lucifer.

They sat in silence, each sipping his drink, for a few moments.

"You're going to have to go to Hades, you know," said Lord Lucifer at last. "If she knows you're alive, she'll just keep making more attempts to kill you . . . and you'll never get her to come out to Port Marrakech."

"I know," said Chandler. "My immediate problem is getting there. Then I'll worry about approaching her."

"Oh, getting there is easy enough," answered Lord Lucifer expansively. "I'm not the Lord of the Underworld for nothing. But what you do once you get there—that's the problem."

"You know what I have to do."

"I'm not making myself clear. I can smuggle you down to Hades easily enough—there's a transport ship for Blue Devils every other day, and depending on how much money you can spread around, we can disguise you as a copilot or navigator, or at least hide you in the cargo hold—but if you have no official status, you'll be picked up the moment you show yourself." He shook his head. "No, let me think further on the matter. There's got to be a better way."

Chandler stared thoughtfully at his beer glass. "Why are you going to all this trouble for me?" he asked at last.

"First, because I like you," answered Lord Lucifer. "And second, because the sooner you leave, the sooner there is, shall we say, a power vacuum at the top of our profession here on Port Marrakech, one which I hope to fill myself."

"Are you a criminal kingpin, a killer, or what?"

"I am an opportunist," answered Lord Lucifer calmly. "The Surgeon's death and your departure present me with an opportunity."

"Whatever your reasons, I want to thank you for your help."

"My dear Mr. Chandler, I have every intention of letting you thank me in a substantial manner before you leave Port Marrakech for Hades."

"How much do you want, and when can I leave?"

"I don't know the answer to either question yet," admitted Lord Lucifer. He stared at Chandler. "Getting you there will be *my* problem. Staying alive until then will be *yours*." He paused. "There are a lot of Blue Devils on Port Marrakech. If she tried to kill you once, she'll very likely try again."

Chandler got to his feet. "I'd better be getting back. When you're ready, leave a message for me at the Wolfman's."

"Not the Green Diamond?"

Chandler shook his head and grinned wryly. "I've lost my faith in their cuisine."

"Poor Charles! I hope he doesn't take it personally." Lord Lucifer suddenly arose. "I'd better escort you back," he said. "It will keep you from getting lost, and it might also add to the longevity of some of my more aggressive subordinates."

Lord Lucifer led the way through the labyrinth of ascending tunnels. Eventually they passed through the chamber where Chandler had killed Boris and his companions; nothing remained but a few bloodstains.

"Here we are," said Lord Lucifer when they reached the small circular chamber beneath the manhole through which Chandler had entered. "Do you know your way from here?"

Chandler nodded. "Yes. My driver should be waiting for me at the Green Diamond."

"Maybe I'll walk over there with you," said Lord Lucifer suddenly. "I never did get around to having my dessert and coffee."

They emerged into the alleyway, then walked the two blocks to the restaurant.

"There's the landcar," said Chandler, gesturing at Gin's vehicle, which was parked near the door to the Green Diamond.

Gin saw Chandler approaching and got out to open the door for him. As Chandler reached the vehicle, Lord Lucifer's voice rang out.

"Chandler—watch out!"

Chandler hit the ground instantly, his projectile weapon already in his hand as he rolled over. Gin was slower in reacting, and screamed an instant later as a laser beam seared the flesh of his left shoulder.

Chandler fired at the source of the beam, and a body that had been hiding behind another vehicle fell heavily to the pavement.

"Thanks," said Chandler, getting to his feet and walking across to the corpse.

"Just dumb luck," answered Lord Lucifer, joining him. "If I'd been looking in any other direction, I'd never have seen the movement." He looked down at the body. It was a human male. "You've got more enemies than you thought, Mr. Chandler."

"You don't think he worked for the Oracle?" asked Chandler.

"If he did, he was the first human I've ever known her to use."

Chandler crouched down and began going through the body's pockets. "Let's find out," he said.

He withdrew an ID packet and frowned.

"You look troubled," commented Lord Lucifer.

"I am," said Chandler. He tossed the packet to Lord Lucifer "He worked for the Democracy."

"So?"

"It was the Democracy that hired the Iceman to bring her out I'm just the subcontractor."

"Then why did they try to kill you?"

"I don't know," answered Chandler. He frowned again. "Something's very wrong here."

PART 2

The
Injun's
Book

9

The dark-haired man hovered three feet above the floor, sprawled comfortably on his airbed, watching an adventure holo that was taking place about four feet away from him.

"Hey, Injun—you got company!" said one of his guards over the speaker system.

Suddenly the holoscreen deactivated, and the door to his cell slid open. A tall, well-dressed man with a shock of white hair walked in.

"So you're Jimmy Two Feathers," said the man, staring at him.

"If I'm not, you're gonna get a hell of a nasty letter from my lawyer in the morning," answered the Injun.

The man smiled. "They told me you had a sense of humor."

The Injun shrugged and waited for him to continue speaking.

"You've got quite a reputation, Jimmy."

"As a comedian?"

The man's smile vanished as he shook his head. "As a thief, an arsonist, an extortionist, a blackmailer, and a murderer."

The Injun shrugged. "I take it you disapprove of versatility?"

"No," said the man. "Just of you."

"You came all the way from Deluros VIII to tell me you disapprove of me?" said the Injun.

"What makes you think I'm from Deluros?"

"I can spot you government types a mile away," answered the Injun. "And you're too well dressed to be from around here."

"What else do you think you know about me?" asked the man.

"You act like you think your shit don't stink. That makes you Military." The Injun paused. "I know I was flying pretty high when they brought me in, but I'll be damned if I can remember killing an officer."

"You didn't."

"What a pity," said the Injun, lying back and relaxing.

"Aren't you interested in why I'm here?" asked the man.

"You'll tell me when you're ready to."

"I'm ready right now." The man paused. "How would you like to get out of here?"

"I suppose I could adjust to it."

"You didn't the last four times."

The Injun shrugged. "A series of misunderstandings."

The man smiled caustically. "You call twenty-seven dead men a series of misunderstandings?"

"Actually, I was performing a valuable social service. Most of them would have wound up in here; look at all the money I saved the government."

"You have no regrets at all, do you?"

"Well, I regret getting caught."

"You're a bright man, Jimmy," said the man. "Why *do* you keep getting caught?"

"You wouldn't be here if you hadn't read my record," answered the Injun. "You know why."

"You're a seed-chewer."

"When I'm on the seed, I feel like I can take on a whole regiment—so sometimes I try to." He grinned wryly. "Next time maybe I should settle for a platoon."

"You've been clean for two years now."

"Yeah, well, the prison chef doesn't serve alphanella seeds with the roast beef, more's the pity."

The man stared at him and shook his head sadly.

"You got a problem?" asked the Injun.

"You're the one with the problem," answered the man. "You're one of the most brilliant criminals of the past quarter century. You commit the insoluble murder or the perfect robbery, and then you start chewing the seed and tell everyone what you've done. I wish I knew what makes someone with your talents just piss his life away."

"Are you here to lecture me or offer me a deal?" asked the Injun in a bored voice.

"I'm here to offer you a deal," answered the man. "You may not like it, though."

"I'm sure I won't—but why don't you tell me about it, anyway, and then I'll tell you what I think of it."

The man nodded. "All right."

"By the way, have you got a name?"

"You may call me 32."

"Well, I was close," said the Injun.

"I beg your pardon?"

The Injun smiled. "You're Covert Operations. I thought you were Military."

"We frequently work in tandem," answered 32 calmly. "May I proceed?"

"Be my guest."

"What would you say if I told you that I have the authority to give you a full pardon, effective immediately?"

"I'd say that's damned generous of you, and let's get the hell out of here."

"There are strings, of course."

"Aren't there always?" said the Injun wryly.

"You would have to come to work for me."

"Why am I not surprised?"

"And you would have to submit to certain surgical alterations."

The Injun frowned. "Just what kind of freak do you plan to turn me into?"

"I assure you that this particular surgery will make no difference whatsoever to your physical appearance."

"Yeah? And just what are your assurances worth?"

"Your freedom."

The Injun stared at him for a moment, then sighed. "Okay, go on."

"The third planet of the Alpha Crepello system is home to a race of aliens known as the Lorhn, which are more commonly called Blue Devils. Over the centuries they have resisted all of our efforts to assimilate them into the Democracy." 32 paused for a moment, then began speaking in lower tones. "On Alpha Crepello III is a human woman named Penelope Bailey, a woman possessed of certain extraordinary talents. We have been trying to get her to return to the Democracy for almost sixteen years. Thus far all of our efforts have failed."

"What makes her so special?"

"She is gifted with the power of precognition," answered 32. "Do you understand what that means?"

"It means I'll never bet against her in a card game."

32 sighed deeply. "I don't think you understand the gravity of the situation. This is a woman who can foresee the outcome of various political and military actions, and our best information is that she has become a renegade, totally opposed to the goals of the Democracy. She is therefore potentially the most serious threat to the existence of the Democracy, and indeed the primacy of the human race, that has ever existed, and as such, her continued presence is unacceptable."

"How many men have you sent after her already?"

"What makes you think we've sent any?" asked 32.

The Injun smiled. "You don't recruit from the jails until your own killers have failed."

32 stared at him for a moment. "We've sent eight men in. We would have been just as happy to bring her out as to terminate her—but new orders have just come down, and that is no longer an option."

"What happened to your eight operatives?"

"Seven are dead."

"And the eighth?"

32 shrugged. "He's still there."

"But you've lost faith in him?"

"No. From everything I've heard about him, he's as good as they come."

"Then why are you giving up on him?"

"Because our policy has changed. As I said, the order came down yesterday that she is to be terminated. The man who is on the scene had orders to try to bring her out alive."

"He's already there. Why not just tell him that there's been a change in orders?"

"He's operating covertly in enemy territory," answered 32. "We don't want to jeopardize his position by attempting to make contact with him." He grimaced ruefully. "Furthermore, he's from the Inner Frontier and has no interest in or loyalty to the Democracy. He's basically a subcontractor whose sole loyalty is to his employer, and it is possible that his employer has reasons of his own for wanting to bring the Oracle out alive, reasons about which we know nothing."

"Then why not just blow his cover, if you think he might screw up the works?"

"If he can actually make contact with her where seven of my finest operatives have failed, I want to know how he managed it. Besides," continued 32, "there is no such thing as a cover when you are operating against someone who can see the future. There is no question in my mind that she knows he's there."

"I don't understand," said the Injun, frowning and running his hand through his unkempt black hair. "If she knows he's there, why hasn't she taken him out? And why are you concerned about contacting him?"

"She can see what *will* happen, but we don't think she can see what's happening *now*," answered 32. "In other words, she knows that he plans to abduct her at some point in the future, but she doesn't know where he is at this very minute."

"You're sure of that?" asked the Injun dubiously. "Maybe an hour ago she knew where he'd be right now."

32 sighed deeply. "We're not sure of anything. We know what her capabilities were when she was six years old, and from this our people have been able to extrapolate what they may have become . . ."

"Then you don't actually *know* a damned thing, do you?" said the Injun.

"No, we don't," admitted 32. "That's why I don't want to expose this man. Thus far it has been impossible to get any of my people close to her; perhaps if he distracts her, if her attention is divided between the two of you, if he seems the more immediate threat, you might have a chance."

"You want a suggestion?"

"I'd be grateful for any suggestions you might care to make," said 32.

"Sue for peace," said the Injun. "Based on what you told me, there's no way you're going to kill this woman. All you can do is make her mad at you."

"Then you are refusing my offer?"

"Who said anything about refusing your offer?" demanded the Injun.

"But—"

"I'd much rather die with a weapon in my hand than locked in a cell." He paused and stared sharply at 32. "Am I going to *have* a hand when you're all through with this surgery?"

"Certainly," answered 32. "I told you: you will look exactly as you do now."

"I know what you told me," said the Injun. "What you *didn't* tell me is what you're going to do."

"We are going to turn you into a walking holograph transmitter," said 32. "Your left eye will be removed and replaced with a prosthetic one. It will appear identical to the one we take from you, and it will be tied into your optic nerve center so that you will be able to see through it—but it will also transmit to me a three-dimensional image of everything you see. Also, a microscopic transmitter and receiver will be embedded inside your ear. Everything you hear will also be audible to me, and I in turn will be able to speak to you without anyone else being able to hear what I say."

"Where will *you* be all this time?"

32 shrugged. "That's undecided at present. If I can land on one of the uninhabited planets in the system, I will. Otherwise, I'll be on Philemon II, the nearest Democracy world, about four light-years removed. You'll be sending and receiving subspace signals; the transmissions will be virtually instantaneous within a range of ten light-years."

"You've selected me because you think I'm good enough to kill her," said the Injun. "So why do you have to monitor me?"

"I may be able to help."

"How? All you'll do is distract me."

"I spent more time with Penelope Bailey than any member of the Democracy except her parents."

"Yeah?" said the Injun. "How much time?"

"Almost six months."

"Sixteen years ago?" The Injun snorted contemptuously. "Forget the surgery and just let me get on with business."

"There is another reason for the surgery," said 32, unperturbed by the Injun's attitude.

"Oh?"

"You will be operating beyond the boundaries of the Democracy," continued 32. "Based on your prior behavior, there is every likelihood that, once there, you will take your ship and head straight for the Inner Frontier—or, if you remain in the Alpha

Crepello system, sooner or later you will be tempted to revert to your addiction."

"And you think being able to whisper platitudes about duty and honor in my ear will stop me?"

"No," said 32. "But I rather suspect that the miniature plasma bomb we plant at the base of your skull, which I can trigger from a distance of up to twenty light-years, will act as a deterrent." He paused. "Now, do we still have a deal?"

The Injun glared at him for a long moment, then nodded. "Yeah, we have a deal, you no-good bastard."

10

"Can you hear me?"

Jimmy Two Feathers grimaced and rolled onto his side.

"Jimmy, wake up. This is 32."

"32 what?" muttered the Injun.

"Wake up, Jimmy. You're coming out of the anesthetic now."

"I'm awake, goddammit! Now leave me alone."

"Sit up, Jimmy."

"Go away."

"I am away, Jimmy. I'm more than five thousand miles from you."

The Injun sat up groggily. "What are you talking about?"

"Open your eyes, Jimmy."

"Don't want to. My head is killing me."

"It will pass."

"It damned well better."

"Now open your eyes, Jimmy."

The Injun opened his eyes and winced as the light struck his pupils—both the real one and the artificial one.

"It's bright," he complained.

"That's just because your pupils are dilated. They'll adjust in a minute or two."

"The operation is finished?" asked the Injun.

"Yes. How do you feel now?"

"Like I've been on a week-long bender. Everything hurts. Especially my head."

"We did a lot of work on your head. Look around the room."

The Injun did as he was instructed, and found himself in a

large hospital room. A nurse, dressed in sterile white, sat in a corner, observing him intently. From the smarting in his left arm, he expected to find a number of tubes and wires tying him into a life support system, but evidently it had already been removed from the room. A number of small monitors were attached to his chest and neck, but they were more awkward than painful.

"Very good," said 32 approvingly. *"Now hold your hand up about six inches in front of your left eye."*

"Which hand?"

"Either one."

The Injun held a hand up.

"The lenses adjust almost instantaneously," noted 32. *"Now turn your head to the left and look out the window."*

"I'm not a puppet," said the Injun.

"Just do what I ask," said 32. *"I want to see how your vision adapts to a sudden change from a darkened room to sunlight."*

"Then what?"

"I don't understand."

"I don't plan to spend the rest of my life jumping through hoops for you," said the Injun.

"We've got to test out your new eye, Jimmy."

The Injun sighed and turned to gaze out the window.

"Excellent!"

"What next?" demanded the Injun in a surly voice.

"Nothing," answered 32. *"Everything appears to be functioning properly. I assume you have no difficulty hearing me?"*

"I wish I did."

"Your surgery doesn't seem to have improved your attitude," said 32 dryly.

"I don't like having a voice inside my head," said the Injun.

"That's not all you've got inside your head. Just remember that and we'll get along fine." The Injun made no reply, and 32 continued speaking. *"Now we've got some private business to discuss. Ask the nurse to leave."*

The Injun turned to the nurse. "He wants you to leave."

"In a moment," she said, walking over and checking the readings on the monitors. She nodded her satisfaction, then left the room without a word.

"You've got her well trained," commented the Injun.

"She was only there in case your implants were malfunctioning. It could be very disconcerting to wake up alone in a room minus

half your vision and with nobody to talk to."

"It's disconcerting just to hear you talking to me."

"You'll have to learn to put up with it, Jimmy." 32 paused. *"Do you see the nightstand to the left of your bed?"*

"Yes."

"Open the top drawer and pull out the envelope that's in it."

The Injun did as he was told.

"Now open it."

"All right. It's open."

"Now let's examine all the material carefully," continued 32. *"The holograph on the top is Penelope Bailey at age six."*

The Injun stared at the image of a thin, blonde little girl, with pale blue eyes. She looked drawn and tired, and most of the color was gone from her cheeks.

"The next holograph is a representation of the way we think she'll look today, barring extreme overweight or anorexia. We can only guess at the style and color of her hair, of course, but based on her bone structure, this is probably pretty accurate."

"You've wasted your artist's time," replied the Injun. "If she's as important as you think, I'm going to have to plow my way through a hell of a lot of people to get to her. I'll know her when I see her."

"Possibly so, possibly not. Even among primitive races, the substitution of an expendable subject for the ruler is not completely unknown. If you run into a woman with brown eyes, or the wrong cheekbones, this may help you."

"Then why the hell do I need a camera in my eye? Either you trust me to spot her or you don't."

"I think you have a chance of reaching her. A chance, not a certainty. I do not necessarily think that you have the skill or intelligence to terminate her without my help—or, quite possibly, even with it. Is that plain enough?"

"Thanks for your confidence."

"Let's be perfectly frank with one another, Jimmy. You accepted this assignment solely because it is the only way you were ever going to get out of your prison again, and you doubtlesss have every intention of reneging on your pact with me if the opportunity presents itself. I chose you because I have lost a number of excellent operatives; you are more adept at deceit and murder than any of them, and you are expendable. Do we understand one another?"

"One of us does," replied the Injun sullenly.

"Then let's get back to business. The next item is your identi-fication packet. We considered trying to change your retinagram and erase your fingerprints, but there was still the matter of your voiceprint, and if they found too many surgical changes, you'd be a marked man the instant you touched down. Therefore, you will retain your real identity, that of Jimmy Two Feathers, but we have changed every existing data base—including the master computer at Deluros VIII—to show that you are a naval offic-er who has been officially attached to our embassy on Alpha Crepello III."

"Just a minute," said the Injun. "There are a lot of people on both sides of the law who know my name and my face. What about them?"

"You will fly directly from here to your destination. The embas-sy staff has been informed that you are working on a highly confidential assignment, and they will be ordered not to question you about it or to discuss your presence among themselves."

"I could still run into a bounty hunter or a pusher on the street."

"I think that's highly unlikely, Jimmy. You've been out of circulation for two years; the average bounty hunter doesn't live that long. Still," he added, "that's one of the reasons for your surgery. If you spot anyone who might recognize you, we will take him off Hades if necessary."

"Hades?"

"That's the informal name for Alpha Crepello III."

"Sounds like my kind of place."

"I very much doubt it," said 32. *"To continue: the next item before you is a map of Hades. As you'll see, it's a relatively under-populated planet for a world that size. There are nineteen major metropolitan areas. The largest is the capital city of Quichancha, which I am certain I am mispronouncing. Next is a street map of Quichancha, with the location of our embassy highlighted."*

"The Oracle lives in Quichancha?" asked the Injun.

"We assume so, but we don't know for certain." 32 paused. *"The next three packets contain all the information we have on Port Marrakech, Port Samarkand, and Port Maracaibo, the three human-populated moons of Hades."*

"What do I need them for, if I'm landing on the planet?"

"We have safe houses on all three moons. Assuming that your mission is successful, you may need a place to hide if your route

back to the embassy is being watched."

The Injun ripped up the three packets.

"What are you doing?" demanded 32.

"Let's stop playing games," said the Injun.

"I don't understand you."

"If I'm good enough to kill the Oracle, I'm too goddamned dangerous for you to let me live. Every last one of those safe houses is going to be filled with people just waiting to blow me away."

"If I want to kill you, Jimmy, all I have to do is trigger the device we've inserted in your skull." 32 sighed. *"I'll have another set of packets on the three moons made up and delivered to you."* He paused. *"There's only one item left. Are you ready to continue?"*

"Yes."

"Then pick it up and study it."

The Injun held up a holograph of a tall, moderately handsome man with auburn hair and pale blue eyes, who appeared to be in his late thirties.

"Who is it?"

"His name is Joshua Jeremiah Chandler."

"Should that mean something to me?"

"You may have known him as the Whistler."

The Injun shook his head. "Nope." He stared at the holograph again. "What's he got to do with the Oracle?"

"He's our distraction." 32 paused. *"He is a top professional, possibly the best on the Inner Frontier. He's operating at a disadvantage: I had a feeling that the termination order would come through, so he, unlike you, was not provided with these maps—but that won't prove much of a hindrance to a man of his abilities. He's currently on Port Marrakech, but if anyone can make it to Hades in one piece, he's the man. If that should happen . . ."*

"You want me to work with him?"

"No."

The Injun frowned. "Then why the hell am I looking at his holograph?"

"We hope that he'll take the Oracle's attention away from you. After all, he's a covert agent who, according to my information, may already have killed one of her operatives on Port Marrakech, which means his presence is probably known to her. However,"

ontinued 32, *"as I mentioned before, his goal is different from
ours."*

"If the Oracle is half of what you think she is, there's no
vay he's going to bring her out," said the Injun with absolute
onviction.

*"I realize that the notion of kidnapping the Oracle seems ludi-
rous,"* admitted 32, *"but to be truthful, so does the thought of
illing her. If she has a weakness, I imagine one is as likely as
ie other."*

"So what are you trying to tell me?"

*"Simply this, Jimmy: we dealt with him in good faith, and I
on't wish to sacrifice him—but if at any point it seems that he
iight actually reach the Oracle before you do, you're going to
ave to kill him."*

11

It took the Injun five hours to clear Customs on Hades, which refused to honor the concept of diplomatic immunity. The Blue Devils questioned him over and over again—more than long enough for them to feed his fingerprints and the retinagram of his right eye through their computers, and their allies' computers, and those computers of their enemies to which they had access—and throughout the long interrogation, 32 kept feeding him the proper answers.

Finally he was allowed to leave, and found a driver from the embassy waiting for him.

"Lieutenant Two Feathers?"

"That's me," answered the Injun, declining to return the young driver's snappy salute.

"I'm here to take you to your quarters at the embassy."

"The sooner the better," grunted the Injun. He looked around. "Where the hell's my luggage?"

"It's still being examined, sir," said the driver. "Another member of the staff will retrieve it when it's been cleared."

"What do they think I'm smuggling, anyway?"

"Nothing, sir. It's just their way of emphasizing their independence from the Democracy." The driver paused. "By the way, I suppose I should introduce myself. I am Daniel Broussard, and am at your disposal for the duration of your stay on Hades."

"Jimmy Two Feathers," replied the Injun.

"That's a curious name, if I may be permitted to say so, sir."

"Cherokee."

"Cherokee? Is that a planet?"

"Not exactly," said the Injun. "Let's get the hell out of here. You can tell me your life story on the way."

"Follow me, sir," said Broussard.

"Just a minute, son," said the Injun.

"Sir?"

"My name is Jimmy. That's what people call me; that's what I respond to. You say 'sir' and my first inclination is to turn around and see who's standing behind me." He paused. "If you get tired of 'Jimmy,' you can call me Injun. I'll answer to either."

"Yes, sir," said Broussard.

"Kid's a real quick study," muttered the Injun under his breath. *"He is to be your liaison, Jimmy. Don't start by offending him."*

"He didn't hear me."

"I beg your pardon, sir . . . Jimmy?" said Broussard.

"Just talking to myself," answered the Injun. "I do it all the time these days. Don't pay me any attention."

"As you wish, sir." Broussard caught himself. "I'm sorry: as you wish, Jimmy."

"Okay. Lead the way."

The Injun followed Broussard through the small spaceport and out into the hot air of Hades, where a land vehicle was waiting for them.

"You're supposed to sit in back," said Broussard as the Injun opened the front door.

"I like it up front. Better view."

"Please, sir—I'll get in trouble if they see you riding up front."

"Who's the enemy, anyway?" muttered the Injun. "The embassy or the Blue Devils?"

"You know who the enemy is. There's no point in making more."

The Injun climbed into the back of the vehicle, and Broussard started driving through twisting streets that suddenly widened and narrowed for no discernible reason. The buildings bore no relation to each other, nor to any other structure the Injun had ever seen. No two looked remotely alike: some were tall, others were squat; some were round, some needle-shaped, some trapezoidal, some possessed so many sides and angles that he doubted there was a mathematical term that could properly describe them.

The street itself was as strange as the buildings. It began as a gleaming, super-hardened ceramic near the spaceport, became a pothole-filled rubble in the midst of what seemed to be a commercial section, constantly changed grades and inclines, and moved from ceramic to dirt to gravel to plastic and back again for no reason that he could discern.

"How the hell do you find your way around this madhouse?"

"It takes getting used to," answered Broussard, swerving to avoid a Blue Devil who was strolling aimlessly in the middle of the street. "I've been here almost two years, and I myself needed a guide for the first ten months or so. None of the buildings are numbered, and none of the streets are identified, not even in their native language." He paused. "Most alien cities have a Human Quarter that makes some sense by our own standards, but we have such a marginal presence here on Hades that our embassy is right in the middle of their financial district. If I were you, I wouldn't wander out alone until I was sure I could find my way back; once you're out of sight of the embassy, you could get lost for weeks."

"The city's not big enough to get that lost in."

"It's not the size but the structure, sir," said Broussard. "Many of these thoroughfares bear a striking resemblance to a mad city planner's notion of a Möbius strip; they keep turning in upon themselves, and though you're sure you've been walking in a direct line for a mile, you suddenly discover that you're right back where you started."

"Where's the embassy from here?" asked the Injun as they passed a building that seemed tall enough to act as a landmark.

"It's no more than half a mile away, though I'll have to cover about five more miles of these streets before we reach it." Broussard grinned. "Actually, you could walk to it much faster than I can drive to it." He paused. "You won't find it too disconcerting once you become acclimated."

"I'm not disconcerted."

"That's surprising," said Broussard. "Most newcomers are."

"You ever chew any seed, son?" asked the Injun.

"No, sir."

"You ought to try it sometime. Then *all* the streets look like this one." He leaned back and relaxed. "It's like coming home."

"You're kidding me, right, sir?" said Broussard, a worried frown on his youthful face.

"Jimmy!"

"Right, Daniel."

They rode in silence through fifty more right angles and obtuse angles and hairpin turns, and finally Broussard pulled into the driveway of the one building that seemed to make any sense.

"Here we are, sir," he announced.

"Doors, windows, everything," said the Injun, looking at the large embassy building. "I wonder how the Oracle likes where *she's* living?"

"Subtlety, Jimmy. Remember: they don't know why you're here."

"You ought to fire any of them who haven't guessed yet," replied the Injun.

"Fire who, sir?" asked Broussard, confused.

"Nothing," replied the Injun. "Let's go inside." He waited until Broussard had entered the building, then muttered: "You keep talking to me and they're going to change their minds and think I'm here for the Cure."

He walked into a large, elegant, tiled foyer. The walls bore portraits of the last three Secretaries of the Democracy including the current holder of the office, plus an artistic rendering of the sprawling, planet-wide city that Deluros VIII had become.

Three uniformed men stood guard before a trio of doors, looking neither right nor left. Broussard escorted him to a large office where a black woman dressed in a severely tailored outfit sat behind a polished chrome desk.

"Yes?" she said, not looking up at him.

"Lieutenant Jimmy Two Feathers, reporting for duty," he said.

"We've been expecting you, Lieutenant," she replied. "You are not on our duty roster, so you might wish to spend some time settling in and getting acquainted with the embassy and its staff."

"Is there anyone I'm supposed to report to?"

She glanced at a computer screen. "No. You are to make your reports to your superiors by your own means. The embassy is to feed and house you and provide you with a guide, and otherwise leave you strictly alone."

She dismissed him with a nod of her head, and Broussard led him out of the office and down a corridor to an airlift.

"Friendly sort, isn't she?" remarked the Injun sardonically.

"She doesn't have to be," answered Broussard as they floated gently up to the third level of the building. "She's Commander Ngoma, the embassy's Chief of Staff." They stepped out into a corridor. "Your quarters are this way, sir," said Broussard, heading off to his left. They passed four doors, then stopped before a fifth. "The computer lock is coded to your military ID number. Since I don't know what it is, I can't open the door for you."

"How does the room get cleaned?" asked the Injun curiously.

"There's a small household robot in each closet. Don't let its appearance startle you—it looks like a cross between a tree stump and a large snake."

"Thanks for warning me," said the Injun. He approached the door and stared at the lock.

"293Y78Q1," said the voice inside his ear.

He touched the appropriate numbers and letters, and the door receded into the paneling.

"Very nice," he said, walking forward. The room was quite long, and very smartly furnished. To his right was a bed with a nightstand, to his left a sitting area with two cushioned chairs and a sofa, and straight ahead of him, facing a window that overlooked the carefully manicured grounds, was a desk with a small computer.

"This is the door to your closet," said Broussard, "and this is the one to the bathroom. Each will slide away as you approach it, and the bathroom can be locked from within."

"Very nice indeed," repeated the Injun. "My most recent accommodation"—he smiled—"was somewhat more confining."

"Any changes or additions to your standing orders will be stored in your computer," continued Broussard. "It can be activated by your voiceprint and ID number."

"Okay, I'm impressed," said the Injun. "Now let's get something to eat."

"The commissary is in the basement, sir. I'll be happy to escort you there." He paused. "There's every likelihood that your luggage will arrive before we're through."

The Injun shook his head. "Aren't there any restaurants in the area?"

"Restaurants, sir?" repeated Broussard, surprised.

"Establishments where people who don't want to eat at home go for dinner," said the Injun sardonically. "Possibly you've heard of the concept?"

"*I* have, but the Blue Devils haven't, sir. To them, eating is a private and personal a function as, well, going to the bathroom is to us."

"You mean there's not a restaurant in the entire city?" demanded the Injun.

"Actually, there are three, sir," answered Broussard. "But they're all in the grubbiest section of the city, a section where the Blue Devils rarely go, and they cater to *all* offworlders, not just humans. I don't think you'd enjoy the experience very much, sir."

"Choose one of the three and let's go. The government will pay for it."

"That might be unwise, sir," said Broussard hesitantly. "We are not exactly the most popular race on the planet. There was an incident between a human and two Canphorites at one of the restaurants just last week . . ."

"I can't get the feel of the city by sitting here in the embassy."

"I'll be happy to drive you around and give you a thorough tour, sir."

"And I can't get it from the inside of a vehicle," continued the Injun. "You don't have to come along if you don't want to. Just tell me how to get to the nearest restaurant."

"I won't let you go alone, and I haven't the authority to prevent you," said Broussard with a sigh. "So I guess I'll have to accompany you, sir."

"Fine. Let's go."

They left the room, walked down the corridor, took the airlift back down to the foyer, and were soon outside in the incredibly hot air of Hades.

"Is it within walking distance?" asked the Injun. "I feel like getting a little exercise."

"Well, yes and no, sir," answered Broussard. "It's probably no more than four hundred yards away in a straight line. But we'll have to walk for almost a mile to reach it."

"A straight line could get mighty lonely on this planet," replied the Injun. "Lead the way."

"Let me suggest one last time that I drive you, sir. You're not used to the heat, and it can sap your strength before you know it."

"This is the best way I know *to* get used to it."

They walked past a large, many-sided building that possessed neither windows nor, apparently, doors, then turned a corner and almost walked through the window of a crafts shop. Seventeen triangles of various woods and metals were on display, and the Injun queried Broussard about them.

"They're not exactly religious symbols," was the answer. "I mean, they can't be equated with crosses. I suppose they're more of an emblem, the way you might display a flag or wear a military insignia. As near as we can tell, each substance and color denotes a different ethnic group, though I really don't know if the group represents a clan, a business, or even a military unit. But it's the most common symbol on Hades." Broussard looked up the street, which contained perhaps forty Blue Devils, some walking purposefully, some window-shopping, a few simply standing still for no discernible reason. "You'll see that about half of them have the triangles, sir. Some wear them as pendants, some attach them to their clothing, some simply tie them around an arm or a leg."

The Injun stared at the nearest of the Blue Devils, then shrugged and continued walking. A sickening odor wafted out to him and he peered into the interior of a building, where he saw the corpses of a number of small, six-legged animals hung on what appeared to be meat hooks.

"Slaughterhouse," explained Broussard. "The Blue Devils like their meat on the high side."

"Stupid place for a slaughterhouse. This looks like a retail area."

"Not really, sir," said Broussard. "They don't cluster their businesses the way humans do. In fact, if there's any order to the way the city was laid out, I've yet to figure it out."

"Are there any businesses or shops around here that are run by humans?"

"No," said Broussard. "The law doesn't forbid us to own a business on Hades, but as I said, we're not very popular here, and except for a medical center, no human enterprise has been able to obtain a license. The restaurants are owned by a Canphorite, a Lodinite, and a Mollut." He pointed to a spherical structure about one hundred yards away. "That's the medical center over there."

"It's too small for a hospital," noted the Injun.

"We have our own medical facilities at the embassy, of course, but this is for nonembassy personnel. There are currently less than one thousand Men on Hades; the center is more than capable of handling those problems that arise beyond the embassy compound."

"You sound like you've been there."

Broussard smiled. "Not as a patient, sir. But the young lady I'm seeing is a doctor there."

"I hope my presence isn't damaging your romance."

"This is my job, sir. If I wasn't with you, I'd be escorting someone else."

"Good. I hate feeling guilty."

They continued walking through the tortuously twisting streets, with Broussard pointing out an occasional landmark or point of interest to the Injun, and finally they arrived at the restaurant.

It was a small building, with an even smaller dining room. There were fifteen tables. Nine were empty, and the other six were occupied by a variety of beings, none of them human.

"As I told you, sir," said Broussard as they seated themselves at a table near the door, "very few humans leave their hotels to eat."

"No problem," answered the Injun. "I wanted to see the city."

They turned to the small holographic menu that hovered above the table and ordered it to list its contents in Terran.

"I wouldn't order the meat, sir," advised Broussard. "It translates as beef, but Hades has no trade agreements with the Democracy, and actually it's their local meat animal. Humans have some difficulty metabolizing it."

"You're not going to tell me that you've all become vegetarians?"

"No. The embassy imports all the food it needs from Port Samarkand—but these restaurants aren't owned by humans, and they don't especially cater to us, so I would consider their meat dishes suspect."

"Well, I appreciate your concern, but I've eaten animals on two dozen worlds, and nothing's ever upset my digestion yet." He stared at the menu again for a moment, then requested the dish he wanted. As soon as it registered, the menu vanished.

"I think you're making a mistake, sir," said Broussard with a worried frown.

The Injun shrugged. "I'll never know if I don't try."

"You're being foolish, Jimmy."

The Injun ignored the voice within his head and engaged Broussard in meaningless small talk, mostly about sports, until their meal arrived.

"Looks pretty awful," said the Injun, staring down at the blue-green piece of meat on his plate.

"We can order something else if you'd like."

"Nothing ventured, nothing gained," muttered the Injun. He took a small mouthful and chewed it thoughtfully. "Tastes about the way it looks."

Broussard turned to his own plate—a large salad—and the Injun took a few more small bites of his meat during the next few minutes, then announced that his experiment in alien cuisine was ended and that he would dine at the embassy for the duration of his stay on Hades.

"You can share some of my salad if you're still hungry," offered Broussard.

"No, thanks. That stuff killed my appetite." The Injun shrugged. "When all is said and done, that's just what a meal is supposed to do. I suppose I could get thin and healthy if I came here every night for a month."

He waited for Broussard to finish, left his thumbprint and ID number with the tiny computer that had generated the menu, waited another minute until the embassy accepted the bill, and then the two of them left the restaurant.

He began complaining about the meal the instant they were outside, and kept it up until they were within thirty yards of the medical center. Then, suddenly, he clutched his stomach, doubled over as if in agony, and began moaning in pain.

Broussard decided that he was too ill to wait for an embassy car and helped him stagger to the medical center.

As he sat, moaning hideously, on the steps outside the building while Broussard raced off to find a doctor, he listened to 32's scathing lecture on the stupidity of eating alien food and managed to fight back a grin of triumph. Then he closed his eyes and collapsed.

12

He felt them lift him onto a stretcher and carry him to an emergency room, then heard them leave in search of a doctor. He cracked open his right eye, looked around, and saw a very worried Broussard standing near him.

He sat up on the table, and as Broussard was about to say something, motioned him to silence. The young man stared at him curiously as he made writing motions in the air, finally nodded in comprehension, and handed him a pocket computer.

The Injun examined the voice-activated machine, then shook his head and made the same motions again. Broussard pulled a pen out of his pocket, found some paper on a nearby table, and handed both to the Injun.

DON'T SAY A WORD, wrote the Injun. AND LOCK THE DOOR.

Broussard read the message, frowned, and did as he was instructed.

NOW FIND SOME COTTON AND SOME ADHESIVE, AND TAPE MY LEFT EYE SHUT.

Broussard searched through a pair of drawers, came up with what was required, and taped the eye closed.

UNDER NO CIRCUMSTANCES ARE YOU TO SPEAK UNTIL I GIVE YOU PERMISSION. IS THAT UNDERSTOOD?

Broussard read the message and nodded, still frowning, then took the paper from the Injun and wrote: WHAT'S GOING ON? WHY CAN'T I SPEAK? WHAT'S WRONG WITH YOUR EYE?

I AM HERE ON A VERY SENSITIVE ASSIGNMENT,

responded the Injun. I AM NOT AT LIBERTY TO TELL YOU THE DETAILS, BUT IT CONCERNS THE ORACLE.

A doctor began pounding on the locked door.

TELL HIM TO WAIT, wrote the Injun. MAKE UP ANY STORY THAT WILL WORK.

Broussard nodded, walked to the door, unlocked it, and stepped out into the hall. He returned a moment later.

ALL RIGHT, he wrote. NOW SUPPOSE YOU TELL ME WHAT'S GOING ON.

The Injun took the pen back. DURING MY ORIENTATION AND BRIEFING PERIOD, WHILE PREPARING FOR THIS ASSIGNMENT, I LOST A DAY SOMEWHERE. I WENT TO BED ONE NIGHT AND WOKE UP IN MY HOTEL ROOM 32 HOURS LATER. BITS AND PIECES OF INFORMATION THAT I'VE BEEN ABLE TO PIECE TOGETHER LEAD ME TO BELIEVE THAT I HAVE BEEN TAMPERED WITH.

IN WHAT WAY? asked Broussard.

I SUSPECT THAT I HAVE HAD A CAMERA AND AN AUDIO TRANSMITTER IMPLANTED INSIDE MY HEAD.

WHY DIDN'T YOU REPORT THIS TO YOUR SUPERIORS AT THE TIME?

BECAUSE I DON'T KNOW WHICH OF THEM IS IN THE EMPLOY OF THE ORACLE. IF I TOLD THE WRONG ONE, I WOULD HAVE BEEN TERMINATED INSTANTLY. I MADE UP MY MIND NOT TO DO ANYTHING ABOUT IT UNTIL I REACHED HADES.

Broussard stared at him for a long moment. WHAT IF YOU'RE WRONG?

IF I'M WRONG, YOU'VE BEEN INCONVENIENCED FOR TEN MINUTES AND I'VE MADE A FOOL OF MYSELF, BUT NO HARM HAS BEEN DONE AND NO FALSE ACCUSATIONS HAVE BEEN MADE. BUT IF I'M RIGHT, THEN OUR COVERT OPERATIONS BRANCH HAS A TRAITOR IN ITS MIDST.

WHY WOULD THEY RIG YOU WITH A CAMERA AND AN AUDIO RECEIVER? asked Broussard.

The Injun shrugged. ANY NUMBER OF REASONS. THE ORACLE COULD BE TESTING HER SECURITY, SHE COULD BE CREATING A FILE ON ALL THE HUMANS ON HADES, SHE COULD MERELY BE HOPING THAT I'LL HAVE ACCESS TO SECRET INFORMATION.

SO WHAT DO WE DO NOW? asked Broussard.

NOW WE GET SOMEONE YOU CAN *TRUST*—MAYBE YOUR LADY FRIEND WHO WORKS HERE—AND WE REMOVE WHATEVER'S BEEN IMPLANTED WHILE WHO-EVER'S AT THE OTHER END STILL THINKS I'M BEING TREATED FOR A BELLYACHE.

Broussard looked thoughtful. SHE'S NOT THE DOCTOR I JUST SPOKE TO, BUT I KNOW SHE'S ON DUTY. He paused. BUT I'D HAVE TO TELL HER WHAT'S GOING ON.

CAN YOU TRUST HER TO KEEP QUIET?

Broussard nodded.

OKAY—GET HER. AND TELL HER SHE'S GOT TO WORK FAST. IT CAN'T TAKE THAT LONG TO PUMP OUT A STOMACH FULL OF BAD FOOD.

Broussard smiled and took the pen back. I'LL HAVE HER MAKE A COUPLE OF STATEMENTS ABOUT SEDATING YOU. THAT SHOULD BUY US A GOOD EIGHT TO TEN HOURS.

The young man turned to leave, but the Injun grabbed him by the arm.

ONE LAST THING, he wrote. I'M ASSUMING A CAM-ERA AND A RECEIVER, BUT THERE COULD BE MORE THINGS IN THERE. TELL HER TO REMOVE ANYTHING SHE FINDS.

Broussard nodded again, then walked to the door and left the emergency room. He was back some ten minutes later with a pretty but grim-faced young woman in tow. She immediately took a pen out of her pocket and wrote a message on a notepad.

I AM DR. JILL HUXLEY. DANIEL HAS EXPLAINED YOUR SITUATION TO ME AND HAS VOUCHED FOR YOUR CREDENTIALS.

THEN LET'S GET ON WITH IT, wrote the Injun.

"You've been a very foolish man, Mr. Two Feathers," she said aloud. "Daniel warned you against eating alien food."

He managed a groan.

"It's nothing life-threatening," she continued while writing on her notepad. "And I've got a couple of patients who are in immediate need of my services. I'm going to sedate you now, and I'll get around to emptying your stomach as soon as I get a chance."

She tore off a sheet and handed it to him.

I WILL HAVE TO MOVE YOU TO AN OPERATING THEATER, it read. AND SINCE THIS IS TO BE DONE IN ABSOLUTE SECRECY, I WILL HAVE TO ASK DANIEL TO ASSIST ME.

Broussard read the message over her shoulder and suddenly looked somewhat ill.

HOW LONG WILL IT TAKE? asked the Injun.

IF YOU HAVE BEEN TAMPERED WITH, IT WILL TAKE ME ABOUT AN HOUR TO RUN A SCAN ON YOUR HEAD AND HAVE THE COMPUTER CONSTRUCT A HOLOGRAPH-IC ANALOG. THE ACTUAL SURGERY WILL LAST ANY-WHERE FROM ONE TO FOUR HOURS, DEPENDING ON HOW DEEPLY EMBEDDED THE DEVICES ARE. IF YOU'RE READY, NOD YOUR HEAD AND I'LL SEND FOR SOME ATTENDANTS TO MOVE YOU.

The Injun nodded, then lay back and waited.

Two husky young men arrived a moment later, transferred him to an operating room, and then departed. Broussard had remained with him, and Jill Huxley arrived almost ten minutes later.

WHAT WAS THE DELAY? asked the Injun.

She held up a pair of treated contact lenses, then placed them in a pocket.

IF YOU'VE GOT A CAMERA IN THERE, IT WON'T STOP FUNCTIONING JUST BECAUSE YOU'RE UNCONSCIOUS. I REALIZE THAT YOUR EYES WILL BE CLOSED INITIALLY, BUT IF I HAVE TO REMOVE THE CAMERA, IT WILL RE-CORD WHAT IS HAPPENING ONCE I OPEN THE EYE THAT CONTAINS IT. ONCE I DETERMINE THAT A CAMERA INDEED EXISTS, I'LL INSERT THE LENSES IN MY EYES, DARKEN THE ROOM, AND OPERATE IN INFRARED LIGHT ONLY.

GOOD THINKING, wrote the Injun. I NEVER CONSIDERED THAT.

THERE'S NO NEED TO ANESTHETIZE YOU UNTIL WE DETERMINE THAT SURGERY IS INDICATED, she continued. THE SCANNING PROCESS ITSELF IS QUITE PAINLESS.

He nodded his agreement, and a moment later she had wheeled him under a large device that looked like a cross between a punch press and an oversized camera.

IT IS ESSENTIAL THAT YOU HOLD STILL FOR THE

NEXT TWENTY SECONDS, she wrote.

He made no reply, but simply handed the notepad back to her and stared up at the machine. It began whirring softly, and deep within its lens a small reddish light glowed faintly. He felt neither discomfort nor pain, and finally the whirring stopped, the light went out, and Broussard wheeled him away.

Jill Huxley gestured him to join her at a bank of computers along the far wall. One by one each screen came to life, displaying readouts that were totally meaningless to him, but finally one of them produced a three-dimensional rendering of his head, with three blinking yellow dots—one in his left eye, one deep inside his right ear, and one at the base of his skull.

HAVE YOU ANY IDEA WHAT THIS ONE MIGHT BE? she asked, pointing to the third dot.

He shrugged. WHATEVER IT IS, IT DOESN'T BELONG THERE. TAKE IT OUT.

She ignored him for the next half hour, creating cross sections of his head on her various machines, checking and cross-checking the best routes to reach the artificial implants.

Finally she picked up the notepad and began writing again.

I CAN REMOVE TWO OF THE DEVICES, BUT THERE MAY BE A PROBLEM WITH THE ONE IN YOUR EYE. IT'S TIED INTO THE OPTIC NERVES SO INTRICATELY THAT I MIGHT CAUSE IRREPARABLE DAMAGE IF I REMOVED IT.

REMOVE IT AND GIVE ME A PROSTHETIC EYE, he answered.

She shook her head. ONCE THE OPTIC NERVES ARE DAMAGED, IT REQUIRES A SPECIALIST TO IMPLANT A FUNCTIONING PROSTHETIC EYE, AND PROSTHESES ARE NOT MY FIELD. She paused and stared at him, then wrote: YOU HAVE A DECISION TO MAKE, MR. TWO FEATHERS. I CAN LEAVE THE CAMERA IN, OR YOU CAN AWAKEN WITH VISION IN ONLY YOUR RIGHT EYE. THERE'S NO THIRD OPTION.

The Injun lowered his head in thought. He didn't especially give a damn whether 32 could see what he was doing or not; his prime concern was to get rid of the explosive device, and secondarily to find a way to silence the voice within his head. But he had sold these two a story, and his answer would have to comply with it if he wanted to retain his vision.

Finally he bent over the notepad and began writing.

YOU'D BETTER LEAVE IT IN. THERE'S NO WAY I CAN REPLACE THE EYE ON HADES, AND MY MISSION MAY PLACE ME IN HAZARDOUS SITUATIONS WHERE DEPTH PERCEPTION IS ESSENTIAL. WHOEVER IMPLANTED IT HAS ALREADY SEEN DANIEL'S FACE AND KNOWS WHAT MY QUARTERS LOOK LIKE. IF I MAKE SURE THAT I SPEND A MINIMAL AMOUNT OF TIME AT THE EMBASSY, I PROBABLY WON'T BE REVEALING ANYTHING THAT THE TRAITOR DOESN'T ALREADY KNOW.

BUT YOU WILL STILL BE TRANSMITTING EVERYTHING YOU SEE TO THE ORACLE, wrote Jill. WON'T THAT TOTALLY NEUTRALIZE YOU?

I'LL WEAR AN EYEPATCH, he wrote, smiling as the thought came to him. I'LL REMOVE IT ONLY IF AND WHEN I REQUIRE THE USE OF BOTH EYES.

ALL RIGHT, she replied. PERHAPS IT'S JUST AS WELL; I WAS UNCOMFORTABLE ABOUT OPERATING IN INFRARED LIGHT. I'LL PREPARE THE ANESTHETIC.

ONE MORE THING, he wrote, grabbing the notepad back from her. IT OCCURS TO ME THAT THE DEVICE AT THE BASE OF MY SKULL MAY HAVE BEEN PLACED THERE AS A MEANS OF CONTROLLING OR DESTROYING ME IF I GET TOO CLOSE TO THE ORACLE. HAVE YOU ANYTHING THAT CAN ANALYZE IT?

I DOUBT IT.

THEN TO BE ON THE SAFE SIDE, GET RID OF IT AS QUICKLY AS POSSIBLE.

SHOULD I GET RID OF THE RECEIVER, TOO? she asked.

NO, he replied. IT'S HARMLESS ONCE IT'S BEEN REMOVED, AND IT MIGHT TELL ME SOMETHING ABOUT THE NATURE—AND EVEN THE IDENTITY—OF THE ENEMY. SAVE IT FOR ME.

She nodded. REMOVE YOUR TUNIC, AND THEN LIE BACK ON THE TABLE. I'M GOING TO INJECT YOU WITH AN ANESTHETIC, WHICH WILL WORK ALMOST INSTANTANEOUSLY.

ONE LAST THING. THAT ALIEN MEAT REALLY *IS* MAKING ME SICK. CAN YOU PUMP MY STOMACH OUT WHILE I'M UNCONSCIOUS?

YES, she wrote. THAT'S PRETTY TERRIBLE STUFF. I'M SURPRISED YOU'RE NOT IN EVEN MORE DISCOMFORT.

He removed his tunic, tossed it to Broussard, who was standing around looking both uncomfortable and useless, and then he lay down on the table.

Suddenly he sat up and gestured for the notepad again.

DON'T SPEAK ONCE YOU'VE REMOVED THE AUDIO TRANSMITTER. THERE'S EVERY POSSIBILITY THAT IT WILL STILL BE FUNCTIONAL.

I'M WELL AWARE OF THAT, she replied.

Then, aloud, she said, "Well, as long as he's sedated, there's no sense bringing him out of it. Let's go to work, and when he wakes up with the granddaddy of all stomachaches, maybe it'll encourage him to be a little more intelligent about his choice of food next time he visits an alien restaurant."

"Sounds good to me, Doctor," replied Broussard, disguising his voice.

Then she leaned over and injected something into the Injun's left arm, and he tried mentally counting backward from 100.

He was unconscious before he hit 98.

13

A voice disturbed the darkness that enveloped him.

"How do you feel?"

The Injun moaned and tried to turn away, then winced as his right ear touched his pillow.

"Wake up, Lieutenant Two Feathers."

"Go away."

"The surgery's over, Lieutenant," said Broussard. "It's time to get up now."

"What time *is* it?"

"Almost morning."

"All right. Give me a minute to clear my head." He lay motionless, trying to remember all the events of the previous evening until they finally came into focus. "How did it go?"

"About as anticipated," answered Broussard. "She removed the transmitter and the explosive, and left the camera in." He paused. "She woke you and checked you out briefly right afterward, then had me move you here for a few more hours."

The Injun sat up abruptly, then moaned and held his head.

"No sudden movements for another day," said Broussard, who was sitting in a chair by the foot of the bed.

"Jesus! It feels like someone's inside my head, hammering to get out."

"Jill said you'd have quite a headache when you woke up."

"Was the thing at the base of my skull a bomb?" asked the Injun.

"Yes."

"Where is it?"

"We dissolved it in acid."

"*Can* you dissolve a bomb in acid?" asked the Injun dubiously.

"You can when it's an organic device, like a plasma bomb," answered Broussard. "The trick was getting it out without triggering it." He smiled. "That's why you've got a headache."

"What about the transmitter?"

"It's in the next room," said Broussard. "I didn't think you'd want it around until we had talked. I can destroy it if you like."

"Not yet," said the Injun. He paused. "Am I on any medication?"

"She loaded you up with antibiotics and glucose before she brought you in here, and you'll be on pain medication for a couple of days."

"Things look different," said the Injun, frowning.

"I took the liberty of putting an eyepatch on you," answered Broussard. "You can remove it whenever you want, but until I knew what you planned to do, it seemed best not to let the person at the other end of the camera know that you were awake and in a hospital room."

"Good thinking," said the Injun approvingly.

"Do you think you're up to some breakfast?"

"Yeah, I could do with some in a few minutes," answered the Injun. "Except for four or five bites of that alien meat, I haven't had anything to eat since I arrived at the embassy yesterday afternoon."

"Speaking of the embassy, I'm going to have to report in to them in the next few minutes, before they start sending out search parties." Broussard paused. "I called them right after we wheeled you out of surgery and gave them some cock-and-bull story about your having a liaison with a girl you had met—but they're going to start getting nervous before long."

"How soon can I get on my feet?"

"Whenever you want."

"Okay," said the Injun. "Give me another hour and then take me back to the embassy."

"I don't think you can walk that far in your current condition, sir," said Broussard. "Perhaps I'd better get the landcar and come back for you."

The Injun nodded, then winced as a bolt of pain shot through his skull.

"Damn!" he said. "How long is this going to keep up?"

"What, sir?"

"Every time I move my head it feels like someone's hitting it with a blunt instrument."

"I really couldn't say, sir. I only know that Jill said there would be some discomfort for a day or two."

"Discomfort to a doctor is the torture of the damned to his patients. Get me the painkiller."

Broussard reached into his pocket and withdrew a small inhaler. "Take one breath of this every four hours."

The Injun grabbed it from him, inserted it into a nostril, and took two deep sniffs. "I haven't got time for a slow recovery."

"Is there anything else I can do for you before I leave for the landcar, sir?"

"Two things. First, where are my clothes?"

Broussard walked to a closet and ordered the door to open. "Right here, sir. And the second thing?"

"Bring me the transmitter—and don't make a sound while you're doing it. Then get the vehicle and pick me up in an hour."

Broussard left the room and returned a moment later with an incredibly miniaturized device, which rested on a soft sponge. He handed it to the Injun, saluted, and left the room.

The Injun waited until the door slid shut, then inserted the device into his left ear.

"Good morning, you son of a bitch," he said.

"How's your stomach feeling today, Jimmy?" asked 32, his voice sounding distant and tinny.

"Never better."

"I trust you've learned your lesson."

"You wouldn't believe all the things I've learned," said the Injun.

There was a long silence.

"Aren't you going to ask?" said the Injun at last.

"Ask what?" replied 32.

"Why you can't see anything?"

"I assume you've got your eyes closed."

"One of 'em, anyway."

"This is a very juvenile display of petulance, Jimmy," said 32. *"I'm here to help you, and I can't do that if I can't see what you're seeing."*

"Actually, *I'm* here to help *you*," replied the Injun. "And I think the first thing I'm going to help you do is renegotiate my contract."

"What are you getting at, Jimmy?"

"We're about to change the ground rules," said the Injun. "How badly do you want the Oracle?"

"Very badly. You know that."

"How much are you willing to pay?"

"We've already got a deal, Jimmy," said 32. *"Your freedom in exchange for the Oracle."*

"My freedom was just the down payment," said the Injun, leaning back carefully against a pillow and wincing again. "Now we're going to start talking money."

"Forget it, Jimmy. I'm not going to let you or anyone else take advantage of the Democracy."

"Who's taking advantage?" said the Injun. "I want an honest day's pay for an honest day's work."

"You've never done an honest day's work in your life," answered 32. *"We have an agreement, and you're going to stick to it."*

"No, I'm afraid not."

"Let me remind you that I possess the ability to terminate our agreement rather forcefully whenever I choose."

"You're welcome to try."

"Why are you talking like this?" demanded 32. *"What's come over you, Jimmy?"*

"Nothing's come over me," answered the Injun. "But a lot has come *out* of me. Want to see?"

He withdrew the transmitter, then faced a wall so that 32 couldn't pinpoint his location from the view out the window, removed his eyepatch with his free hand, and stared at the tiny object.

"Look familiar?" he asked.

There was no response, and he realized that even if 32 was speaking, he couldn't hear it until he reinserted the transmitter into his ear. He covered his eye once again and then carefully put the transmitter back in place. 32 was just coming to the end of a long string of obscenities.

"I'd show you the bomb, too, but it's already been destroyed." The Injun grinned again. "Are you ready to talk price?"

"That's extortion, and I don't deal with extortionists."

"No, you just wire them for sight, sound, and extermination."

"You go after the Oracle on our original terms or you're a dead man, Jimmy."

"I can't tell you how frightened that makes me feel."

"I'm not kidding, Jimmy. You may be able to hide for an hour or a day or possibly even a week, but I promise you'll never get off that planet."

"Maybe I don't want to."

"What are you talking about?"

"The reason we're going to negotiate a price, no matter how loudly you protest," said the Injun, "is because you're not the only game in town."

"Who else is there?"

"I figure there are at least two other players," answered the Injun. "First of all, there's the guy who's coming to take her out."

"You don't even know who he is."

"You've already told me the name he uses, and if he makes it here, he won't be that hard to spot." He paused. "Once he learns that the Democracy wants him dead, I figure he ought to be more than happy to pay me to learn the identity of the man who double-crossed him."

"Who's the other party?"

"I would have thought that would be obvious," replied the Injun. "There's the Oracle."

"You'd sell your own race out? I don't believe it!"

"I've got nothing against her," answered the Injun. "She's never done me any harm—which is more than I can say for some members of my own race."

"This is more than extortion!" snapped 32 furiously. *"It's treason!"*

"No," said the Injun. "It's business." He paused. "Now, I can transact it with you, or I can transact it with someone else. That's the only decision you've got to make—and you've got exactly five minutes in which to make it. If we reach an agreement in that time, I'll return to the embassy and go to work for you. If not, I guarantee you won't find me before I find the Whistler and the Oracle."

32 made no reply, and the Injun started counting down the seconds in his mind.

"Four minutes," he announced.

Still there was no reply.

"Three minutes."

"How much do you want?" asked 32 in strained tones.

"I'm a reasonable man," said the Injun. "You keep telling me that the Oracle is probably the greatest potential threat the Democracy has ever faced. I don't think ten million credits is out of line."

"Ten million? You're crazy!"

"Come on," said the Injun easily. "You spend billions of credits waging wars against races that are no threat to you at all. I would think you'd jump at the chance to be rid of the Oracle for only ten million."

There was a lengthy pause.

"Payable upon completion of the job?"

The Injun laughed aloud. "I've lost my faith in the Democracy. I want half down, and the other half where I can get it when the job's done."

"Give me a bank and an account number, and I'll have five million credits transferred there by tomorrow morning."

"I'm not that dumb even when I'm on the seed," said the Injun. "It'll go through so many middlemen that you'll lose track of it before it's halfway to its destination—and I don't go to work until it's where I want it to be." He gave 32 the first step of the money route.

"What assurances do I have that you'll go through with it once the money's in place?"

"None," answered the Injun. "Consider it an act of faith." He paused. "Have we got a deal?"

There was a short pause. *"I'll have to think it over."*

"Think fast. You've got less than a minute left."

"Will you reinsert the transmitter so that I can monitor your progress?"

"Not a chance. I work alone."

Another pause.

"All right. It's a deal."

But, thought the Injun with a grin as he tossed the transmitter into an atomizer and began getting dressed, *we didn't shake on it.*

14

The Injun lay back on his bed, staring at various two- and three-dimensional prints on the beige walls and wishing that the embassy had hired a bolder decorator. When the throbbing in his right ear and at the base of his skull finally began to subside, he decided to begin working.

"Computer, activate," he ordered.

The computer on his desk hummed to life.

"Computer, do you know who I am?"

"You are Lieutenant James Two Feathers."

"Do you know the nature of my assignment on Hades?"

"No, I do not."

"Is anyone currently monitoring my room?"

"No."

"Is anyone currently monitoring my conversation with you?" he continued.

"No."

"Have I the authority to keep it that way?"

"I do not understand, Lieutenant Two Feathers," answered the computer. "You must word your questions more precisely."

"Is there a way that I can prevent anyone from monitoring this room?"

"No."

"Can you warn me if and when the room *is* being monitored?"

"Yes."

"I order you to do so."

"Order received and enacted."

"Good." The Injun paused, trying to formulate his request properly. "I don't want anyone to know what information I am about to request of you. Is there a way to make this and all future conversations between you and me private, so that no one else can access them?"

"Yes."

"How do I go about it?"

"You must instruct me to seal your work under a Priority Restriction."

"Please seal all my work under a Priority Restriction."

"Order received and enacted."

"All right," said the Injun. "Now let's get to work." He paused as another surge of pain shot through his inner ear, then continued speaking after it had passed. "I have two missions on Hades. One is to assassinate the human woman known as the Oracle. The other is to prevent a man who is somewhere within the Alpha Crepello system from reaching her before I do. If I make contact with him, there is a possibility that I may have to kill him. Will your programming allow you to help me?"

"Yes," replied the computer. "Helping you accomplish your mission will not set up any ethical conflicts within me."

"Good. Do you have any information in your memory banks concerning a mercenary or bounty hunter who uses the professional name of the Whistler?"

"No."

"He comes from the Inner Frontier. Can you access a computer that may have some information about him?"

"Possibly."

Silence.

"Well?" demanded the Injun.

"You made no request, Lieutenant Two Feathers."

"Try to access a computer that can supply you with data about the Whistler, and if you are successful, transmit that information to me."

"Working . . ." There was a three-minute silence, during which time the Injun lay absolutely still and hoped the pain within his head would diminish. It had just begun to subside slightly when the computer spoke again. "The man known as the Whistler is actually Joshua Jeremiah Chandler. He is thirty-eight years old. He is six feet two inches tall, weighs 178 pounds, and has auburn hair and blue eyes. He has no distinguishing scars or birthmarks. His home planet is Boyson III, which is known locally as The Frenchman's World. He is a bounty hunter who has made twenty-seven reported kills and has brought in eleven living fugitives. It is assumed that he has made even more unreported kills, but the number cannot be ascertained."

"Impressive," said the Injun. "Can you supply me with a photograph or holograph of him?"

"Yes."

The Injun waited for a few seconds, then grimaced. "Please do so."

Instantly a holograph of Chandler, taken from his passport, flashed on the small screen.

"I'm too far away to see it," said the Injun. "Make it larger."

Suddenly an image of Chandler's holograph, some four feet on a side, popped into existence just above the desk. The Injun studied the pale blue eyes, the high cheekbones, the humorless expression, trying without success to get some feel of the man from his image.

"Do you know if he's landed on Hades yet?"

"No."

"No, he hasn't landed?"

"No, I do not know."

"Don't all humans have to report to the embassy?"

"Yes," answered the computer. "But my understanding is that residents of the Inner Frontier do not recognize the authority of the Democracy. Therefore, it is possible that he has landed without reporting his presence to the embassy."

"Can you check it out with Spaceport Security?"

"No. I am denied access to the spaceport computer."

"I see," said the Injun. He paused, still trying to order his thoughts. "His assignment is to kidnap the human woman known as the Oracle. What, in your opinion, is his most likely course of action?"

"He will come to Hades, gain access to her, and forcibly remove her from the planet."

The Injun grimaced again. "Let's take this one step at a time. If he wanted to come to Hades and keep his presence unknown, how would he do so?"

"He would not report his presence to the embassy."

"That would just keep his presence unknown to *you*. How would he keep it unknown to the Blue Devils?"

"He has two options," answered the computer. "Either he will have to keep his arrival secret from the Spaceport Security system, or he will have to disguise his identity."

"How many humans have managed to avoid Spaceport Security?"

"I have insufficient data to answer that question."

"How many are you aware of?"

"None."

"Then let's assume it can't be done, and that he'll be disguised," said the Injun. "What type of disguise is least likely to be penetrated by Spaceport Security?"

"I have insufficient data to answer that question."

"You mean nobody's ever done it?"

"If it has been done successfully, by its very nature I am not aware of it," answered the computer.

The Injun paused while he digested the information, then spoke again. "Hypothesize that he'll accomplish it. Where will he go next?"

"I have insufficient data to answer that question."

"You are a goddamned pain in the ass!" snapped the Injun. "All right, let me restate it: if a human doesn't stay at the embassy, where is he most likely to stay?"

"There are four hotels that accept humans," answered the computer. "None of their names can be pronounced or spelled in Terran. They are code-named Blue House, Red House, White House, and Green House by members of the embassy staff."

"They don't cater exclusively to humans, I take it?"

"That is correct."

"Now hypothesize that he'll stay in one of the hotels. Let's assume Blue House. His next step will be to determine where to find the Oracle. How will he go about this?"

"First, he will use the vidphone directory. Then he will ask at the embassy. Then . . ."

"Stop!" commanded the Injun.

The computer was instantly silent.

"He doesn't want his presence known, remember? Asking the embassy is like waving a flag."

"I do not understand the reference."

"Look," said the Injun irritably, "there are certain facts that you must take into consideration for this hypothesis. First, the Whistler is here illegally, and if his presence is discovered, he will either be imprisoned or deported, or possibly even executed. Second, he may already be aware of the fact that the Democracy does not want him to succeed in his mission and has ordered his death. Third, the Oracle is under the protection of the Blue Devils, and they will almost certainly be suspicious of anyone who asks questions about her. Now, taking his need for absolute secrecy into account, how do you think he will go about locating her?"

"I have insufficient data to respond to that question."

"Why?" exploded the Injun, sitting up in frustration and groaning at the sudden sharp pain inside his head.

"While I have the ability to shield certain files against scrutiny, I myself have not been programmed to initiate covert activities."

"I'm just asking you to hypothesize, damn it!"

"I am incapable of attempting this hypothesis."

The Injun lay back on the bed, propped his head up against a pillow, closed his eyes, and waited for the pain to pass.

"You're driving me crazy!" he muttered at last.

The machine made no response.

"Okay," said the Injun as the pain subsided again. "Let's skip the Whistler for a while and concentrate on the Oracle. What information do you have on her?"

"The Oracle is known to exist."

There was a long pause.

"That's *it*?" said the Injun unbelievingly as his whole body tensed in frustration and the pain returned.

"That is my only verifiable information. Everything else in my data banks is supposition or hypothesis."

"Give it to me, anyway."

"The Oracle is believed to be Penelope Bailey, age twenty-two. The Oracle is believed to be in the company of an alien being known as the Mock Turtle. The Oracle is believed to be a political renegade, and an enemy of the Democracy. The Oracle is believed to possess the power of precognition; if the supposition that she is Penelope Bailey is true, then the Oracle is known to possess the power of precognition. The Oracle is believed to have resided on Alpha Crepello III for between twelve and fourteen years. The Oracle is not believed to be a member of the government of Alpha Crepello III, but is believed to have considerable influence over its decisions."

The Injun waited to make sure the computer was through, then spoke again:

"Does the Oracle reside in Quichancha?"

"I have insufficient data to answer that question."

The Injun paused for a moment, considering his next question. "Does the Oracle ever grant audiences to humans?"

"No."

"Does the Oracle ever grant audiences to members of alien races, other than the Blue Devils?"

"I have insufficient data to answer that question."

"That means you don't know of any such audiences?"

"That is correct."

"Has the Oracle left Hades at any time during the past twelve years?"

"I have insufficient data to answer that question."

"All right," said the Injun. "Let's assume that she came here twelve or thirteen years ago and hasn't seen a member of any race except the Blue Devils since then. Do you possess any information to the contrary?"

"That is correct."

"Are there any spaceports on Hades other than the one in Quichancha?"

"No."

The Injun analyzed all the information he had been given, and suddenly smiled. "Then I know how *I'm* going to find her. I wonder if the Whistler is smart enough to figure it out."

The machine made no reply.

"Are you denied all access to the spaceport computer, or just to its security functions?"

"I am denied access to all aspects of Spaceport Security."

"What about shipping and receiving?"

"I do not understand the question."

"Can you access cargo manifests from the spaceport's shipping docks?"

"Yes, provided the manifests do not include items associated with planetary security."

"This is almost too simple," said the Injun. "What this embassy needs is more killers and less bureaucrats." He smiled again. "Computer, access the manifests of all goods received in the past two weeks."

"Working . . . accessed, with the stated exceptions."

"Good. Now go through them and access a list of all human foodstuffs that have been imported from Hades' moons."

"Working . . . accessed."

"Now eliminate all those items that were ordered by the embassy or the four hotels that cater to humans."

"Working . . . eliminated."

"Now eliminate all those items that were ordered by the three restaurants in Quichancha."

"Working . . . eliminated."

"How many items remain?" asked the Injun.

"Four."

"Were all four items in the same shipment?"

"No. They were in two shipments, spaced ten days apart."

"To whom were they consigned?"

"To Vrief Domo," answered the computer.

"Who or what is Vrief Domo?"

"A native of Alpha Crepello III."

"A Blue Devil?"

"That is correct."

"I *knew* she couldn't make a steady diet of that goddamned native meat!" exclaimed the Injun triumphantly. "Computer, can you show me what Vrief Domo looks like?"

"Yes."

Silence.

"Then do so, damn it!" said the Injun.

A holograph of a Blue Devil replaced that of Chandler.

"Shit!" muttered the Injun. "They all look alike to me." He paused. "What data do you possess on him?"

"Vrief Domo is employed by the government of Alpha Crepello III."

"The planetary government, not the government of Quichancha?" interrupted the Injun.

"That is correct."

"What are his duties?"

"Unknown."

"Where is his place of business?"

"The House of Rule."

"The House of Rule?" repeated the Injun, frowning. "What's that?"

"The House of Rule is the complex of buildings from which Alpha Crepello III is governed."

The Injun considered this, then shook his head. "It's got to be crawling with security." He paused. "You must know something else about him. Give me everything you have."

"Once every ten days Vrief Domo accepts a shipment of human foodstuffs at the Quichancha spaceport. That is the only information I possess about him."

"Where does he take it?"

"Working . . ." There was a lengthy silence. "Unknown."

"Do you know where he lives?"

"No."

"Can you find out where he lives?"

"Working . . . yes."

"Is his residence in Quichancha?"

"Yes."

"What's the address?"

"Quichancha has no addresses in human terms."

"Can you pinpoint his residence on a map of the city?"

"Yes."

The Injun waited patiently.

"Then so do, goddammit!"

The holograph of Vrief Domo was replaced by a three-dimensional grid of the city, with a tiny flashing dot pinpointing the Blue Devil's living quarters.

"I want a hard copy of this."

"Working . . . done."

"And I also want a hard copy of Vrief Domo's holograph. A two-dimensional representation is acceptable."

"Working . . . done."

"Where are they?" asked the Injun.

"My printer is in the large right-hand drawer of your desk. You will find the hard copies there."

"How far is the embassy from Vrief Domo's quarters?"

"Approximately 1,173 meters."

"Approximately?"

"1,173.239 meters, to be exact."

"Is that in a straight line, or following the streets?"

"A straight line."

"How far is it via the streets?"

"The shortest route is approximately 4.2 kilometers."

"Very good, computer. Make sure no one can access what we've just discussed."

"You have already placed all your interactions with me under a Priority Restriction."

"I was just reminding you."

"I am incapable of forgetting."

"Fine. Deactivate."

The computer went dead, and the Injun got to his feet and walked over to the desk. He opened the right-hand drawer and pulled out his two hard copies. He carefully folded the map and put it into a pocket of his tunic, then held up the picture of Vrief Domo, his first tangible link to the Oracle.

"Gotcha, you son of a bitch!" he said.

If his head hadn't begun throbbing again, he might even have felt sorry for the Blue Devil.

15

The Injun waited for two days.

By that time the pain had subsided, and he had made discreet inquiries to make sure that his five million credits was in the pipeline. 32 was still tracing it, of course, but the Injun was confident that it would become more and more difficult with every transaction until it was finally impossible.

He had the computer match the handful of incoming humans against the embassy's list of anticipated arrivals, and wasn't surprised when they checked out. If the Whistler was half as good as he was supposed to be, it was going to take more than an embassy computer to find him.

Finally, when he felt well enough, he summoned Broussard to his quarters.

"How are you today, sir?" asked the young man, entering the room a moment later.

"Much better."

"I'm glad to hear it."

"Really?" asked the Injun with a smile. "If I were you, I'd be heartbroken to hear it. I'm about to cut into your time with your doctor."

"This is my job, sir."

"Well, it's time for me to get to work on *my* job. Pull up a chair."

Broussard walked to a corner of the room, picked up a chair, and carried it over to the bed.

"Now sit down and get comfortable," said the Injun.

Broussard sat on the chair and grinned wryly. "Well, the sitting part is easy, sir."

"Who the hell furnished this place? You wouldn't think some thing this dull would also be uncomfortable."

"I've often wondered that myself, sir," admitted Broussard.

The Indian looked amused, and then his face became serious "So much for small talk. We've got more important things to discuss."

"The Oracle?" suggested Broussard.

"Yes."

"Before we speak further, perhaps we should go to a secure room."

"Not necessary," said the Injun. "I ordered the computer to let me know the instant anyone attempts to monitor us." He tossed the map to Broussard. "Take a look at this and see if it makes any sense to you."

Broussard studied the map carefully for a moment, then looked up.

"I take it that you want to reach the location that's been highlighted?"

"Right."

"On foot or by vehicle?"

"I'm not sure yet," said the Injun.

"By day or at night?"

"It makes no difference."

"Yes, it does, sir."

"Oh? Why?"

"Because the current temperature is fifty-seven degrees Celsius, and there's no way you can walk there and back without dehydrating and probably suffering heatstroke," answered Broussard "You may be feeling better, but it's still only been two days since you underwent major surgery."

"What will the temperature be tonight?" asked the Injun.

"Perhaps forty-four degrees Celsius, which is still formidable,' answered Broussard.

The Injun grimaced. "Then I guess we drive." He paused. "Too damned bad. Your vehicle is pretty easy to identify."

"That's an area inhabited almost exclusively by Blue Devils,' said Broussard. "A human walking through it would be even more conspicuous."

"Have you got a safe house anywhere around there?"

"I don't think so. We can ask the computer."

The Injun shook his head. "Don't bother," he said. "I already asked. The computer's not aware of any. I just thought there might be things that you didn't tell it."

Broussard looked puzzled.

"Any computer that can be built can be breached," explained the Injun.

"Not this one, sir."

"I admire your confidence," said the Injun dryly. "But I've got half a dozen friends who could invade it in less than two hours."

"I sincerely doubt that, sir," replied Broussard firmly.

"I'm sure you do," said the Injun, unimpressed. "I'm not here to argue the point. I just want to know if there's a nearby safe house."

"To the best of my knowledge, we don't have one in Quichancha. I believe we have four on the entire planet, all in other cities." Broussard fidgeted uneasily. "May I ask why you want to know?"

"There is every possibility that I am going to have to do some very unpleasant things to a Blue Devil," answered the Injun. "I'd rather not have to do them in a building that's filled with other Blue Devils. I'd much rather take him to a secure location first."

"Is murder a possibility?"

"If he doesn't tell me what I want to know, it's an absolute certainty," said the Injun. He paused thoughtfully. "It probably will be, anyway. I don't want him reporting what I know or identifying me to the Oracle, and I don't want him around when the Whistler shows up."

"The Whistler? Who's that?"

"I'm afraid that's restricted information."

Broussard frowned. "You could cause some problems for the embassy, sir. If you kill a Blue Devil—and I assume this one is in some way connected to the Oracle—they're going to assume the embassy ordered it, or at least sanctioned it."

"Embassies exist to confront problems," replied the Injun with no show of concern. "They'll find a way."

"I don't know, sir," said Broussard doubtfully. "It would be extremely difficult to convince the Blue Devils that we didn't at least have prior knowledge of the killing, and that implies either consent or approval." He paused. "After all, I drive an embassy vehicle, and as you pointed out before, it will stand out in a residential area."

"So get an unmarked vehicle."

"I'd have to put through a request for funds, and even if my request was approved, there's still every likelihood that it could be traced to the embassy."

"I don't mean to sound insensitive," said the Injun, "but I really don't give a damn how much trouble I cause the embassy. My assignment is more important."

"You don't understand, sir," said Broussard. "Even if I agreed with you, that's all the more reason for not involving the embassy. It will simply put the Oracle on the alert."

"Just killing the Blue Devil will do that," said the Injun. Suddenly a plan began to take shape in his mind. "Unless . . ."

He fell silent for a moment, and Broussard waited patiently for him to continue.

"I think I've got a way to protect both our asses," he announced at last.

"Yours and mine, sir?" asked Broussard, puzzled.

The Injun shook his head. "Mine and the embassy's. Can you get your hands on some seed?"

"Seed, sir?"

"Alphanella seeds."

"They're illegal on every planet in the Democracy."

"Allow me to point out to you that we're not *in* the Democracy."

"They're illegal on Hades, too."

"You haven't answered my question," noted the Injun. "Can you get some seed?"

"It's possible," said Broussard reluctantly.

"Within the embassy?"

Broussard shook his head. "No. But there's a woman in Red House . . ."

"User or seller?"

"A user."

"Good," said the Injun. "Confiscate half a dozen seeds."

"What's the purpose of this, sir?" asked Broussard.

"Whether they trace the killing to the embassy or not, they're going to know I'm after the Oracle the second I kill the Blue Devil."

"What have the seeds got to do with anything?" persisted Broussard.

"If I take out most of the residents of the building and leave a couple of half-chewed seeds on the premises, the embassy could claim that I was a hopped-up chewer who'd gone on a binge and offer a reward for me, giving out a phony ID and hologram, which will get *them* off the hook while still giving me freedom of movement, and in the meantime it might hide my real reason for being there, at least temporarily." He paused. "I'd have to do it at night, and I'd have to go there on foot. It wouldn't do to have an embassy vehicle being seen transporting a maniac to the scene of the crime." The Injun frowned. "I'll still need your help, though. I can't read or speak the language, and I've got to hit *my* Blue Devil's quarters first, before I kill the rest of them. I don't want him escaping if he hears any noise elsewhere in the building."

Broussard considered what he had heard for a long moment, then shook his head. "No chance, sir," he said at last. "The embassy will never be a party to this. You're speaking about blithely killing dozens of innocent beings simply for the sake of misdirecting the Oracle."

The Injun shrugged. "They're just aliens."

"The ambassador would point out that on this planet *we're* the aliens."

"Spare me his platitudes," said the Injun. "The Democracy's at war with the Oracle, and in a war, sometimes civilians get hurt."

"I don't know anything about the Oracle," admitted Broussard, "but I *do* know that the Democracy's not at war with Hades, and your proposed actions could precipitate one." He paused. "I know the way the bureaucracy works. They'll kick it all the way up to Deluros VIII, and even if their transmissions aren't intercepted, your Blue Devil will probably have died of old age or disease before they make a decision."

"Well, that's that," said the Injun. "I can't do it without the embassy's complicity. I might get my hands on the seed, and I might find the Blue Devil I'm after, and I might kill enough other Blue Devils to confuse the Oracle—but if the embassy won't support the cover story, I'll have both sides hunting for my scalp with no place to hide." He sighed deeply. "I guess we go to Plan B."

"Just killing the one Blue Devil?" asked Broussard.

"Yeah," said the Injun. He frowned. "I hate to do it, though. Once he's dead, there's no way the Oracle can mistake what's going on." He paused, considering the situation. "And if he doesn't talk," he added, "I'm going to eliminate my only link to the Oracle." He shook his head unhappily. "I just wish they didn't all look so much alike."

"If you *could* follow him, would you prefer it, sir?" asked Broussard.

"Much." The Injun looked at Broussard. "Why? What do you have in mind?"

"There may be a way, sir."

"Yeah?" said the Injun. "If you can come up with one, you've just made my life a hell of a lot easier."

"I don't think so, sir," said Broussard seriously.

16

Port Marrakech, Port Samarkand, and Port Maracaibo were all high in the night sky as the Injun emerged from the unlit landcar half a mile from his destination.

"This is as close as I can go without attracting attention, sir," said Broussard apologetically. "I'll wait here for you."

The Injun nodded absently and tried to get his bearings. The suddenly broadening, suddenly narrowing, always twisting streets looked a lot different in person than they did on a map, and he already felt mildly disoriented.

He had a small lithium-powered flashlight in the pocket of his tunic, and his first inclination was to pull out the map and double-check his position, but Men with maps weren't supposed to be here, and the light would only broadcast his presence.

He had wanted to approach his destination via alleyways, but there weren't any. His next notion was to go underground and make his way via the sewer system, but they had no map of it, and he didn't relish trying to find his way with no maps and no landmarks. So, keeping as near to the irregular buildings as he could, he began walking slowly and silently through the incredibly hot night. The humidity was minimal, but between the heat, the effort he was expending, and the tension, both his skin and clothes were soaked with perspiration before he had traveled more than one hundred yards.

He was fast approaching a very sharp corner, and suddenly he could hear voices—*alien* voices—somewhere up ahead of him. He turned and looked for the landcar, but it was lost in the shadows.

The voices grew clearer and louder, until he estimated that they were no more than thirty yards from the corner. He decided to duck into the doorway of the nearest building until they passed, then discovered that it didn't *have* a doorway. He backtracked a few steps, found a small alcove between that building and the one he had just passed, and darted into it. Then he crouched down and waited.

Five Blue Devils suddenly came into view as they turned the corner. One of them had an extremely high-pitched voice, but he couldn't discern any other difference among them. Four of them wore the triangles he had seen on his first day in Quichancha, and all five wore what appeared to be stoles made of some metallic fiber wrapped about their torsos.

As they reached a spot in the street opposite his hiding place, two of them got into what seemed to be an argument, and suddenly all five stopped walking. Voices grew strident, postures grew aggressive, and they remained where they were, gesticulating wildly.

The Injun felt his calves and thighs cramping up after a few minutes. He was horribly uncomfortable, his legs aching, his body pouring sweat, but he didn't dare move while the aliens were there. It would be bad enough to be seen walking through this section of the city, but to be found *skulking* would be infinitely worse.

Finally he could stand the pain no longer, and he carefully leaned forward, momentarily assuming the position of a runner in the starting blocks, alternately stretching each leg out behind him. When he was through, he carefully brought one leg beneath him and moved to a kneeling position.

The Blue Devils were still arguing, but a moment later one of them made a gesture that the Injun couldn't comprehend, and two of them stalked off into the darkness. The remaining three spoke among themselves for another minute and then continued walking in the direction they had been going.

The Injun waited for almost three minutes, long enough to make sure that none of them were coming back, and then carefully stood erect, stuck his head out, looked in both directions, and quickly walked to the corner.

As the map had shown, the street made a 160-degree turn, almost doubling back on itself, and simultaneously narrowed to a point where it was less than ten feet wide. The Injun felt very claustrophobic as he kept walking and the street kept narrowing. Within another fifty yards he had to walk sideways, with his back pressed against a wall, to pass between buildings on the opposite sides of the alien street.

Then it broadened again, not slowly and gradually, but instantly, and in a single stride he went from a street so narrow that it seemed like a corridor to a thoroughfare so wide that he thought for a moment that he had turned the wrong way and wound up in a public square.

There was no artificial illumination, nor, with the three moons overhead, was any needed. It was almost bright enough to read by the moonlight, and he realized that he had almost three hundred yards to walk before the street narrowed again, three hundred yards in which there were no parked vehicles, no lampposts, no benches, no trash atomizers, nothing to hide behind, and he would be the only living, moving thing.

He didn't like the odds of crossing those three hundred yards without being seen, and he stopped, looking for some less exposed route. His first thought was to go via the rooftops, but very few of the buildings were remotely similar in height and structure. The sewers were out, too: even if he had a map, which he didn't, he couldn't spot a manhole and didn't know how to go about finding an entrance to them.

Finally he decided that there was no alternative to simply walking as quickly and silently as he could, and this he proceeded to do, staying as close to the buildings on the left side of the street as possible. When he had covered slightly more than half the distance, he saw a Blue Devil staring at him from a third- or fourth-story window.

Fighting the urge to run, he looked up, saluted, and continued walking. He expected to hear outraged screams, or sirens, or approaching footsteps, or *something,* but nothing happened, and in another ninety seconds he had turned another corner and found himself on a street that, for a change, seemed neither too wide nor too narrow.

He stepped into some deep shadows as two more Blue Devils came into view, and was prepared to wait, motionless, until they had passed him, but instead they entered a small building, and he began walking again. Then another pair of Blue Devils began approaching, and he once again hid in the shadows until they had walked by.

For some reason this stretch of the street had much more activity than he had encountered thus far, but fortunately the buildings and shadows afforded him instant hiding places. Four more groups of Blue Devils and one single being caused him to duck out of sight before he made it the final two hundred yards to his destination, but eventually he arrived at the building he sought.

And couldn't find a door.

Whispering a curse to himself, he began circling the structure, looking for some means of ingress. He finally came upon a miscolored section and leaned tentatively against it.

Nothing happened.

He pushed harder, with no results. Finally he stood back a few feet and waved a hand, hoping that some hidden scanner might react to the motion. Still nothing.

He walked once more around the building and came back to the miscolored section, convinced that it was the entrance. He stood a few feet away from it, trying to determine how to trigger the locking mechanism. Obviously it didn't react to force, or to motion. He chanced shining his flashlight on it for a second, just long enough to make sure that there were no buttons, buzzer, bells, or computer locks.

Next he looked around the ground, hoping he might find some mechanism there, but he couldn't see anything remotely promising.

Vrief Domo lived on the third level. He looked up, wondering if he could scale the building, and decided that he couldn't.

He spent another five minutes trying to figure out how to gain entrance to the building, and couldn't come up with an answer. At last he leaned against a wall next to the miscolored portion, mentally exhausted—and almost fell over backward when a four-foot-wide section of the wall slid behind the miscolored part of the building.

He looked around quickly, before the wall slid back and plunged the interior of the building into total darkness, and found a narrow staircase. He shone his light on it just long enough to fix the height of each stair in his mind and then slowly, carefully began ascending. Fourteen stairs later he reached a landing, felt around for the railing, couldn't find one, flashed his light again for an instant, and discovered that the stairwell ended on the second level.

Deciding that he hated alien buildings even more than he hated 32, he stood still and tried to reason things out. As far as he could determine, there was only one door to the building, the one he had inadvertently triggered. If that was so, this was the only set of stairs leading up from the ground floor. Therefore, everyone living on a higher level had to come to this point before proceeding. Then what did they do?

He activated his flashlight again and examined the landing more carefully. There were four doors, each more familiar in shape than the one downstairs. Three of them possessed various markings; the fourth was absolutely plain.

Realizing that it was just as likely that there was only one apartment on this level and three stairwells leading up, he nonetheless decided to try the unmarked door. It slid up as he approached it, revealing another narrow staircase, and he decided to keep his light on. After all, if someone was coming down while he was going up, having his light in his pocket wasn't going to keep his presence secret for very long, anyway.

When he reached the next landing—he was annoyed but not surprised to find that it took thirty-one stairs to reach it—he came to five doors, four marked and one plain.

Now he pulled out the map once more, turned it over, and looked at the symbols Broussard had drawn on the back.

The teardrop signified the domicile of a communal or family group of young Blue Devils, old enough to leave home but still bound together by some social custom that was beyond the comprehension of human psychologists. That eliminated the door on the left; Vrief Domo was a mature Blue Devil with a responsible position in the government.

He shone his light on the next door: there were seven symbols he didn't understand and one that Broussard had duplicated. It looked like a broken dagger, or perhaps a very twisted cane. Broussard hadn't explained it, but had said that it was the most common symbol, and that for reasons that were too esoteric to go into, it wouldn't be on the door he wanted.

That left the two right-hand doors. Each possessed the symbol that looked like a crescent moon, the one that Broussard said would signify a government employee.

The Injun was barely able to resist the urge to curse. *Two* government employees! How the hell was he going to know which was the one he wanted? They looked alike, sounded alike, dressed alike— and if he chose the wrong one, he'd waste so much time before he discovered his error that the Whistler could wind up so far ahead of him that he'd never catch up.

Think, Redskin, he told himself silently. *Think!*

He studied both sets of symbols, trying to find something, anything, that matched the other symbols Broussard had said might be on Vrief Domo's door. There weren't any.

All right, he decided. *Let's try it the other way around.*

He had a list of eleven symbols that would definitely not be on the door of the Blue Devil he wanted. He couldn't find any of them on the second door from the right.

He turned his light on the right-hand door, carefully studying each symbol—and then he found it: the off-balance trapezoid with two right angles that denoted a member of the military. Both Blue Devils worked for the government—but Vrief Domo was a civil servant.

The Injun turned his attention to the second door from the right—Vrief Domo's door. He had been prepared to spend hours decoding a computer lock, but instead all he found was a large keyhole, so large that he could insert his finger all the way through it. It took him less than thirty seconds to spring the latch, and then he was inside the Blue Devil's quarters, his body tensed, listening for any sign that his quarry might be awake.

He remained absolutely still for almost a minute. Moonlight filtered in through the single window, and his right eye gradually adjusted to the semi-darkness. He hadn't wanted to remove the eyepatch from his prosthetic left eye, hadn't wanted 32 to have any idea of what he was doing, but he needed his depth perception, and he took the patch off and put it into a pocket.

He took a tentative step into the room, then another, searching for the object he sought. He carefully examined the furniture, both the functional pieces and the totally incomprehensible ones, but he couldn't find it.

There were three doorways leading from the room, in addition to the one through which he had entered. The smell of spoiling meat wafted out from the doorway on his right, and he knew that it must be the kitchen. He quickly walked to it, considered using his flashlight once he determined that the room was empty, and then decided that he'd have too much difficulty readjusting to the darkness once he left the room.

The kitchen was small, filled with gadgets that he had never seen before, and arranged in a way that made no sense whatsoever. A slab of meat lay on a counter that had been constructed no more than eighteen inches above the floor. Chairs faced the walls, spices were piled on the floor in a corner, there was what seemed to be a sink with seven spigots, and there was nothing that remotely seemed to resemble a stove or a refrigerator. A large hectagonal chart was tacked on the wall at an odd angle; he studied it for a moment, but couldn't begin to guess whether it was a calendar, a recipe, or something else.

Finally he returned to the room that he had originally entered and tried to figure out which of the other two doorways led to the sleeping Vrief Domo. He paused, undecided, for almost a minute. Then he heard a gurgle of water running through a pipe off to his left and immediately walked through the left-hand doorway.

He found himself in a large room, and this time he had no choice but to use his flashlight, as there were no windows, and the room was set at such an angle that none of the moonlight from the first room reached it. Now that he could see clearly, he took the eyepatch out of his pocket and put it back over his left eye to prevent 32 from monitoring his actions.

The walls were made of a beautiful alien hardwood that was streaked with various shades of brown and gold, and had intricate designs carved on each panel. The floor was covered by a handwoven carpet; at first he thought the fabric was metallic, but then he realized that it was a finely spun silk. There was a strong smell of chemicals in the air, and there were four large, hand-painted ceramic basins, each with drains at the bottom and gold-plated pipes running into the walls. He couldn't tell which constituted a sink, which was a commode, and which served as a tub—and he had absolutely no idea what the fourth basin was for—but there was no question in his mind that he was in a Blue Devil bathroom. There were six fixtures on the walls, none of which seemed at all functional to him, all of which glistened with a plating that seemed like a dull chrome but on closer inspection proved to be a hand-rubbed alloy, not unlike pewter.

You guys take your ablutions seriously, I'll give you that, he thought wryly.

There was a series of small porcelain boxes stacked against one of the walls, and he knelt down, placed the flashlight in his teeth, and began opening them one by one.

He found what he was looking for in the third box: a large triangle, the same type that he had seen so many of the Blue Devils wearing in the street.

He reached into another pocket and pulled out the small vial that Broussard had supplied him, opened it, and, using a clean cloth that had been supplied for this purpose, moistened it and then carefully rubbed it on the surface of the triangle. He waited a moment until i dried, then replaced the triangle in the box, put the other two boxes back the way he had found them, walked to the doorway, and shu off the flashlight.

He waited almost two full minutes for his eyes to adjust to the filtered moonlight, then, enormously relieved that he wouldn' have to enter the sleeping Blue Devil's bedroom, carefully walked across the main room of the apartment and gently opened the door pulling it shut behind him. He reached into the enormous keyhole and manipulated the lock back into place.

He had no difficulty finding his way back to ground level, and a moment later he was in the street, darting from shadow to shadow hugging the wall as he reached the incredibly broad section, and then carefully squeezing between buildings as the street narrowed to less than a meter.

Broussard was waiting for him, and he entered the vehicle with an enormous feeling of relief.

"You did it?" asked Broussard.

"Yeah," replied the Injun. "You'd just better be right about it."

"I am," answered Broussard confidently. "There were micro scopic particles of a unique uranium isotope in that solution; some of them have to have stuck to his triangle. The radiation won't do him any lasting damage, but with the equipment we've got back at the embassy, we'll be able to trace him anywhere he goes." He paused. "We'll just wait for him to pick up his next shipment of human foodstuffs at the spaceport and then follow him right to the Oracle."

"Sounds good to me," said the Injun. "Now let's get the hell out of here."

"Right," said Broussard, speeding off down a crazily twisting street.

"Take it easy," cautioned the Injun. "I didn't risk my life back there to die in a goddamned traffic accident."

"I'm sorry, sir. I guess I'm a little excited." Broussard paused. " would think you'd be running on pure adrenaline right about now."

"This was just the first step. The next one might be a little more difficult."

"Following the Blue Devil? No problem at all, sir."

"The problem comes when we're all through following him," said the Injun, and suddenly his feelings of triumph and exultation faded away as he wondered exactly what he would do once he found himself in the presence of the Oracle. Parlor tricks like the one he had pulled off tonight certainly wouldn't fool her, and he realized that it was time to begin considering exactly what *would* let him get close enough to her to accomplish his mission.

Then, as he relaxed and felt the tension finally leave his muscles, an old craving returned—and with it, the germ of a plan.

17

The Injun staked out the cargo area of the spaceport for four days with no success.

On the fifth morning, Vrief Domo finally showed up.

"He's here, sir," announced Broussard, pointing to a blinking indicator on the control panel grid.

"Damned near time," said the Injun, leaning forward from the landcar's backseat to look at the blinking light. "I was starting to think the Oracle had gone on a hunger strike."

"He's approaching the cargo dock."

"How long will it take us to find out what he's picked up?"

"We're tied into the embassy computer, and it in turn is monitoring the spaceport's cargo manifests. I think we should have corroboration before he leaves the gate."

"Just be ready to move out fast," said the Injun.

Broussard nodded without replying and concentrated on the panel.

"Okay," he announced after another two minutes. "He's made his pickup, and he's on his way out."

"Follow him."

"The embassy computer hasn't verified that he's picked up food-stuffs yet. He could be carrying almost anything."

"Follow him, anyway," ordered the Injun. "If he leaves the spaceport, there's no need for us to stay here—and if he's got food for the Oracle, I don't want to lose him." He paused. "Let him get a kilometer ahead of us."

"I don't dare, sir," said Broussard. "The way these streets wind, that could give him a ten-minute lead."

"So what?"

"If the Oracle's not in the city, and he leaves Quichancha ten minutes before we do, he could get so far ahead of us that we lose his signal."

"All right," said the Injun. "But stay far enough behind so he doesn't spot us. If he thinks he's being followed, he could lead us all over the goddamned planet, or right into a trap."

"I'll do my best, sir," said Broussard, moving the car into the heavy spaceport traffic and keeping a watchful eye on his panel. Another light blinked. "The computer just confirmed it!" announced Broussard excitedly. "He picked up human food at the cargo dock."

The Injun made no comment, and Broussard began concentrating on his panel, making certain that he didn't lose Vrief Domo's vehicle on the small grid.

The Blue Devil didn't seem to be in much of a hurry. He passed through a residential area, then turned to the south.

"He's going to see her right now," said the Injun as the city came to a surprisingly abrupt end and they suddenly found themselves in the vast expanse of red desert that had given the planet its name.

"He could be going almost anywhere," responded Broussard, concentrating on the narrow road that seemed so out of place on the red sand.

The Injun shook his head. "He's going to see *her*," he repeated.

"How do you know?"

"We know she doesn't live in the city, and we know that he's transporting food to her." The Injun paused. "I hope you've got more fuel than he does. I'd hate to think of losing him out here—and even more, I hate to think of roasting to death in this goddamned landcar. It must be sixty degrees Celsius outside."

"It's not a problem, sir," answered Broussard. "This vehicle has an auxiliary power plant that utilizes solar batteries. The one place we *won't* get stranded is the desert."

"He's not going to stay in the desert for long."

"Oh?" said Broussard dubiously.

"If he was headed to the next city, it would have been more practical to ship the food via public transportation. His destination is somewhere up ahead, not too far away—and it won't be in the desert, because any structure that was built here would stand out like a sore thumb." He pointed to some large rock outcroppings about sixteen kilometers to the southeast. "My guess is that he's heading *there*."

"It makes sense when you say it that way, sir," admitted Broussard. "But . . ."

"But you think it's too pat?"

"Well, frankly, yes."

The Injun smiled. "The simpler something is, the less can go wrong with it. That applies equally to machines and hideouts."

Broussard shrugged. "You're the expert."

The Injun leaned forward again, checked the blinking light on the grid, then laid a hand gently on Broussard's shoulder. "Come to a stop."

"But we'll lose him. He's already eight or nine miles ahead of us."

"Believe me, he's going to stop at those rocks up ahead," said the Injun. "But we're starting to raise a cloud of dust from all the sand that's blown onto the road, and I don't want him to see it."

"All right," said Broussard, reluctantly slowing the vehicle to a dead stop.

"Pull off the road."

Broussard shook his head. "I don't dare, sir. We'll sink into the sand."

"It's *that* soft?"

"And that deep."

"I wonder how they ever managed to keep the road itself from sinking?" asked the Injun, curious.

"Beats the hell out of me, sir." Broussard pulled out a pair of small Antarrean cigars and offered one to the Injun. "Care for a smoke, sir?"

"Filthy habit."

"Would you rather I didn't smoke?" asked Broussard.

The Injun shrugged. "Suit yourself. I figure everyone's allowed at least one weakness."

Broussard stared at the cigars for a long moment, then sighed and replaced them in his tunic.

"How long do you intend to remain here, sir?"

"How far ahead of us is he now?"

Broussard checked the grid. "About twelve kilometers."

"I suppose we might as well get going again," said the Injun as the last of the dust cloud dissipated. "If we start raising too much dust, stop. Even if we lose him on the screen, we'll catch up with him at the rocks up ahead."

The vehicle began moving forward, and when they were within six kilometers of the rocky outcroppings, Broussard announced that Vrief Domo's vehicle had stopped.

"It's somewhere in that field of rocks, as you said, sir."

"There's gotta be some buildings hidden in there," said the Injun. "Is that grid of yours good enough to tell us which one he enters?"

"No problem," answered Broussard. "I can pinpoint his location whenever you want."

The Injun considered this, then shook his head. "Not good enough. If this is her headquarters, there could be half a dozen structures, and Domo could have business in three or four of them. I need to know where he drops off the food." He paused. "Does the road run through the rocks, or around them?"

"Around them."

"Can you tell if there's more than one building in the rocks?"

"To be honest, sir, I didn't know there were *any* buildings there."

The Injun sighed. "Too bad. I guess we do it the hard way."

"The hard way?"

"Get me as close to the rocks as you can and let me off. I've got to find out if there's more than one building, and if there is, I have to figure out which one the Oracle is in."

"That won't be as hard as you think, sir," said Broussard. "The grid detaches from the control panel. You can take it with you."

"I'm going to carry that thing over uneven terrain in this unholy heat without being spotted by the best-protected person on the planet, and you don't think it'll be hard?" said the Injun wryly.

"I merely meant that—"

"Never mind, never mind," said the Injun. "Just get me to the edge of the rocks."

"It's about three kilometers from one end to the other," said Broussard as they approached the outcroppings. "Then the desert starts again. Shall I wait for you here or on the far side?"

"Right here. I don't think we've been spotted yet. Why take any chances?"

"Actually, sir," said Broussard thoughtfully, "I suppose it doesn't really matter where I wait for you. If the Oracle's got the gift of precognition, as most members of the embassy seem to believe, then she knows you're here to terminate her."

"No, she doesn't," said the Injun confidently.

Broussard frowned. "But—"

"She can't foresee what was never going to happen, and I have no intention of confronting her today. I just want to know where to find her." He stared at Broussard. "You look unconvinced."

"Whether you confront her today or tomorrow or next week, the end result is the same: you mean to do her harm at some point in the future. So why wouldn't she dispose of you right now, before you can threaten her?"

"There has to be a limit to her powers," answered the Injun. "The fact that I'm still alive means we're still beyond it."

"She might simply be waiting for you to approach on foot," suggested Broussard.

"She might be," agreed the Injun. "But I don't think so. If planning to kill her was enough to elicit a response from her, she could have killed me, or had me killed, half a dozen times since I landed. I have a feeling that she either can't foresee anything but an immediate physical threat to her, or else she's so secure in her powers that she's not concerned *until* she's threatened. Either way," he concluded with a wry smile, "I've got to find out exactly where she is before I can threaten her."

"How do you even approach someone who can see the future?"

The Injun smiled. "When the time comes, you'll be the first to know."

"You seem awfully sure of yourself, sir," said Broussard.

"This is my business, and I'm damned good at it." The Injun glanced out the window. "Start slowing down, then stop behind that big rock that's coming up on the right."

Broussard did as he was instructed.

"Good," said the Injun, detaching the grid, opening the door, and wincing as he stepped out into the oppressive heat. He took a few tentative steps along the side of the road, then turned back to Broussard. "The ground's a lot harder here. Pull off the road and move alongside the rock. If anyone else comes along, they'll pass right by and never know you were here."

Broussard nodded and edged the vehicle off the road, and the Injun began climbing to the top of a rocky outcropping. He couldn't see anything out of the ordinary, but he checked the grid and found that Domo's position had not changed appreciably in the past few minutes, which implied there had to be *something* hidden back there among the rocks and boulders.

He had gone almost half a mile, keeping well off the road and hiding among the myriad outcroppings, when he finally saw the first building. It resembled nothing more than a purple glass pyramid some twenty feet on a side, and he was more annoyed than surprised to note that it possessed neither windows nor a discernible door. He looked at the grid again and found that he was still half a mile away from Vrief Domo.

He continued his slow, cautious approach, and finally he came to it. He didn't have to check the grid or search for Domo's vehicle to know he had reached his goal. Nestled in a small depression beneath a huge outcropping was a building—palace would have described it better, as would fortress, except that both words seemed somehow inadequate—that covered the equivalent of a Quichancha city block.

The structure was irregular and many-sided. Walls rose to enormous heights and then angled back down for no apparent reason. The roof was a hodgepodge of colored quartz and a shining metal that seemed to shimmer with all the colors of the spectrum. A private road, covered by some incredibly hard plastic that showed no sign of melting in the heat, led up to a huge triangular door that he assumed was a garage for numerous vehicles. Here and there were artifacts that looked like fountains, but none of them seemed to have any water, and he had no idea what function they fulfilled.

The building was beautifully camouflaged: between the rocks and the depression, there was no way to spot it from overhead, and a huge row of boulders had been positioned in such a way as to shield it from the view of passing vehicles. Only in one location could a driver turn off the road and slip his landcar between two of the boulders and then onto the plastic surface.

Half a dozen Blue Devils were walking in intricate individual patterns around the grounds. They didn't seem to be carrying any weapons, and the Injun couldn't tell if they were guards, residents of the huge building, or were simply carrying out some duty so alien that he couldn't begin to comprehend it.

The grid was going wild, and, afraid that it might start beeping as well as blinking, he quickly deactivated it. He was still wearing his eyepatch; he wanted very badly to remove it, to get a more thorough view of the building and its surroundings, but he was afraid that 32 would record the image and bring in some expert to identify the rock formations at this particular point, and he hadn't gone to all the trouble of finding the Oracle's hideout just to broadcast it to 32 and his whole department.

He squatted down in the shadow of a large overhang and spent the next ten minutes studying the layout, and taking holographs with the tiny camera he had brought along for the purpose. When he finally felt himself beginning to dehydrate from the heat, he carefully retreated, still staying well clear of the road, until he came to the spot where Broussard had hidden the vehicle.

"God, it's hot out there!" he panted, leaning back and luxuriating in the conditioned air of the vehicle.

"People weren't built to live in this kind of heat," agreed Broussard. "Sometimes I think even the Blue Devils look uncomfortable in this weather." He paused. "Did you find her?"

"I think so."

"You *think* so?" repeated Broussard.

"I didn't see her," answered the Injun, "but I'll be awfully surprised if she's not there."

"Did you find a way in?"

"I'm working on it."

"What now?"

The Injun leaned back comfortably, clasped his hands behind his head, and shut his eyes.

"Now we go back to Quichancha and wait."

"Wait for what?" asked Broussard.

"For any number of things," said the Injun serenely. "For certain funds to be transferred. For the Whistler to show up. For the Oracle to make another mistake."

"*Another* mistake?"

The Injun nodded. "She should have killed me this afternoon. I was unarmed and on foot, and I couldn't have run fifty yards in that heat." He paused. "She has her limitations. She can't see far enough ahead to know that the next time I come back I'm going to kill her."

"I still don't see how you plan to do it, sir," said Broussard, putting the vehicle in motion and starting to head back toward Quichancha.

The Injun smiled tranquilly. "Neither does she."

"But you *do* have a plan?"

"Absolutely."

"Would you care to share it with me?"

"You'll know it when the time comes," answered the Injun.

"If I know it, won't the Oracle know it, too?"

"Very likely."

"Then she'll be able to prevent it."

The Injun shook his head. "Knowing it won't do her the least bit of good."

"I don't understand, sir," said Broussard.

"Neither will she," said the Injun, smiling again. "I almost feel sorry for her."

PART 3

———

———

———

———

———

———

———

———

———

———

The Jade Queen's Book

18

Chandler remained in his rooming house for three days following the attempts on his life, leaving only to have dinner each night at the Wolfman's restaurant. He considered meeting with some of the Surgeon's former clientele and going through the motions of soliciting business, but decided against it. After all, both the Oracle and the Democracy had tried to kill him; there didn't seem to be any reason to try to maintain his cover.

On the fourth night, as he entered the restaurant accompanied by Gin, who had resumed his duties though his injured shoulder was still heavily bandaged, the Wolfman spotted him and immediately approached him.

"Follow me, please," he said, leading them to a small circular room at the back of the restaurant, where Lord Lucifer sat at a hexagonal table.

"Good evening, Mr. Chandler," said Lord Lucifer.

"Good evening," replied Chandler, looking around the room as Gin seated himself at the table. Finally he took a small device out of his pocket and pressed it against a wall, where it remained when he took his hand away.

"What's that?" asked the Wolfman.

"An anti-eavesdropping device," answered Chandler. "It'll scramble any signals that might leave this room."

"You're a very careful man, Mr. Chandler," said Lord Lucifer.

"That's how I stay alive."

"Can I bring you anything, Whistler?" asked the Wolfman. "I just got in a shipment of Cygnian cognac."

"Later."

"Dinner, perhaps?"

"We'll let you know."

The Wolfman shrugged and went back into the restaurant while Chandler seated himself at the table.

"Well?" said Chandler, facing the dapper criminal.

"Finding a way to smuggle you onto Hades is proving to be more difficult than I thought," replied Lord Lucifer. "Since Boma's death the Blue Devils have taken additional security measures on their shuttle flights. It can be done, of course, but it will take a lot more time and planning than I had anticipated." He paused and smiled. "She's definitely not very anxious to see you in the flesh, Mr. Chandler."

"If she's everything she's supposed to be, I don't imagine she's losing any sleep over the prospect," replied Chandler. "This is probably the Blue Devils' idea." He stopped speaking, struck by a sudden thought.

"What is it, Mr. Chandler?" asked Lord Lucifer, staring at him intently.

"Consider what I just said," answered Chandler. "There's no reason why a woman who can foresee the future should be worried about me trying to kill her. Therefore, this *has* to be the Blue Devils' idea." He stared at Lord Lucifer. "What does that imply to you?"

"That they don't want you to reach her."

"Of course they don't," said Chandler impatiently. "But why not? They know the extent of her power—it's what's kept them out of the Democracy—so why should this worry them?"

"I see!" said Lord Lucifer, suddenly grinning.

"Well, I don't see a damned thing," interjected Gin. "Would someone please tell me what you two think you know?"

Chandler turned to the driver. "I've been hired to bring her out, and to kill her only as a last resort. I haven't figured out how to kill her yet, and they have no reason to think she can be killed. What does that imply to you?"

Gin shrugged. "I don't know," he said, confused. "What *should* it imply?"

"That they're afraid she'll leave voluntarily with Mr. Chandler," said Lord Lucifer.

"I've been operating on the assumption that she's remained on Hades by choice," added Chandler. "But what if that assumption was false?"

"You've told me about her," said Gin. "How could they hold someone with her powers against her will?"

"You lock her in an electrified cell, surround it with a force field, and leave two guards on duty, and all the foresight in the world isn't going to do her a bit of good," said Chandler. "If every possible future has her incarcerated against her will, then that's where she'll stay."

"It still doesn't make sense," protested Gin. "If she can see the future, why would she let herself be locked up to begin with?"

Chandler shrugged. "Who knows? She was only eight years old when she came to Hades. Maybe her powers weren't that well developed then. She arrived with an alien called the Mock Turtle—maybe he betrayed her. Maybe she simply didn't understand what they intended to do with her." He paused. "Or maybe they were all bosom buddies until the day she decided to leave, and they realized that without her they were going to be assimilated into the Democracy."

"Or maybe you're dead wrong," said Gin, unconvinced.

"Maybe," said Chandler. "But let's assume for the sake of argument that I'm right." He paused again. "It would also explain why the Democracy wants me dead. If they think there's a chance she'll come out with me, they'll just have to go to the trouble of tracking her down again, and I gather she wasn't an easy lady to find." He paused. "Look at it from their point of view: the Blue Devils aren't much of a military threat, and they haven't made any major alliances with the Democracy's enemies. If they can't kill her, this is probably as safe a place to keep her as any. If she leaves, she could go to the Canphor Twins or Lodin XI or some other world that *can* make war on the Democracy."

"I still think you're making a mistake," said Gin adamantly.

"Prove it."

"Easy," said the driver. "If she wants you to rescue her, why did she send the Blue Devil to kill you?"

"She didn't. That was *his* idea—his or his government's."

"Then how did he know who you were and where to find you?"

"A very good point," said Lord Lucifer. He turned to Chandler. "Have you an answer?"

"There are no answers when we're dealing with such minimal information, just suppositions," said Chandler. "But suppose she could foresee that Boma couldn't kill me, that I'd spot the glass in the food—and suppose further that she knew it would lead me to the

very conclusion I've just reached." He paused. "Wouldn't that b
the best way she had of telling me that she was willing to leave?"

"That's a lot of supposing," said Gin dubiously. "I sure wouldn
risk my life on it."

"I don't plan to risk *my* life on it, either," answered Chandle
"Not yet, anyway." He fell silent for a moment, collecting hi
thoughts. "Still, I've got a gut feeling that I'm right. I think a new
course of action is called for."

"What did you have in mind, Mr. Chandler?" asked Lor
Lucifer.

"Well, we seem to be in agreement that I can't go to Hades righ
now, not if they're searching every shuttle."

"Then what do you plan to do?"

"I would think the answer was obvious," answered Chandler. "I
I can't go in after her, the only alternative is to get her to com
to me."

"She'll never come up here," said Lord Lucifer. "If she wants t
leave with you, the Blue Devils will never let her. And if you'
wrong and she wants you dead, she's got enough agents on Po
Marrakech to do the job for her."

"I have no intention of remaining on Port Marrakech," sai
Chandler. "The Blue Devils know who I am, and the Democrac
is also trying to kill me."

"Then I still don't understand what you're going to do," sai
Lord Lucifer, frowning.

"There are two other moons. Which one has the most Blue Devil
on it?"

"Port Maracaibo," offered Gin. "Port Samarkand is mostly farm
and processing plants."

"Then the Whistler is going to be captured by that famed oppo
tunist, Lord Lucifer, who will incarcerate him in the tunnels beneat
the Platinum Quarter until someone pays a ransom of, oh, not t
price myself too cheaply, ten million credits." Chandler smile
"No one will pay it, of course. The Democracy wants me out c
the way, the Blue Devils want me out of the way, and the Icema
isn't about to dip into his own pocket to rescue me." He pause
"And tomorrow, a man with a fresh and totally untraceable identit
will show up on Port Maracaibo. He'll dwell in total obscurit
shunning the spotlight there every bit as much as the Whistle
sought it on Port Marrakech, and before a month has gone b
he'll have wrought such havoc among the Oracle's agents that th

Blue Devils themselves will insist that she take a hand in finding and capturing him."

"You really think they'll send her to Port Maracaibo to find you?" asked Lord Lucifer.

"They're not going to be willing to live in a state of terror forever," replied Chandler, "and they're certainly not going to declare war against the moons and give the Democracy any cause for moving in to protect its human population. Sooner or later they're going to decide that their best bet is to send the Oracle to Port Maracaibo to save them."

"And if they decide she's too valuable to risk losing?" persisted Lord Lucifer.

"Then," answered Chandler wryly, "I've still got four months to think of something else."

"I don't mean to be insulting, Mr. Chandler, but that's a pretty feeble answer."

"It was facetious," admitted Chandler. "Actually, if I can't draw her up to Port Maracaibo, I think my chances of getting her out may actually be enhanced."

"You lost me again," said Gin.

"I'm afraid I don't quite follow you, either," added Lord Lucifer.

"If she's totally committed to the Blue Devils, she'll come after me the instant I start putting pressure on them. She probably considers herself invulnerable, so from her point of view there's no risk involved; it's just a matter of tending to security. And if she actually wants to leave Hades and they let her come anyway, then they feel they can control her, and I've overestimated her power." He paused. "But if they're afraid to let her come to Port Maracaibo, then her power is every bit as awesome as I've been led to believe it is and they don't dare risk giving her any freedom of action at all. If that's the case, all I have to do is figure out a way to open one door for her and she'll do the rest."

Lord Lucifer smiled. "You make it sound a lot simpler than I think it will prove to be."

"Well, if it was easy, someone would have gotten to her before now," admitted Chandler. He paused. "I don't know about anyone else, but I think I'm ready for that cognac."

"Sounds good to me," agreed Gin.

Chandler turned to the driver. "Why don't you go and tell the Wolfman to bring it in?"

"Sure thing, Whistler," said Gin. He got up from the table and left the room.

"Find out everything you can about him," said Chandler, lowering his voice.

"About Gin?" repeated Lord Lucifer. "He's been around for years."

"Do it anyway."

"Do you have some reason to suspect he might be in the employ of the Oracle?"

"If she's got any humans working for her, I'm not aware of it."

"Neither am I," admitted Lord Lucifer. He frowned. "Then why are you suspicious of him?"

"The Oracle's not the only one trying to kill me, remember?"

"But Gin was almost killed by a Democracy assassin," protested Lord Lucifer.

"And he spent two days in the hospital with a shoulder burn," responded Chandler. "He should have been out on the street the next morning. They knew he was my driver; they may have gotten to him while he was being patched up. If they did, I want to know who he reports to."

"I'll take care of it," promised Lord Lucifer. He paused thoughtfully. "Still, I think your fears are groundless. Look at him—the man practically worships you."

"If I recall my theology, Judas practically worshipped Jesus too," answered Chandler wryly.

"Duly noted," said Lord Lucifer. "By the way, it occurs to me that you could use a contact on Port Maracaibo."

"You have one in mind, no doubt?" suggested Chandler.

"The very best," answered Lord Lucifer. "But I see Gin is returning with our cognac, so perhaps we'd best discuss it later."

"Right," agreed Chandler.

"Good stuff," said Gin, entering the room with a bottle and three glasses on a tray. "I had a little taste out there, just to make sure it was as represented." He filled the glasses and passed them around. "Let me propose a toast, Mr. Chandler."

"Be my guest."

"To the Oracle," said Lord Lucifer. "She has certainly made our lives more interesting."

"I'll drink to that," said Chandler, raising his glass to his lips. "Let's just hope she hasn't also made them briefer."

19

There were major differences between Port Maracaibo and Port Marrakech, although they had been terraformed by the same team and possessed almost identical atmospheres, gravities, and climates.

The structures on Port Maracaibo were less exotic, more rectangular, less formal, more closely clustered in the residential areas. The city—which like its counterpart on Port Marrakech bore the name of the moon—had been carefully planned: its streets were laid out in a grid, its commercial center had clearly defined borders, and a series of public coaches, powered by superconductivity, skimmed a few inches above the streets between the city center and the outlying areas.

Chandler sat in a coach, studying a map of the city he had picked up while passing through Customs. From time to time he looked up to make sure that no one was watching him, but he didn't seriously expect that he was being followed. Before leaving Port Marrakech he had dyed his auburn hair a dark brown, put brown-tinted contact lenses into his eyes, and had left all his weaponry on Port Marrakech. His new features perfectly matched the passport that Lord Lucifer had supplied him, and he hadn't set off any alarms while going through Spaceport Security. He was just a down-on-his-luck traveler, hoping to find work on the farthest of Hades' three moons.

His new name was Preston Grange, and Lord Lucifer had even arranged to give him a history that included four arrests and a pair of convictions for minor crimes. He probably couldn't stand the

kind of scrutiny he would receive if he were arrested, but then, i
he were arrested he had more pressing problems to worry about
anyway.

The address Lord Luficer had given him was on Cleopatr
Street. He hunted it up on the map, realized that he had t
change coaches in order to reach it, and walked to a door. A
electronic sensor picked up the heat from his body, relayed i
to the coach's brain, and the coach came to a stop at the nex
corner.

Chandler stepped out, looked for a public transit sign on th
next cross street, and stood in front of it. A moment later he wa
in another coach, and a few minutes after that he was standing o
Cleopatra Street. He checked a number and began walking towar
the address he had been given.

The area quickly turned shabby and a bit run-down: bars
nightclubs, and drug dens lined the street, and brightly dresse
men and women lingered in doorways, some beckoning, som
engaged in whispered conversations, some merely staring out a
the street in complete boredom.

Finally he came to number 719, a small, unobtrusive build
ing stuck between an all-night restaurant and a sleazy night
club promising acts that would shock any race in the galaxy
bar none.

He opened the door and found himself in a small octagona
foyer with no other doors. There was a small device on on
wall, about five feet above the floor, and a recorded, slightl
mechanical voice instructed him to peer into it. He did as h
was told, and was soon staring at a hologram of a stunningl
beautiful blonde woman doing a sensuous dance. The hologran
vanished after thirty seconds, and the voice informed him that hi
retinagram had been taken, analyzed, and cleared.

"Please step forward," said the voice.

Chandler approached the wall, which slid aside to let him pas
through, then moved back into place.

He followed a narrow corridor and emerged into a luxuri
ous parlor, filled with plush furnishings, erotic paintings an
holograms, and even a bronze sculpture of the same woma
who had appeared in the little holo he had seen in the foy
er.

The room was filled with women in various states of undress
including a pair who were totally nude. There were four me

resent—a huge, well-muscled bouncer and three well-dressed
en who were obviously clients.

A seductively clad woman detached herself from a group of
milarly dressed young women and approached Chandler.

"Welcome to The Womb, the finest brothel on the three
oons," she said. "May I help you?"

"I'm looking for the Jade Queen," replied Chandler.

"Is she expecting you?"

"I believe so."

"And your name is . . . ?"

He stared at her. "Just tell her that Lord Lucifer sent me."

"Won't you make yourself comfortable?" said the woman. "I'll
e back shortly."

She left the room, and Chandler idly inspected some of the erot-
 artwork that hung on the walls. She returned a moment later.

"Follow me, please," she said.

Chandler fell into step behind her as she led him into an airlift,
scended two levels, walked down a narrow corridor, then stopped
hen she came to the very last door.

"She's in there."

"Thanks."

"Perhaps I'll see you later?" suggested the woman.

"I doubt it."

She shrugged and walked away, and Chandler turned to face
e door. He heard the whirring of a holo camera and felt the
rief, always slightly unpleasant sensation of having his reti-
a scanned, and then the door receded and he entered a huge
ctagonal chamber, furnished with artwork and exotic artifacts
om more than a dozen worlds. The carpet rippled with a life
f its own, and a golden love seat designed for beings that bore
o resemblance to humanity hovered inches above the ground
ff to his left. Dominating the room was a huge window that
oked out upon sights far more alien and savage than the jun-
les of The Frenchman's World; Chandler looked for the holo
rojector that was casting the incredibly real images, but couldn't
ot it.

Seated behind a large desk that allowed her to observe both the
oor and the window was a woman, no longer youthful but not
uite middle-aged, carrying a few pounds more than she should
ave, but carrying them well. She wore a jade necklace and a
air of rings with matching stones, and a golden outfit trimmed

with the delicate feathers of some alien bird. Her eyes were large, green, and rather wide-set; her nose small and straight; her lips thin and painted an iridescent orange. Her hair was brown, but streaked with shades of gold and red, carefully coiffed and piled high atop her head.

"What can I do for you, Mr. . . . ?" she said in a voice that was just a little lower and a little deeper than he had expected.

"Grange," he replied. "Preston Grange."

"That idiot!" she snapped contemptuously.

"I beg your pardon?"

"He's sent three Preston Granges to Port Maracaibo in the past four years. How long does he think he can keep getting away with it?"

"Serves me right for trusting anyone else," said Chandler. "I'll change it tomorrow."

"Just out of curiosity, what is your name?" she asked.

"Chandler."

"Do some people call you the Whistler?"

"From time to time."

She nodded, as if to herself. "I *thought* it was you. Your fame precedes you, Mr. Chandler."

"So, it would appear, does my alias," he added wryly.

"No problem," she said. "You'll have a new identity before you leave my office." She paused, then indicated a chair facing the desk. "Have a seat." He did as she bade him. "Can I get you something to drink?"

"No, thanks."

"Something to make you happier, perhaps, or mentally sharper?"

He shook his head.

She shrugged. "As you wish," she said, walking to the cabinet and helping herself to a pair of small round pills. She stood perfectly still for a moment, as if waiting for the effect, whatever it was, to begin, then sat down opposite him.

"Write down the name you want to use so that there won't be any discrepancy in the way it's spelled. I'll need your signature for the ID documents, anyway."

"Have you got a piece of paper?" he asked, withdrawing a pen from a pocket of his tunic.

She opened the top drawer of her desk and handed him a monogrammed sheet of stationery.

"All right," said Chandler, scribbling on the paper. "This is it."

She took the sheet back from him and studied it. "Julio Juan Javier?"

Chandler smiled. "It's so alliterative that no one will ever believe it's not a real name given by a doting mother with terrible taste. No one would use a name like that as a cover."

She shrugged. "All right. You'll be Javier by tomorrow morning." She paused for a moment. "I'll start calling you that right now. I don't want to get in the habit of calling you Chandler or Whistler and having it slip out at an inopportune time."

"And what do I call you?" asked Chandler.

"My professional name is the Jade Queen. You may call me Jade."

"May I assume that you own this place, Jade?"

"I own every building and business for two blocks in each direction," she answered bluntly.

"I'm impressed," said Chandler.

"You should be."

"What's your connection to Lord Lucifer?"

"Since he sent you here, there's no sense hiding it from you," she replied. "I suppose you could say that he's my counterpart on Port Marrakech. Each of us has created an empire by preying upon the foolish, the gullible, and the greedy." She paused. "His holdings do not extend to Port Maracaibo, and mine do not extend to Port Marrakech. But," she added, "each of us would like to establish a foothold on Hades itself, so it is in our best interest to help you in any way we can."

"Good," said Chandler. "I'll take all the help I can get."

"From what I hear, you'll need plenty," said Jade. "Does anyone else know you're here?"

"Just my driver, a man named Gin. He's back on Port Marrakech, under Lord Lucifer's watchful eye."

"Have you some reason to be suspicious of him?" she asked.

"No."

"Then why—?"

"I just don't have a very trusting nature."

She nodded her approval. "You'll live a lot longer that way." She paused. "You're sure he's the only person other than Lord Lucifer who knows you're here?"

"Except for you."

"How long do you plan to stay here?"

"I'm not sure yet," answered Chandler. "Possibly a month, hopefully much less."

"Well, if you want me to help you while you're on Port Maracaibo, perhaps you'd better tell me what you'll be doing here."

"You might be better off not knowing," he suggested. "Once I tell you, you're legally culpable."

"Mr. Javier," said Jade, "I own half the officials on this moon, and I rent the other half. If you want my help, you're going to have to tell me what you intend to do. Otherwise, we can't do business."

Chandler paused for a moment, then nodded his acquiescence. "All right," he replied. "I've come to Port Maracaibo to kill Blue Devils."

"If you hate Blue Devils, there were plenty of them on Port Marrakech."

"I wasn't interested in killing those Blue Devils."

"So I gather," she said. "Why do you want to kill these particular Blue Devils?"

"I hope to elicit a response."

"I don't understand," said Jade. "What kind of response? Hatred? Fear? Panic?"

"All three."

"That's no answer. Why is it important that the Blue Devils on Port Maracaibo should feel fear or panic?"

"Because if they do, I hope they will make an attempt to prevent what I'm doing."

She stared at him for a moment. "You think they'll summon the Oracle to come to Port Maracaibo and hunt you down, don't you?"

"That's right."

"That may not be the brightest idea you've ever had," said Jade. "She's supposed to be virtually invulnerable. How do you propose to kill her?"

"She's much more valuable alive than dead," said Chandler. "There isn't a government or military organization in the galaxy that wouldn't give its eyeteeth to get its hands on her. After all, how can you lose an election or a war when she's on your side, telling you what to do next?" He paused. "The Democracy has been after her for sixteen years. I've been paid to bring her out, and to kill her only if there is no possible way of taking her away from Hades."

"And you think that if you kill enough Blue Devils, she'll come to Port Maracaibo?"

"It's a possibility."

Jade looked dubious. "Why should she?"

"Because she'll be the only one who can stop me, and eventually the Blue Devils are going to get tired of being decimated."

"What I meant was, what does she care about Blue Devils? Why should she leave Hades, where even the Fleet doesn't dare attack her?"

"Because I have reason to believe that she *wants* to leave Hades, that in fact she may be incarcerated there against her will."

"Oh?"

He explained his chain of reasoning to her, as he had done to Lord Lucifer two days earlier.

"So actually, you'll be more encouraged if she doesn't come to Port Maracaibo than if she does?" said Jade.

"If I'm reading the situation correctly, yes."

"How long will you give her?" continued Jade. "How many Blue Devils will you have to kill before you decide that she *isn't* coming?"

"I don't know," admitted Chandler. "I imagine it'll depend on how much confusion I can cause here, and how much I can disrupt any lines of communication that exist between her and Port Maracaibo."

"I still don't know why you had to come here to do it, though."

"My identity was known to too many people on Port Marrakech," he answered. "Sooner or later the Blue Devils would have figured out who was behind the killings, and they would have come after me themselves. It makes much more sense to start on a new world with a fresh identity; they're only going to use her as a last resort, once they themselves have failed to find out who's responsible for the murders and the disruptions."

Jade got up, walked to a wet bar, poured herself a Cygnian cognac, and turned to face him. "Well, you certainly have your work cut out for you, Julio Juan Javier." She sipped her drink. "Where do *I* come in?"

"I'm an outsider here," answered Chandler, "and I plan to keep it that way. Given a week or so, I could learn my way around the city, find out where the Blue Devils congregate, and set up a number of hideouts—but a lot of Men and Blue Devils would see me, and some of them might remember me, and the only way to make this an effective campaign of terror is for my identity to be completely concealed. In fact, I'd be just as happy if the Blue Devils think I'm one of them. Therefore, I need a guide, someone who can tell me where to go, or better still, provide me with some form of private transportation, and I need a place to return to when I'm done. One of the bedrooms at The Womb would serve my purposes, because that way if anyone ever *does* track me back here, you'll be able to vouch that I'd been here all night." He paused. "And there's another reason I need you."

"Oh?"

"I'm going to have to kill a number of alien beings. It's strictly business, and I have no more use for them than they have for me. But it would be less wasteful and more useful if you could direct me toward those Blue Devils who might be in contact with the Oracle or whatever forces she controls. Since the object of this operation is to wreak enough havoc and cause enough disruption that the Blue Devils are forced to bring the Oracle here to confront me, then my most effective course of action is to kill those Blue Devils who might have some connection to her, or at least to the government of Hades."

"I see," said Jade, nodding thoughtfully.

"By the way, I'm going to need some weapons. Can you get them for me?"

"No problem."

Chandler paused. "There's one more thing you should know," he added.

"Oh? And what is that?"

"Someone in the Democracy doesn't want me to fulfill my contract. I don't know if they don't want me to bring her out, or if they don't want me to kill her—but this person, or these people, whichever the case may be, tried to kill me back on Port Marrakech."

"Is the Democracy your employer?" asked Jade.

"I think so."

"You *think* so?"

"I'm just a subcontractor," he answered. "I've never dealt directly with the person who's paying for this."

Jade frowned. "One thing puzzles me," she said, returning to her chair and sitting down once more. "If the Democracy is your employer, why don't they just call you off?"

"I don't know for a fact that the Democracy *is* my employer— and at any rate, I'm not working directly for it."

"Let me try it a different way," continued Jade. "If they don't want you to fulfill your mission, why are you going ahead with it?"

"Because I'm a businessman, not a patriot," answered Chandler. "I was paid half the money up front, and I don't get the other half until I complete the contract."

"You're a foolish man," said Jade. "Whatever they're paying you, it isn't worth going up against the Oracle."

"Then you're an equally foolish woman for helping me," replied Chandler.

"There's a difference," she said. "There's an entire world for the taking. *My* gain is commensurate with the risk. Yours isn't."

"Half a world," he corrected her.

"You're referring to Lord Lucifer, of course?"

Chandler nodded.

"He's out of the equation," said Jade, her expression as cold and hard as Chandler's own. "Or did you really think you were the only killer in this room?"

20

Jade ushered Chandler to a large, luxurious room next to her own. It possessed an ornate airbed, hand-carved furniture from the Domar system, and the same holographic display she had in her office.

"I'll pass the word that I've got a special friend living here, and everyone will leave you alone," she said.

"Won't they want to see who your special friend is?" asked Chandler.

"What's wrong with that?" she retorted. "The more people who know you're here, the better. We'll even have all your meals brought up here. The trick is not to let anyone see you leave." She paused. "That's a false closet," she continued, indicating one of four identical mirrored doors lining one of the walls. "I'll rig it to respond to your retinagram, so it will open whenever you approach it and stay open for, shall we say, twenty seconds? Behind it is an airlift that will take you down to my garage. You'll enter and leave the building through it, and no one will know you're gone."

"I saw a number of doors down the corridor," said Chandler. "How much business gets transacted on this floor?"

"Almost none, unless we're overcrowded. Some of the girls sleep up here when they're too tired or too busy to go home. It would probably be a good idea for you to meet a few of them and try to make friends with them; the more people who can vouch that you spend all your time up here, the better."

"It sounds good," he replied. "I'll need to take a tour of the city tomorrow."

"I'll be off duty just before sunrise," she said. "We'll leave then." She paused. "I'd better fetch you the first time, until you learn your way around." Jade walked to the door. "I'll see you in a few hours."

He offered no reply, and she left the room.

Chandler took a Dryshower, shaved, and then lay down on the bed. He was asleep almost instantly, but some internal clock woke him up about twenty minutes before Jade was due back, and he was dressed and ready for her when she appeared.

"You look pleased with yourself," he noted as she entered the room, dressed in a more practical outfit, and handed him the weapons he had requested. "I take it the whorehouse did a good night's business."

"Actually, it was only average," she replied. "But *I* did a good night's business." She tossed two small packets onto the bed.

"What are these?"

"The top one contains your new ID papers and passport."

"Thanks," he said, studying them with an expert eye. "That was fast."

"You're paying for it."

"And what's in the other one?"

"Take a look."

He picked it up and opened it, withdrawing a sheet of paper on which were written a trio of incomprehensible alien symbols.

"What is it?" he asked.

"One of The Womb's clients works for the Planetary Defense Department," she replied.

"I didn't know you had one."

"When you live on a moon, and you're outnumbered hundreds to one by a hostile population on the planet that you're orbiting, you'd damned well *better* have one," she said. "Oh, we couldn't win a war with the Blue Devils. In fact, we probably couldn't last ten minutes if they attacked us. But we monitor all their transmissions, and if we ever have cause to believe that an attack is being planned, we'll send for the Navy." She paused. "Anyway, this client specializes in translating and decoding the Blue Devils' transmissions. And *that*," she concluded, gesturing toward the paper, "is the way the Blue Devils refer to the Oracle in their own language."

"How did you get him to write this down?"

"First, I got him a little drunk," said Jade with a smile. "And then I appealed to his ego, which, alas, is the most massive thing about him. By the time he wakes up in the morning, he won't even remember he wrote it."

"All right," said Chandler. "Now I know how to spell the Oracle's name on Hades. So what?"

"Well," said Jade, "it seems to me that if you're trying to elicit a response, to use your own words, you can elicit it a lot faster if you'll leave this symbol on each of your victims."

Chandler considered her suggestion. "Not bad," he admitted.

"It's damned good," replied Jade. "If they think the Oracle's responsible for the killings, she'll *have* to try to capture you to prove she's innocent. And if they think she's being set up, they're going to want her to stop you from killing them with such impunity." She flashed him a triumphant smile. "They might even think you're trying to elicit a response so that we're justified in bringing in the Fleet."

"*That* ought to shake them up," agreed Chandler. "I'd like you to do something else for me."

"What?"

"Contact the guy who gave this to you and see if he knows which Blue Devil is sending those messages—and also see if he can identify any other Blue Devils who work for the Oracle, or if he knows the location from which they're being sent. I think we'll get a much quicker response if I go after those Blue Devils who are in communication with her."

"I'll make a point of finding out next time he's here."

"How often does he show up here?" asked Chandler.

She shrugged. "It varies."

Chandler shook his head. "Not good enough. He could stay away for weeks."

"All right," said Jade. "I'll invite him to lunch after I show you around the city."

"Will he come?"

She smiled. "If *I* invite him, he'll come." She paused. "Well," she said at last, "are you ready to go?"

"Lead the way."

She walked to the false closet, waited for it to open, and led him inside. A moment later they floated gently down to the basement level on the heavy air currents. There were two vehicles parked there: an elegant, chrome and gold groundcar that, like the public coaches, was capable of skimming just above the ground, but also possessed wheels for those streets that hadn't been treated for superconductivity; and a very old, very nondescript vehicle that had seen better days and even better decades, but which would arouse almost no interest. She entered the latter, and he climbed into the front seat beside her.

"What do you think of it?" she asked.

"It belongs in a home for the elderly."

"It might surprise you, Javier," she replied with a smile. "I've had the whole thing rebuilt and customized beneath this exterior. It's twice as fast as the showpiece over there," she continued, indicating the groundcar.

"Interesting," commented Chandler.

"Practical," answered Jade. "It doesn't draw attention the way the other one does, and as a result I can maintain my privacy when I have to go out."

She pulled out of the garage and drove up a ramp to the street, then turned north.

"You've got to watch out for these damned coaches," she commented, moving to the side of the street to allow a coach to pass her. "They're omnipresent, and they're responsible for eighty percent of the accidents in the city."

"Where are we going?" asked Chandler.

"Blue Devil heaven."

"That's what it's called?"

"It's what it *ought* to be called," replied Jade. "It's the area where most of the Blue Devils congregate. There are a few shops, but no restaurants, no nightclubs, no whorehouses, nothing but apartment buildings. They're a strange race, Javier—I've been on Port Maracaibo for eleven years, and I *still* don't know what the hell they're doing here. They're not part of the economy, they don't work, they don't organize politically, they don't interact with Men . . . they just hang around on street corners like a bunch of surly human teenagers."

"They must immigrate here for *some* reason," said Chandler.

"I suppose so," she agreed. "But I'll be damned if anyone I know can tell you what it is."

"Maybe they just want some token presence here in case they ever try to reclaim the moons, some legal justification to prove they've never really relinquished them."

She shook her head. "That's a good, logical, human reason—so it's probably not valid." She looked ahead. "Here it comes," she announced. "Once we cross this big street coming up, we'r in their neighborhood."

Chandler looked out the window and studied the area. Most c the buildings had been built for human residents and had falle into various states of disrepair. Blue Devils lined the streets most of them simply standing and staring, a few walking pur posefully.

"What do they do for entertainment?" asked Chandler. "Hav they got anything akin to holos or theaters?"

"Damned if I know."

"I thought you'd been living here for eleven years."

"We don't bother them, they don't bother us," answered Jade "Both races prefer it that way."

"Drive by the heart of their commercial district," said Chandler "I want to take a look at it."

She turned left for a block, then continued going north. I another moment they came to a single block that was line with shops and stores, almost half of which were grocery mar kets.

"Go slower," said Chandler.

Jade slowed the vehicle's pace.

"It won't work," she said.

"What won't?"

"Destroying some grocery stores," she answered. "They'r not like us. You're just as likely to disrupt them by killing some innocuous-looking Blue Devil who's standing on a cor ner, minding his own business."

"I'll do both if I have to," he replied. "I'd much rather fin out which Blue Devils have some connection to the Oracle though."

"I *told* you I'd get your information," she said irritably. "In cas it's escaped your notice, I haven't been out of your presence sinc you first said you wanted it."

"I'm sorry," he said. "It's just that I find the thought of killing hundreds of Blue Devils wasteful. I'd rather kill two or three wh matter to the Oracle and get the same response."

"A moral assassin," she said with an amused smile.

"Not everyone gets into this business because they like to kil people," he replied.

"Then why do you do it?"

"Because I find *all* forms of business distasteful," answered Chandler. "This one pays me enough so that I don't have to work very often."

"I suppose there's a twisted kind of logic to that," said Jade.

"Let's leave this part of the city," he said after a few more minutes had passed. "Go back to The Womb and then just start driving around that general area. I want to get the feel of it, and to make sure I can find my way back in the dark."

She headed for The Womb, spent another twenty minutes crisscrossing the vicinity, and finally pulled into the sunken garage.

"I'm going to leave you here and try to get some more information," said Jade. "Once you get back up to your room, just tell the computer what you want to eat and it will transmit the order to our kitchen."

"You've got a kitchen?" he asked, surprised.

"Well, actually it's in the restaurant next door, but the buildings are connected. In the meantime, I'll see what I can find out about the transmissions." She seemed about to open the door, then paused. "Can I ask you a question, Javier?"

"Go ahead."

"Just what is it that makes the Oracle so valuable to the Democracy?" asked Jade. "We've all heard of her, but no one knows exactly who she is or what she does."

"She sees the future."

"Second sight?"

"More than that. If all she could do was see what was going to happen next, I think everyone except gamblers and stockbrokers would leave her alone."

"What else does she do?"

"She not only sees the future, she manipulates it," answered Chandler. "She sees every possible future, every permutation, and she tries to make the one she wants come to pass."

"You're kidding!"

"No, I'm not."

"If she's got the power to make anything happen that she can envision, why hasn't she conquered the galaxy by now?"

He shrugged. "It's a big galaxy. And I think her power has its limits."

"What limits?"

"I don't know," he admitted. "But if she didn't have them, she *would* have conquered the galaxy by now—or at least changed it a hell of a lot more than she has."

"Just the same," said Jade, "I hope they're paying you enough."

"Sometimes I wonder about that myself," he said, getting out of the vehicle.

He floated up to his room, ordered a meal, decided that it was a good thing the brothel wasn't depending on the quality of its food to make a profit, then lay back on his airbed and watched a prerecorded game of murderball on the holo.

Jade entered the room just as the game, and its few remaining participants, had headed into overtime.

"How did you do?" he asked, getting to his feet.

"Well, I've got your first victim for you," she said. "And with a little luck, I may have the Oracle's location by tomorrow morning."

"Oh?"

She nodded. "My friend is putting a tracer on their transmissions. He'll be able to pinpoint the exact location on Hades that they're being sent to."

Chandler considered the possibilities for a moment, then grimaced. "I don't know if that will be of much use to us," he said. "It's probably relayed half a dozen times before it reaches her." He paused. "But I'd like to know where it's sent from."

"We're working on it," answered Jade. "In the meantime, you've got your own work cut out for you."

"What do you mean?"

"The Blue Devil you want—the one who sent the transmission my friend told me about—is named Kraef Timo. I don't know what his function is, but it must be something pretty damned important."

"What makes you think so?" asked Chandler.

"He's got half a dozen bodyguards."

"How could your friend possibly know that? I thought he just checked transmissions."

"I have other friends," said Jade. "And one of them is a local policeman who's on my payroll. Once I got Kraef Timo's name, I asked him to run it through his computer, just to see if there was anything on him. And it turns out that they arrested Timo on a very minor violation about five months ago—it never even went to court—but when they went to his quarters to bring him in, he had to call off his bodyguards or there'd have been a real bloodbath."

"Very interesting," said Chandler. "Where do I find this Timo?"

"He's one of the few Blue Devils who doesn't live in their sector," said Jade. "He's got a suite of rooms at the Uncut Diamond—that's a hotel about ten blocks from here."

"I assume his bodyguards stay there with him?"

"Yes, they do."

"Is Timo likely to be there after dark?"

She shrugged. "Since nobody knows what he does, nobody knows his hours." She paused. "Are you really sure you want to go up against six armed Blue Devils?"

"I can think of things I'd rather do."

"But you're going to do it anyway?"

"I can't think of a better way to start putting some pressure on her."

"Maybe I can get another name from my friend, someone who sends transmissions and *doesn't* have a walking arsenal following him around."

He shook his head. "The bodyguards are precisely what makes this one such a desirable target. Why don't you come back for me in about six hours?"

"What are you going to do in the meantime?" she asked.

"Take a nap," he said, reclining on the airbed. "I've got a busy night ahead of me."

He closed his eyes, and a moment later he was sound asleep.

Jade stared at him for a long moment, then left his room and returned to her own. And sat down. And for the first time, tried to decide whether she really *wanted* the Oracle to come to Port Maracaibo looking for Chandler and his confederates.

21

Chandler awoke just after sunset, ordered dinner, and spent the next half hour watching various sporting events on the holoscreen. Then Jade entered his room and approached him.

"Are you ready?" she asked.

He shook his head. "Let's wait another two or three hours. I want to give Timo's bodyguards a little time to get sleepy."

"Good," said Jade, pulling up a chair and sitting down. "Because we have to talk."

"What about?"

"About the Oracle."

Chandler stared at her. "Go ahead," he said. "I'm listening."

"Why are you trying to lure her to Port Maracaibo?"

"I told you why," said Chandler.

"I know what you told me," she said. "Now I want you to tell me something else."

"What?"

"How do you know this is *your* idea?"

"She's no telepath," he replied. "The man who hired me actually spent some time with her some years ago."

"She doesn't have to be a telepath," persisted Jade.

"I don't think I follow you."

"You told me yourself: she can see an infinite number of futures, and manipulate things so that the future she wants will come to pass. Maybe she chose the one future in which you came to Port Maracaibo and devised this particular plan."

"I doubt it," said Chandler. "But even if it's true, so what? My job is to bring her out."

"What if she doesn't *want* to go with you?" said Jade. "What if she just needs an excuse to leave Hades?"

"For what reason?"

"How should I know what reason?" responded Jade. "I just want to know how you can be sure she's not pulling your strings right this moment."

He sighed. "The answer to that is that I don't know. I don't think she is. I don't think she has that kind of power, or, if she does have it, then I don't think she can be held anywhere, even Hades, against her will. But even if she *is* manipulating me into getting her off Hades, why should I care about it? She's just making my job easier."

"I don't know," said Jade. "But I feel very uneasy about it. If she's manipulating *you*, then she's manipulating *me*, too, and I don't like being manipulated."

"I don't know exactly what we can do about it either way," replied Chandler.

"We can quit right now."

"Not a chance," he said. "I've got a contract to fulfill."

"How do you know that she isn't planning to go to war with the Democracy? Maybe Kraef Timo is the only voice in opposition to hers, and she's manipulating us into killing him."

"If she can do that from 300,000 miles away," answered Chandler, "why doesn't she just choose a future in which he chokes to death on his food, or trips down a flight of stairs and breaks his neck?"

"I don't know," admitted Jade. Her face hardened. "In fact, the more I think about this situation, the more things I don't know."

"Look," said Chandler. "Either we've got free will or we don't. If we do, then we're doing the right thing. If we don't, then we can't do anything else, anyway. So what's the point of worrying about it?"

"Because we can stop right now if we decide to."

He smiled. "And how will you know that the Oracle didn't change her mind and choose a future in which we stopped?"

She wearily leaned back on the chair. "Where does it end?"

"Second-guessing Fate?" asked Chandler. "Never. That's why it's a good idea not to start."

"Doesn't it bother you to think that your actions, your very thoughts, might not be your own?" she asked.

"But they *are* my own. Even if we're being manipulated, the Oracle didn't choose these thoughts and put them into my mind. She just arranged things so that these were the ones I'd think and act upon." He paused. "Besides, I don't see any viable alternative. If I assume she's controlling me, then she's controlling me whether I kill Kraef Timo or walk away from him."

Jade considered his statement. "Well, it's a practical approach," she conceded. "But it's not very satisfying. I think an animal in the forest might have that same viewpoint."

"I spend most of my life with animals in the forest," replied Chandler. "Very few of them have high blood pressure or heart attacks. Maybe they know something we don't know."

"They don't *know* anything," said Jade. "They just react."

"They stay warm and dry and well fed," he noted. "When all is said and done, that's all most humans are really trying to do."

"You're not a very comforting person to talk to, Javier," she said. "I come to you with serious doubts, and you give me a lecture on animals."

"I'm not in the comfort business."

"I know. I suppose I'll have to make my decision without any help from you."

"What decision?"

"Whether I should help you or stop you," Jade said bluntly.

"I'd very much like your help, though I can accomplish my mission without it," said Chandler with equal bluntness. "I'd strongly advise you not to try to stop me."

She stared at him for a long moment. "I still have to make up my mind," she said at last.

"Let me know when you do."

"You'll be the first to know."

She got up and left the room.

Chandler waited another twenty minutes, then got up and walked to the false closet. It opened after scanning his retina and registering it against its data base, and a moment later he was standing in the sunken garage. He decided against borrowing Jade's vehicle, since he didn't know Port Maracaibo's traffic laws and also had no idea where he could leave it while he went about his business.

He walked over to a gentle incline, followed it up to a door at ground level, opened it, and a moment later found himself in a small alley behind The Womb. He followed it for two blocks, then turned onto a main street, asked a passerby how to find the Uncut Diamond, and caught a coach that seemed to be going in the right direction.

He was annoyed that Jade had forced him to change his schedule: he'd have been much move comfortable visiting Kraef Timo after midnight, when the Blue Devil's bodyguards had relaxed and a couple of them had perhaps gone off to bed. But if she decided to oppose him, there was no telling how she might go about it, and bringing in some hired killers was certainly not beyond her capabilities.

The coach passed the Uncut Diamond, a small, rather ordinary-looking hotel, and he got off at the next street, then walked back to the main entrance. He felt no need to keep to the shadows or hide his presence, since nobody here knew him, anyway.

He walked into a darkened cocktail lounge off to the left of the registration desk, was struck by the rancid odor of alien intoxicants, realized that he was one of the few humans in the room, and dialed a beer on the computer menu. He nursed it for about fifteen minutes, keeping an eye on the hotel entrance. Though the hotel catered almost exclusively to aliens, no Blue Devils entered or left—he hadn't really expected to see any—and he decided that it was time to find out where Kraef Timo's suite was located.

There was no guest register, nor could he have read one if there was. The house vidphones were out of the question, too; he was sure the desk wouldn't release the room number, and asking would just alert Timo to his presence. The hotel was only five floors tall; he could simply check each floor for Blue Devils, but it was unlikely that any of Timo's bodyguards were posted outside the suite.

Finally he walked over to a public vidphone booth, entered it, checked the directory, and found a restaurant down the street that delivered around the clock. He quickly punched out its combination, then smiled into the camera when the connection was made.

"This is Mr. Timo at the Uncut Diamond," he said. "I've been displeased with room service the last two nights. Can I get a sandwich and a beer sent over?"

The man at the other end took his order and asked for his room number.

"It's in some alien script," answered Chandler. "But you can't miss it. It's the third door to the right of the lift, on the seventh floor."

He hung up, walked back to the cocktail lounge, and waited. Half an hour later a young man carrying a bag that obviously contained food entered the hotel, walked to the airlift, stepped into it, and stepped right back out, frowning. Chandler left the lounge and slowly approached the airlift as the young man walked to the desk and exchanged a few words with the Lodinite clerk. The two of them arrived together and floated up to the fourth level in silence.

The deliveryman turned to his left, checking the numbers on the doors, and Chandler waited a few seconds, then began following him at a leisurely pace.

The man stopped at a door, touched a sensor, and waited for it to slide open. Chandler saw a Blue Devil approach the deliveryman, after which the two exchanged heated words for a minute or two, and finally the man left and returned to the airlift.

Chandler leaned against a wall until he was sure the man wasn't going to come back and make a second attempt to deliver his package and get his money. Then he walked silently down the corridor, stopped in front of Timo's door, and reached out to touch the sensor.

The door opened instantly, and a powerful-looking Blue Devil appeared.

"I told you to go away!" it said in thickly accented Terran.

Chandler reached out and slit his throat without a word, then leaped into the room. Three Blue Devils were seated in odd-looking chairs. He killed all three with a sonic pistol before they realized he was there.

A laser beam missed his ear by inches, and he hurled himself to the floor, rolling and firing back as he did so. A Blue Devil shrieked in agony and staggered across the room, an ugly green fluid trickling from its ears. He fired again and the alien fell motionless to the floor.

"Who are you?" demanded another voice, less heavily accented but definitely not human. "What do you want?"

The voice seemed to be coming from a bedroom off to his left, and, changing his sonic pistol for a laser gun, he fired a beam that seared through the wall at a height of about four feet.

"Who are you?" repeated the voice. "Why does she want me dead?"

Chandler felt a brief surge of satisfaction: the *she* that the alien mentioned could only be the Oracle, which meant that he had indeed chosen the proper target. For a moment he considered trying to take Timo alive and grilling it thoroughly about the Oracle and her plans, but he recalled that Boma, the Blue Devil they had questioned on Port Marrakech, took its own life rather than reveal any information about the Oracle, and with at least one more bodyguard unaccounted for, Chandler didn't think the risk was worth it.

He fired through the wall once more, lower this time, and heard a body fall to the floor.

He waited a full minute for another sound, a movement, any indication of life within the bedroom, then cautiously approached it. When he reached the doorway he peered in and saw a Blue Devil lying on the floor, a huge burn mark running the length of its torso.

He entered the room, turned the corpse on its back, and looked for some sign or symbol of identification. As he was examining the body, he saw a sudden motion out of the corner of his eye, and as he turned to face the final bodyguard, a blue foot kicked the weapon out of his hand.

The huge Blue Devil leaned forward, reaching out for Chandler. He responded with two quick kicks against the Blue Devil's leg joints, and as the surprised creature was struggling to maintain its balance, Chandler made a quick slashing motion with his hand, then stood back as blood spurted out of the bodyguard's throat. It rasped hoarsely once, glared at Chandler for a moment, and died.

Chandler locked the door to the corridor and spent the next few minutes making sure there were no more Blue Devils around, then withdrew a small knife, made the Oracle's mark on each corpse, and began thoroughly inspecting the suite, looking for anything, however insignificant, that might tell him something more about the Oracle and her organization.

He was rummaging through the very last compartment when Jade walked in, a pistol in her hand.

"You've had a busy night," she said, glancing briefly at the corpse-strewn floor.

"How did *you* get in here?" he demanded.

"I own this building."

"What are you doing here?"

"I came to stop you," said Jade.

"Why?"

"Because I hadn't decided whether or not I wanted you to kill these Blue Devils—and on *my* world, nobody kills anyone unless I give my permission." She paused, then continued speaking with a cold fury. "You said you'd wait in your room for two more hours. You lied to me."

"I changed my mind," he said.

"You lied to me, and that's all that matters," she replied. "It could be that, for various reasons, you didn't want me to come along. It could be that you're simply a liar by nature. Or it could be because *she* made you lie."

"You're getting paranoid about her," said Chandler.

"How can you be paranoid about someone with the ability to shape the future?" she retorted. "You can underestimate her capacity for harm, but I hardly think you can *over*estimate it." She stared at him. "However, that's not the issue here. You lied to me, and you killed seven Blue Devils without my permission. That's tantamount to disobeying me."

"How can I disobey you?" said Chandler irritably. "That implies that I take orders from you—and nobody gives me orders."

"There are only two options for you while you're on Port Maracaibo," said Jade. "First, you can clear your plans with me and obtain my permission."

"And what's the second?"

She pointed the pistol at him. "I can kill you."

22

"Put that away," said Chandler. "You want to expand your operations to Hades, and I'm the only man who can make that possible. We're still on the same side."

"If you're on *my* side, you don't sneak off and commit murders without my approval."

They heard the sound of footsteps outside the door as a very heavy-footed alien walked to its room.

"This is neither the time nor the place to discuss this," said Chandler. "These bodies aren't going to stay undiscovered all night." He paused. "Timo and one of his bodyguards were in one of the bedrooms. For all I know, they sent for help before I killed them."

Jade considered his statement, then nodded. "All right," she said, lowering her pistol. "We'll continue this discussion back at The Womb."

They walked quickly to the airlift, floated down to the lobby together, then left the building.

"Did you bring your vehicle?" he asked.

"It's around the corner," she replied.

They entered the landcar and drove back to The Womb in silence. She pulled into the sunken garage, and a moment later they ascended to his room and immediately went to her quarters.

"Well, what now?" she asked.

"Now we choose another target."

She shook her head. "I'm not helping you until I know that I'm not being manipulated into it."

Chandler shrugged. "Then I'll have to do it myself."

"Without my help, all you'll be doing is slaughtering a bunch of innocent Blue Devils who may not have any connection to the Oracle at all."

"I won't have to kill that many of them," responded Chandler. "If I put the Oracle's insignia on each victim, she'll either come up here to stop me in a couple of weeks, or I'll know she can't leave Hades and I'll have to go after her." He paused. "But it would save me a lot of trouble if I knew who worked for her or communicated with her."

"Not until I sort things out," said Jade adamantly.

"The only thing you have to know is that whether I kill her or take her out, you're going to get rich—or, rather, richer," said Chandler. "As for the rest of it, we simply don't have enough information. You could consider the problem halfway to eternity, and you still wouldn't know if we're doing what she wants or acting on our own."

"There's one piece of information that you haven't considered."

"Oh? What is that?"

"You told me that the Democracy tried to kill you back on Port Marrakech. Why?"

"I don't know. Probably they didn't want me to fulfill my mission."

"*Which* mission?" asked Jade. "Bringing her out, or killing her?"

"I don't know."

"Well, it's something you ought to consider," she continued. "If they've managed to learn something about the Oracle since you were hired, something that makes them think she's too dangerous to be allowed to live, then the last thing you want to do is bring her out alive."

"By the same token," he replied, "if you're convinced she can manipulate you and me without our knowing it, she can probably manipulate *them*."

"But why would she have them try to kill you if you were going to bring her out?"

"Any number of reasons," answered Chandler. "First, she may be very happy where she is. Second, she may have arranged the attempt on my life, knowing I'd survive it, as a way of making me move my base of operations from Port Marrakech to Port Maracaibo, where I'd have a better chance of convincing the

Blue Devils to bring her to me. Third, there's every likelihood that she's carrying a grudge against the man who hired me; maybe with me dead, he'd have to come here and try to fulfill the contract himself." He paused. "There's no way to know until I come face-to-face with her."

"By that time it'll probably be too late," said Jade. "I don't know if she can control events from Hades, but everything you've told me leads me to believe she can control them when she's in the same room with you."

"I haven't come to kill her," answered Chandler. "She'll know that."

"But you *will* kill her if you have to," said Jade. "She'll know *that,* too."

"Unless I know for a fact that she's amenable to coming away with me, I'll probably *have* to kill her. She's too dangerous to try to deal with."

"She'll know that."

"Then I'll have to put her in such a position where knowing it doesn't do her any good."

"There's no possible way to do that."

"We'll see," replied Chandler with more confidence than he felt. He paused. "Do you have anything more to say?"

"Not at the moment."

"Then if you don't mind, I'm going to go get something to eat."

"You'd better have something sent to your room," she said. "You'll want whoever delivers it to be able to testify that you were there."

He nodded, then left her suite and returned to his own quarters. He ordered a sandwich and an imported beer, and watched the artificial scenery through his window while he waited for the meal to arrive.

The vidphone flashed, and he activated it.

"Yes?" he said.

The image of a Blue Devil appeared above the phone.

"It won't work, Whistler."

"What are you talking about?"

"Go home, Whistler," said the Blue Devil. *"Go home and stay alive."*

It broke the connection.

He immediately returned to Jade's suite, where he found her sitting at her desk, staring at a computer with a frown on her face.

"What's the matter?" she asked, looking up.

"It worked," he said. "Much faster than I thought it would."

"What worked?"

"I've just been warned off."

"By the Oracle?" asked Jade.

"In essence," he replied. "By some Blue Devil."

"How did they find you so quickly?"

He shrugged. "For all I know they've been watching me since I landed here."

"And you led them right to The Womb?"

"Not on purpose," said Chandler. "Besides, they contacted *me*, not you. They know who's responsible for what happened at the Uncut Diamond. They have no reason to suspect you of any complicity."

"If they saw you at the Uncut Diamond, then they saw *me*, too. What exactly did this Blue Devil say?"

"That what I was doing wouldn't work." He paused. "That's her way of telling me to go in after her."

"You're jumping to conclusions."

"I don't think so."

"Maybe the Blue Devils are trying to scare you off before they have to bring the Oracle to Port Maracaibo."

Chandler shook his head. "This has the Oracle's signature on it, believe me."

"What makes you so sure?"

"Because if she wanted me dead, the Blue Devils know where I am. They'd have sent me a bullet or a laser beam, not a vidphone call." He paused. "But if she wants me to bring her out, this is exactly the way she'd tell me."

"You killed seven Blue Devils tonight," said Jade. "Why wouldn't they retaliate regardless of her wishes?"

"Because she told them not to," said Chandler. "And because she and she alone has manipulated things to keep them from being assimilated by the Democracy."

"That doesn't make any sense," said Jade. "First you make her sound like a prisoner, and now you're telling me that they're afraid to disobey her orders."

"Maybe the two aren't mutually exclusive," suggested Chandler. "Maybe as long as she gives them valid information, they let her live . . . and if she ever misleads them, they'll kill her. Under those circumstances, they'd give her the benefit of the doubt, because the alternative would be to kill her and they don't want to do that if there are any other options. Besides, look at her message: it sounds like she's dealing from strength and trying to frighten me off."

Jade was silent for almost a full minute. Finally she looked directly into Chandler's eyes.

"You can't go," she said.

Chandler frowned. "More doubts?"

"While you were in your room, I tied into the master computer on Deluros."

"And?"

"And I told it to locate any information that was available about the Oracle," she continued. "It qualified its information by saying that it was only valid if she had once been known as the Soothsayer—but some of the details matched what you've told me about her."

"What point are you trying to make?" asked Chandler.

"When she was eight years old, she was able to kill some of the best bounty hunters on the Inner Frontier," said Jade. "And that was when she was just a little girl. She's a grown woman now, and it's reasonable to assume that she's even more powerful now than she was then." She looked across her desk at Chandler. "She killed eight armed bounty hunters in a single afternoon on a planet called Killhaven. I don't want any part of her—it's not worth the risk."

"If she was easier to kidnap or kill, the rewards wouldn't be this great."

"Don't you see?" said Jade in frustration. "This woman has the power to hold the Democracy at bay. Those Blue Devils aren't even cold yet and she already knows you killed them. If she's being kept on Hades against her will, then I say: good for the Blue Devils, and let's leave her there." She paused. "The Blue Devil who contacted you gave you good advice: go home."

"I've got a job to do first," said Chandler. "Besides, aren't you curious to see her and find out what she can really do? *I* am."

"I don't want to be the one who turns her loose on the galaxy."

"You don't have to have anything to do with it," he said. "I just need to find some way to get to the planet without being detected."

"*You* aren't going to have anything to do with it, either."

"Don't try to stop me," he said ominously.

"I won't let her escape from Hades," she replied firmly.

"You don't have a choice."

"Of course I do," she said, producing her pistol. "I told yo
once: you're not the only killer in this room. I let you live befor
but I'm afraid now you've left me with no alternative."

"You really intend to kill me?" he asked.

"I do."

"How do you know that this isn't what the Oracle wants?"

Jade frowned, as if considering the question, and in that instan
as her concentration wavered, he made a swift motion with hi
hand. She grunted and dropped her pistol as a knife buried itse
in her throat.

Chandler walked over to her. "I'm sorry," he said. "But yo
were going to kill me."

"You're a fool," she whispered hoarsely. "You've destroyed u
all." Then she slumped over and died.

He left her where she was sitting, pausing only long enough
retrieve his knife, then returned to his room, took the airlift dow
to the garage, and walked out into the Port Maracaibo night.

PART 4

The
Iceman's
Book

23

The Iceman took the shuttle down to Philemon II, made his way to the large hexagonal building that was his destination, and flashed his temporary pass at the door. Once inside he walked directly to the information computer, queried it briefly, and walked to an airlift. He was required to display his pass again and undergo a retina scan, after which he descended almost two hundred feet below ground level.

He stepped out into a maze of shining, brightly lit corridors, waited for an armed soldier to approach him, displayed his pass a third time, and was ushered to a small waiting room. He barely had time to light a small cigar when a door slid back and another soldier stepped through.

"He'll see you now, Mr. Mendoza."

The Iceman walked to the door, then entered a large office as the soldier moved aside and the door closed behind him.

"Carlos!" said 32, looking up from his chrome desk and smiling. The wall behind him was filled with the memorabilia of a lifetime devoted to government service, including a personally inscribed holograph of the current Secretary of the Democracy. "It's been a long time."

"Twenty-four years, give or take a month," replied the Iceman.

"You haven't changed much."

"Maybe you'd better have your eyesight tested," said the Iceman. "I'm a sixty-five-year-old man with a potbelly and an artificial leg."

32 smiled. "No, you haven't changed at all, Carlos," he said. "Always a little too blunt, always inclined to disregard a well-

meant social lie." He uttered a terse command to his computer and a chair floated over. "Won't you have a seat?"

The Iceman sat down. "How about a drink?"

"Name it."

"Whatever's wet. Unless you've changed more radically than I think, you haven't got anything cheap lying around."

32 chuckled in acknowledgment. "How about some Alphard brandy?"

"Sounds good," said the Iceman.

32 walked to a wall that appeared to be covered with book-shelves, pressed a certain spot on it, and a section of the holo-graphic projection vanished, to be replaced by a well-stocked bar. He filled two glasses with brandy, handed one to the Iceman, and returned to his desk.

"Thanks," said the Iceman.

"It's from a new vineyard," said 32, straightening the glow-ing fabric of his expensively tailored tunic, which had wrinkled slightly when he sat down. "I'm anxious to have your reaction."

The Iceman shrugged. "What the hell," he said. "*I've* got all day. Let me know when you want to talk business."

"You never believed in small talk, did you?" said 32 wryly.

"It's your money," replied the Iceman. "Chatter all you want. But when you're through, I hope you'll get around to telling me why you promised me three million credits if I'd come to Philemon II."

"I didn't think you'd come for less," said 32 frankly. "It's my understanding that you've become a very wealthy man."

"I get by."

"But you were still willing to come for three million credits," noted 32.

"It's a lot of money, just to take a trip."

"There's more where that came from."

"I'm listening," said the Iceman.

"We've got a serious situation on our hands, Carlos," said 32.

"Who's 'we'?"

"You know who I work for."

"All right, you've got a serious situation on your hands. What has that got to do with me?"

"Well, to be perfectly candid, Carlos, you're working for me."

The Iceman smiled. "So *you* sent Bettina Bailey, or whoever she really was, to Last Chance." He paused. "I knew *someone* in he Democracy sent her, but I didn't know who."

"I sent her," confirmed 32. "And you accepted her commis-
ion."

"I'm working on it."

"To be more precise, Joshua Jeremiah Chandler, alias the Whis-
ler, is working on it. Am I correct?"

The Iceman stared levelly at him. "I see no reason to lie about
t. He's younger and stronger and a hell of a lot quicker than
am."

"But I hired *you*."

"In point of fact, *you* didn't hire anyone. Your operative did—
nd I sent the best man for the job."

"Well, it may interest you to know that the best man for the
ob has gone off the deep end," said 32.

"I very much doubt that."

"Have you been in contact with him since he reached the Alpha
Crepello system?"

"No. But I didn't expect to be, not this soon." The Iceman
rained his glass, then relit his cigar, which had gone out.

"I'd be surprised if he ever contacts you again," said 32. "Do
ou know what he did when he landed on Port Marrakech?"

"Port Marrakech?"

"One of Alpha Crepello III's terraformed moons."

"Suppose you tell me," said the Iceman.

"He murdered the best assassin on the moon and took over his
usiness. Then he moved his base of operations to Port Maracaibo,
vhere two nights ago he killed the woman who ran most of
he brothels and rackets on *that* moon." 32 paused. "Damn it,
Carlos—the man has become the criminal kingpin of both moons,
nd *I* financed him!"

The Iceman shook his head. "You're not telling me every-
hing."

"I certainly am. What he's done is a matter of record."

"I know the Whistler. He has no intention of leaving his home
vorld; in fact, he only takes assignments to pay for that jungle
vorld he lives on."

"I tell you, the man has turned," insisted 32. "He's in business
or himself now."

"Slow down a minute," said the Iceman. "He began just the
vay I'd have begun. He set himself up on the first moon. This
vould assuage any fears Penelope had that he had come after her,

and would make it easier for him to buy information about her
Obviously he was successful. But if he was, there was no reason
for him to move to the second moon."

"He's turned renegade."

The Iceman shook his head again. "He wasn't on the first
moon long enough to consolidate his holdings. Something made
him change his base of operations." He stared at 32. "Something
you're going to have to tell me about if this conversation is to
proceed any further."

32 stared at him, then sighed deeply. "Someone tried to kill
him."

"One of your men?"

"No. But one of the Democracy's. We're not the only department concerned with the Oracle."

"Come on," said the Iceman disbelievingly. "They were your
men and you decided it was the most efficient way to eliminate
him." He paused. "So the Whistler found out you were trying to
terminate him, and he moved to another moon. The only thing
that surprises me is that he didn't change his identity."

"He did."

"Then how do you know he was there?"

"He killed a woman known as the Jade Queen. A number of
people who worked for her gave us his description."

"I assume you haven't picked him up?"

"He's vanished completely," said 32. "But it's just a matter of
time before he surfaces again. He hasn't had time to establish his
authority there yet."

The Iceman looked amused. "The years haven't made you any
wiser, I see."

"Where do *you* think he'll show up?"

"He's probably on Alpha Crepello III by now."

"Then why did he kill the Jade Queen?"

"I have no idea."

"I don't buy it," said 32. "Every move he's made since arriving
has been directed toward taking over the criminal networks of
those two moons."

"Have it your way," said the Iceman nonchalantly. "I didn't
come here to argue with you."

"You came here because I paid you to."

"That's right," agreed the Iceman. "And for three million credits, the very least I can do is listen to your ramblings politely."

"Look," said 32 irritably. "I told you we had a problem. Even if you're right about his reaching Alpha Crepello, we *still* have a problem."

"I'm still listening."

"Word has come down that we don't want to risk bringing the Oracle out. My new orders are to terminate her."

"I wish you luck," said the Iceman.

"I need more than luck," said 32. "I need results." He paused. "Will the Whistler kill her?"

"Only if he can't find a way to bring her out," answered the Iceman. "In case it's slipped your mind, that's what you paid for."

"Can you contact him and tell him the situation has changed?" asked 32. "After what happened on Port Marrakech, I doubt that he'll believe me, even though I had nothing to do with the attempt on his life."

"I doubt it," said the Iceman thoughtfully. "If he's on the planet, he'll stay undercover until he reaches her. Your best bet is to send someone else in after her and hope your new operative reaches her first."

"I've sent eight men in," said 32. "The first seven were killed."

"What about the eighth?"

32 grimaced. "The eighth was a criminal that I had released from jail. Brilliant planner, brutal killer." 32 paused. "I had him wired all the way—camera in his eye, transmitter in his ear, even a bomb in his skull to keep him in line."

"And?"

"The son of a bitch found a way to disconnect me!" said 32 furiously. "He's already held me up for more money, and he's operating without any guidance or constraint!"

The Iceman grinned. "I like him already."

"He's also got orders to kill your man if he shows up on Hades."

"Hades?"

"That's the trade name for Alpha Crepello III."

"Why is he supposed to kill the Whistler?"

"Because the Democracy has decided that it would rather have her dead than alive and abroad in the galaxy."

"It won't work," said the Iceman after some thought. "The Whistler's as good as they come. Your man won't lay a finger on him."

"I don't care if he kills him or not!" snapped 32.

"Then I'm at a loss to understand your problem."

"Damn it, Carlos—I've got two men down there. One of them is going to try to bring her out, and if she's willing to go with him, then that's the last thing we want. The other knows that ten million credits have been deposited in some secret account that even *I* haven't been able to trace, and he knows he's facing a death sentence if we get our hands on him." He paused, trying to regain his composure. "My assignment is to terminate the Oracle, and I have no reason to believe either of the men on Hades will accomplish that."

"You could be right," agreed the Iceman calmly. "It looks like you've wasted a lot of money."

"It's partly your fault," said 32.

"Oh? How do you figure that?"

"There's only one man who knows Penelope Bailey well enough to do the job. You were the one I hired, Carlos; if you took the money, you should have done the job yourself."

"I'm a fat old man with a limp," answered the Iceman. "I got you the best there is."

"He may be the best assassin, but he doesn't *know* her. *You* do."

"Look," said the Iceman. "I want her dead even more than you do. She killed someone I cared about, and she cost me my leg." He put his cigar out. "But I also know her capacity for harm. She's potentially the most dangerous being in the whole damned galaxy, maybe in the history of the galaxy, so I passed up a chance for personal vengeance to hire you the man most likely to get the job done."

"Well, he's not getting it done. He's killing criminals and taking over their operations."

"I'll bet you the three million you promised me that he's either on Hades or en route to it."

"But even if you're right, he's not going to try to kill her."

"Not at first," acknowledged the Iceman.

"You know her capacities," said 32. "If she knows he's there, and she isn't willing to leave with him, what are his chances of killing her?"

"Just about nil."

"My own man might be able to sneak up on her," continued 32, "but he has no reason to. He's been paid plenty, and he has no reason ever to contact me again."

"You *can't* sneak up on her," said the Iceman. "She doesn't have to see you to know you're there. She can see what's going to happen next, and if she doesn't like it, she can change it."

"You see?" said 32. "That's the kind of thing that the Whistler and Jimmy Two Feathers don't know! That's why I need *you*!"

"Jimmy Two Feathers?" repeated the Iceman, surprised. "You sent the Injun in after her?"

"You know him?"

"I know *of* him. He's a seed-chewer."

"That's why I had him wired."

"Well, you can forget about him," said the Iceman. "If he's not under your control, he's floating off in limbo somewhere."

"There are no seeds on Hades."

The Iceman stared at him. "You really believe that, don't you?"

"We monitor every cargo shipment to Hades."

"If there's a planet they can't smuggle seed to, it hasn't been discovered yet."

"That's neither here nor there," said 32. "If he's on the seed, that's all the more reason why you have to go in."

"I don't have to do anything," said the Iceman. "You're paying me three million credits to listen to you, nothing more."

"There's lots more."

"I'm a rich man. I don't need it."

"And there's the chance for vengeance."

"You don't take vengeance on a hurricane or an ion storm," said the Iceman. "They're forces of nature. If you survive an encounter with them, you count yourself lucky and you make sure that it never happens again." He paused. "Penelope's the same thing— a force of nature. I'd love to see somebody kill her, I don't think it can happen, and I'm not dumb enough to volunteer. I had my shot at her when I was a lot younger and stronger, and I was lucky to come away alive."

"You sound very cool and dispassionate," said 32. "But I researched you thoroughly, Carlos. You followed every lead you could get your hands on for fourteen years. You traveled all over the Inner Frontier looking for her. That's not the behavior of a man who's afraid to face her again."

"In the beginning I hunted her with a passion," admitted the Iceman. "I won't deny it. But a man can't survive on hatred for fourteen years. After a while the blood cools and the passion fades, and toward the end I was hunting her more out of curiosity than hatred. I wanted to find out what she had become, how she had managed to stay hidden all these years, what her plans were."

"She's only two systems away from here," said 32. "And you still don't know the answers to your questions."

"When she's ready to move, we'll all know."

32 finished his brandy and looked across the desk at the Iceman. "We can't afford to find out," he said. "We've got to kill her now."

"Maybe all she wants is to be left alone."

"If *you* had those powers, would you want to be left alone to live in obscurity?" demanded 32.

"No, but . . ."

"But what?"

"But I'm human," said the Iceman. "She probably isn't, not anymore."

"That's all the more reason to terminate her."

"If you say so."

"Ten million credits," said 32.

The Iceman made no answer, but stared at some fixed point on the wall.

"Well?" said 32.

"Be quiet," said the Iceman. "I'm thinking."

"Computing expenses?"

"I said be quiet!"

32 looked at the Iceman, then shrugged and was silent.

The Iceman remained motionless for almost a minute, then turned back to 32.

"You've got a big problem on your hands," he said.

"That's what I've been explaining to you."

The Iceman shook his head. "It's not the one you think."

"What are you talking about?"

"It's been so long since I've seen her that I tend to forget what she can do," said the Iceman. "You've got two men on Hades . . ."

"One that we know of."

"Take my word, you've got two there," said the Iceman.

"All right, for the sake of argument," said 32. "What has that got to do with anything?"

"Why are they still alive?"

32 looked confused. "I don't think I understand the question."

"Why didn't the Injun's ship crash when it landed? Why was the Whistler able to kill whoever it was he killed on the moons?"

"You think she *wants* them alive?" asked 32. "Why?"

"There's only one reason I can think of," answered the Iceman. "She's being held against her will and wants them to bring her out."

"Against her will?" repeated 32. "How is that possible?"

"I don't know . . . but I know if she didn't want to leave, the Injun wouldn't have been alive long enough to get your tampering undone. The surgeon would have sneezed or flinched at the wrong moment, and he'd never have survived." He paused. "You were right. If you can't call the Whistler off, you'll have to kill him. And probably the Injun, too. If she wants to leave Hades, then you've got to stop her."

"My orders are to kill her."

"Fuck your orders," said the Iceman. "You had her when she was six years old and you couldn't keep her even then. I tried to kill her when she was eight, and I failed. But now, somehow, the inhabitants of Hades have actually managed to keep her there against her will all these years, even though her powers have doubtless matured." He stared at 32. "You let her off that planet and there will be hell to pay. She doesn't need a navy to conquer a world; all she has to do is choose the one future out of a million in which its star explodes or a meteor plows into it. Give her an army of five thousand men and she would win any battle against any force in the galaxy, just by picking and choosing which outcome she wants for each skirmish. She probably can't be killed, but she *can* be contained—they're containing her right now."

"If you're right, then these are the perfect conditions under which to assassinate her," persisted 32.

"You still don't understand," said the Iceman. "Let's say she's locked up in a cell. If you tried to shoot her, she'd cough or sneeze or twitch or do something that would bring about the one future in which you blew the lock off the door."

"We've still got to try."

"*No!*" snapped the Iceman. "Once and for all, try to understand what I'm saying to you: they've found a way to contain her. We'd be crazy to tamper with it."

"But we can't just sit back and do nothing!" protested 32.

"We could have, before you hired me and sent the Injun after her," said the Iceman. "But like I said, you've got a big problem on your hands. The first one of them to reach her is going to free her, whether he means to or not." He paused for a very long moment. "Put the ten million in my account," he said reluctantly. "I'm going to have to go in after them."

"I thought you didn't want any part of it."

"I don't," said the Iceman. "But I'm the only one who can call the Whistler off. He'll kill anyone else you send."

"What about the Injun?"

"If he's on the seed, he's off in dreamland somewhere—and if he tries to kill the Whistler, you can bury what's left of him."

"But if he's clean, and he can't find the Whistler, he'll be going after the Oracle."

"Then I'll have to find him and stop him."

"As you pointed out, you're a fat old man with one leg," said 32. "What makes you think you *can* stop him?"

"He won't know why I'm there, and he has no reason to kill me," answered the Iceman. "And hopefully I'll have the Whistler on my side." He stared grimly across the desk at 32. "You've only got one other alternative."

"What is it?"

"Blow up the whole damned planet—and do it with unmanned ships that have been programmed thousands of light-years away."

"We can't kill two hundred million Blue Devils just to get rid of someone who *might* constitute a threat!" protested 32.

"We've done a lot worse in the past," said the Iceman.

"I will not go down in history as a genocidal maniac!"

The Iceman sighed. "Then I'll have to go to Hades and try to find the Whistler and the Injun before *they* find *her*."

"What makes you think she'll let you land?"

"I'll find a way. That's part of what you're paying me for."

32 considered all he had heard for a long moment, then shook his head in confusion. "I just don't know," he said at last. "When you lay it out, it *sounds* reasonable . . ." He sighed. "But when all is said and done, I'm supposed to have her assassinated, and here we are, talking about how to keep the two assassins from reaching her."

"It's up to you," said the Iceman. "I'm an old man. I imagine I can live out my life before she turns the Democracy inside out." He got to his feet. "I'm going back up to my ship. I'll stay locked in orbit for ten more hours. I'm sure you've recorded our conversation; play it to whoever can change your orders. If I don't hear from you by then, I'll assume you're still going to try to kill her, and I'll go back to Last Chance."

It didn't take ten hours, or even eight.

Five hours later the Democracy transferred ten million credits to the Iceman's account on Last Chance.

And ten minutes after that, the Iceman activated his ship and took off for Hades, wondering whether he would live long enough to spend a single credit of his money.

24

As he approached the planet, his radio came to life.

"You are approaching Alpha Crepello III," said an accente[
voice. "Please identify yourself."

"This is the *Space Mouse,* registration number 932K1P23, fiv[
Galactic Standard days out of Last Chance, via Philemon I[
Carlos Mendoza commanding."

"Alpha Crepello III is closed to all unauthorized visitors."

"Let me speak to whoever is in charge," said the Iceman.

"That is impossible."

"I have vital information to convey to him."

"What is the nature of your information?"

"My information is not for underlings," replied the Iceman. '
must speak to your superior."

"I have explained that this is impossible."

"Then give me your name and military identification number,
said the Iceman. "I want to know who to blame when your com
mander asks why he was not contacted."

There was a momentary silence. "Please wait," said the voic
at last.

The Iceman allowed himself the luxury of a smile and opene
a container of beer while he waited for his demand to get passe
up the chain of command to someone who would finally accep
responsibility.

It took eleven minutes.

Then the image of a Blue Devil, its outfit bedecked with gli[
tering stones that the Iceman took to be medals, appeared on hi
viewscreen.

"I am Praed Tropo," said the Blue Devil.

"You're in charge?"

"I am in a position of authority. What information have you for me?"

"It's very sensitive," answered the Iceman. "I'd much rather tell you in person."

"You are not allowed to land on Alpha Crepello III."

"Not even to save the Oracle's life?" asked the Iceman.

There was no change in the Blue Devil's expression, but its voice seemed to drop half an octave. "Continue," it said.

"There is a human assassin, currently on Alpha Crepello III, who has been hired to terminate the Oracle. This assassin does not work for the Democracy; in fact, the Democracy, which does not want to be involved in an interplanetary incident, has assigned me the task of stopping him. To do this, I will need your assistance."

"The Oracle is in no danger," replied Praed Tropo. "She cannot be harmed."

"The Democracy controls more than fifty thousand worlds, and this is the best assassin on any of them," said the Iceman. "Are you sure you care to take that chance?"

"If he is the best assassin, how do you propose to stop him?"

"I don't," answered the Iceman. "I am an old man, well past my prime. But I know his methods, and I can identify him. I hope to enlist your aid in apprehending him."

"Transmit his holograph and retinagram to us, and we will attend to him," said Praed Tropo.

"I have accepted a commission of ten million credits to apprehend him," said the Iceman. "This money is payable only upon the successful completion of my assignment, and the Democracy will have no reason to pay me if I turn the job over to you. Either we work together, or I return to Last Chance and your Oracle can take her chances."

"Why should I believe you?" demanded Praed Tropo.

"You can authenticate my story with the man who hired me," said the Iceman.

"Why should I believe *any* Man?"

He'd been waiting for that question. Now it was time to play his trump card, the offer on which he was willing to wager his life.

"I will be happy to put myself in your custody until you are convinced that I am telling the truth. Surely you have the equivalent of a lie detector; I will willingly submit to interrogation while monitored by any such mechanism."

"I will need time to consider this," said Praed Tropo.

"I understand," said the Iceman. "But you must understand that every minute you delay works in the assassin's favor."

And the less time you have to come up with a question I'm unprepared for, the better.

This time the silence lasted for less than thirty seconds.

"We will transmit landing coordinates to your ship," said Praed Tropo. "All weapons systems must be disarmed or you will be destroyed."

"I have no weapons systems," answered the Iceman.

"We are transmitting now."

The Iceman touched down at a military spaceport some forty minutes later, stepped out into the incredibly hot air of Hades, and was immediately taken into custody by a squadron of Blue Devils. They marched him into a nearby building, where Praed Tropo was waiting for him.

"You realize that if we discover that you have lied to us, you will be imprisoned and quite probably executed," was Praed Tropo's greeting to him.

"I do," answered the Iceman. "But once you find out I'm telling you the truth, I trust that you'll be willing to work with me."

"We shall see."

"Look," said the Iceman. "I'm just an independent business-man, trying to become more independent. Personally, I don't care whether your Oracle lives a million years or dies tomorrow."

"What is that to me?" said Praed Tropo.

"I'm trying to tell you that you can trust me because I'm motivated by the most basic human emotion: greed. I have no reason to lie to you, and every reason to tell you the truth."

"If you are indeed telling the truth, you have nothing to worry about, Mendoza," replied Praed Tropo. "Follow me."

Praed Tropo began walking down a corridor, and the Iceman, still accompanied by the squadron of Blue Devils, fell into step behind him. It wasn't like any corridor the Iceman had ever seen before: it was as if it had been designed by a drunken architect and built by madmen. The ceiling rose to a height of fifteen feet, then dropped to the point where they all had to bend over to keep from bumping their heads, then rose again. It zigged and zagged for no discernible purpose, passing no doorways or rooms along the way, and finally, when he was convinced that they had completed a very erratic circle and were about to wind up where they had started, it abruptly terminated in a large room.

The walls were set at oblique angles to each other, and the ceiling rose and fell like a wave on a turbulent ocean. At the far end of the room was a row of machines, none of which bore any resemblance to anything with which the Iceman was familiar, and near one of them was a chair. Not a chair constructed for human use, but as he stared at it, the Iceman decided that a Blue Devil would probably be just as uncomfortable on it as he would.

He was led to the chair and told to sit down. Then Praed Tropo placed a small metal disk on the back of his neck and another on his left wrist. Four Blue Devils trained their weapons on him.

"We are now prepared to interrogate you," said the Blue Devil. "If you should lie, you will receive a near-lethal correction that will affect your nerve centers. Do you understand?"

"Yes," replied the Iceman.

"Should you attempt to escape before the interrogation is completed, you will be shot. Do you understand?"

"Yes."

"Very well," said Praed Tropo. "What is your name?"

"Carlos Mendoza."

"What is your home planet?"

"Last Chance."

"We have no record of a Last Chance."

"It's official name is Madison IV."

"Why are you here, Mendoza?"

Here it comes, thought the Iceman. *Keep calm, don't get excited, and choose your words very carefully. Do it right and you can beat this machine.*

"I have come to Alpha Crepello III to prevent an assassin named Chandler from carrying out his assignment."

He waited for a jolt, and relaxed when it didn't occur.

"What is Chandler's assignment?"

"He is a hired killer who has come for the Oracle."

"How do you know this?"

Careful.

"I am on intimate terms with the man who hired him."

"And who hired you to prevent him from carrying out his assignment?"

"A high-level official in the Democracy. I don't know his real name, but his code name is 32. He is currently stationed on Philemon II. He has offered to pay me ten million credits if I accomplish my mission."

"How did this Chandler manage to land on Alpha Crepello III?" asked Praed Tropo.

"I don't know."

"Where is he now?"

"I don't know."

"But you know that he has definitely been commissioned to assassinate the Oracle?"

Pause. Take a deep breath. Construct your answer precisely. Think.

"I know that when the circumstances are right, he will try to kill her."

The Iceman half expected to be jolted by a near-lethal shock, but nothing happened.

"Have you met this Chandler personally?" continued Praed Tropo.

"Yes."

"And you can identify him?"

"Yes."

"What good is that to us if he is the master of disguise you claim him to be?"

"I know his methods. I'll know him when I see him."

"You are absolutely sure of this?" said Praed Tropo. "There is no doubt in your mind?"

"I am absolutely sure of it," repeated the Iceman. "There is no doubt whatsoever in my mind." He paused. "If that answers your questions, can you disconnect me from this device now? I'm very uneasy being attached to it, and I'm afraid that it may misinterpret my nervousness as false answers."

"You'll be disconnected when I am through questioning you," answered Praed Tropo. "And not until then."

He asked the Iceman the same set of questions three more times, then had him supply a list of Chandler's known victims.

"He sounds quite formidable," admitted the Blue Devil at last.

"He's supposed to be the best," said the Iceman.

"I still do not understand why the Democracy is attempting to stop him. It would seem to be in their best interest to have him assassinate the Oracle. It is she and she alone who has kept us independent."

The Iceman's first inclination was to remain silent, since no question had been asked. Then he realized that he had better make some response, before the question could be worded in a lethal way.

"I assure you that the Democracy does not want Chandler to succeed in his mission. It is my understanding that they attempted to kill him on Port Marrakech, but he survived."

Praed Tropo stared at him for a long moment.

"I will ask you once more, directly: has the Democracy hired this assassin to kill the Oracle?"

"This" assassin. Concentrate on "this." They don't mean the Injun. They've never heard of the Injun. "This" assassin is the Whistler. Only the Whistler. And I'm the one who told him to kill her if he couldn't bring her out. The Democracy knew nothing about it. They wanted her alive. And he's only talking about the Whistler. Not the Injun. Only the Whistler, and I told him to, not the Democracy.

"You seem hesitant to answer," said Praed Tropo. "Has the Democracy hired this assassin to kill the Oracle?"

"No," said the Iceman.

"Once more: has the Democracy hired Chandler to kill the Oracle?"

"No."

That's it. You've learned everything you can from me. There's no sense asking about the Oracle. I'm just a small-time informer. How could I know about her? Probably I don't even know she's a human rather than a Blue Devil. Why would I know the Oracle? Nobody would even have told me about her powers. Just don't ask about her, and I've won. Just don't ask about the Oracle . . .

"Have you any loyalty to the Democracy?" asked Praed Tropo.

"None."

"If they asked you to lie for them, would you?"

"It all depends."

"On what does it depend?"

"On what benefits I would derive from lying."

"Economic benefits?"

"That's right."

"And have you lied to me?"

He means during this interrogation. He's not referring to anything I said on the ship. That's obvious. He means have I lied while I was hooked up to the machine. The question only applies to this interrogation, only to the machine.

"No."

Praed Tropo checked the machine and then nodded to one of his underlings, who removed the disks from the Iceman's neck and wrist.

The Iceman stood up, suddenly realized just how uncomfortable the chair had been, and stretched the knots out of his muscles.

"Satisfied?" he said.

"For the moment," replied Praed Tropo.

"Then we'd better get busy, because Chandler's got a hell of a head start on us."

"Head start?"

"An advantage," explained the Iceman. "He's been here for days. For all I know, he's within striking distance of the Oracle right now."

"The Oracle is in no danger," answered Praed Tropo.

"I've already told you that this man is the best assassin in the Democracy."

"It makes no difference. The Oracle cannot be killed."

The Iceman saw an opportunity to display his ignorance of the Oracle, and took it. "*Any* Blue Devil can be killed."

Praed Tropo's face contorted into what the Iceman assumed was a look of amusement. "She is not of my race," it said, "but of yours."

"Then what's she doing on Alpha Crepello III?"

"That is not for you to know."

"Well, if she's human, that's all the more reason to protect her," said the Iceman. "If there's one thing Chandler knows how to do, it's kill humans."

"He cannot kill her," repeated Praed Tropo.

"If you're so damned sure of that, why did you let me land?" asked the Iceman.

"Because an assassin is loose on the planet, and he must be apprehended."

The Iceman forced a puzzled frown to his face. "But if you're convinced he can't kill the Oracle, why—?"

"Because he can kill those members of my race who are in daily contact with the Oracle."

"What makes the Oracle so immune to assassination?"

Praed Tropo ignored the question and ushered him back down

the long, crazily winding corridor to the building's entrance. Then it stopped and turned to the Iceman.

"We have no human foodstuffs here. You will be escorted to your ship, where you will bring supplies sufficient for three days."

"What if it takes more than three days to apprehend Chandler?"

"Then I will reassess the situation."

"Just a minute," said the Iceman. "If you don't have any human food, what does the Oracle eat?"

"We have no food for *you*," answered Praed Tropo.

You're operating under deep cover, Whistler, so the odds are you can't find out who delivers her food. But if the Injun isn't lost in some seed-chewer's dreamworld, he'll have figured it out by now. And that means he's closer to her than you are, and I can expect him to show up first—if he's stayed off the seed.

And that means that if I have to sacrifice one of you, it will probably be the Injun, who I'll claim to be you—which is just as well, because it's been years since I was good enough to kill you, if indeed I ever was. I just wish I knew what the hell the Injun looks like.

"Once I get my food, what then?" he asked aloud.

"Then I will take you to a place where we can call up the holographs of every human known to be on the planet," answered Praed Tropo, "and if Chandler is among them, we will arrest and incarcerate him."

"What if he's not among them, or if I identify his holograph but we can't find him?"

"Then we will alert our security forces, and when he approaches the Oracle, we will apprehend him."

"May I make a suggestion?" said the Iceman.

"You may."

"Chandler's too good at his trade to be taken that easily. Maybe I'll spot his holograph and maybe I won't, but the odds are that he's already working his way to wherever it is that the Oracle resides. And he won't approach her directly: only a fool would do that on a planet where every human is suspect." *Only a fool, or perhaps a gimpy old man who's so far past his prime that he can no longer operate covertly,* he amended silently.

"What is the point you are making, Mendoza?" asked Praed Tropo.

"He's a cautious man," continued the Iceman. "He won't make a move until he knows the function and schedule of every Blue Devil who guards the Oracle." The Iceman paused. "Now, if you beef up your security forces around her, he'll just outwait you. I don't know how much he's being paid for this job, but it's got to be enough so that he can spend a year or two waiting for the right opportunity." He turned to Praed Tropo. "But he knows *me*, and he has no reason to distrust me. If you'll put me in a conspicuous position somewhere near the Oracle's headquarters, I think he'll contact me before he acts."

"Why should he?"

"Because I have no business being here, and he'll be curious. He'll want to know if we're business rivals, or if I bear some new instructions from his employer, or just what reason I have for being on the planet."

"How will this benefit us?" asked Praed Tropo. "You are an old man; he is a professional assassin. How can you possibly take him into custody?"

"I can't," answered the Iceman. "But there is a chance that I can *lead* him into custody. I can tell him that there's been a change in plans and that we have to go to some predetermined place to discuss it—a place where you will be waiting for him."

"Why should he believe you?" queried the Blue Devil.

"Why shouldn't he?"

"Because, as you say, you have no business being on Alpha Crepello III. Your presence alone may serve to alarm him."

"It's a possibility," admitted the Iceman. "But what can he do? You assure me that the Oracle is invulnerable. If my plan works, you'll have him in custody an hour later. If it doesn't, if my presence alarms him, he'll almost certainly go back into hiding, and then your task will be no different than it is now, except that you'll know the general area that he's hiding in."

"And what if he kills you?" asked Praed Tropo.

"I'm getting paid a lot of money to take that chance."

"I will have to consider your proposition very carefully," said Praed Tropo. "I do not like giving you such freedom of action."

"If we're going to work together," said the Iceman, "we're going to have to trust each other."

"You are a Man," replied Praed Tropo. "That is reason enough not to trust you."

"But your own machine confirmed that I was telling the truth."

"You answered my questions truthfully," acknowledged the Blue Devil. "But it is possible that I did not ask the right questions. You are a Man, and yet you have allied yourself with an alien race to kill another Man. There is no question in my mind that had I not given you permission to land your ship, you would have sought some covert means to land on Alpha Crepello III. This assassin knows and trusts you, and you plan to deceive him and lead him into our hands. How am I to know what other motivations you might have, what other reasons you might possess for being here?"

You're smarter than you look, Tropo. Any minute now you're going to think of asking the Oracle what to do about Chandler. You'll be afraid to bother her with what you still think of as a wild-goose chase, but eventually—maybe tomorrow, maybe the day after that—you'll muster up the courage, and when you do there's every likelihood that you'll mention my name. I'm afraid you're destined for an early death, Praed Tropo.

"Well, if you come up with a better plan, let me know," said the Iceman.

"I shall."

"Just don't take too long. Remember: this man is an accomplished killer, and he's been on the planet long enough to pinpoint the Oracle's location. A lot of lives depend on our moving quickly."

Including mine.

25

Praed Tropo still had not decided what course of action to take by the end of the day, and the Iceman requested permission to spend the night aboard his ship, which was cooler and possessed a comfortable human bed. The Blue Devil at first objected, but finally gave his permission.

Once he had climbed aboard and triggered his security system, he activated his subspace radio.

"32 here," said the voice at the other end.

"It's me," said the Iceman. "And you'd damned well better be right about this frequency being beyond their capacity to pick up."

"It is. Where are you—on one of the moons?"

"I'm on Hades."

"You're on Hades itself?" exclaimed 32, surprised. "I *knew* I had the right man when I sent that woman out to approach you! You should never have farmed out the job."

"Then you'd have been trying to kill *me*," replied the Iceman dryly.

There was an awkward pause.

"Have you learned anything yet?" asked 32.

"I haven't found out anything about the Whistler, if that's what you mean."

"What about Jimmy Two Feathers?"

"I don't know where he is, but if he's kept off the seed, I know where he'll show up."

"He's not the one we're worried about. He'll either assassinate the Oracle, or he'll fail and probably get himself killed. It's Chandler we've got to stop."

"May I point out that I've only been on the damned planet for three or four hours?" said the Iceman. "If he was *that* easy to stop, I wouldn't have hired him, and you wouldn't have had to hire me."

"I'm sorry," said 32 with a marked lack of sincerity. "It's just that we're very anxious about this whole project."

" 'We'?" repeated the Iceman. "Have you got some kind of pool going on who lives and who dies?"

"Just be careful," admonished 32. "If we did have a pool, the Oracle would be the favorite."

"I know," said the Iceman. "But if you'll let me speak to one of your demolition experts, maybe I can lower the odds."

"I'll get one in here right away."

"The sooner the better. I still don't trust this frequency."

The expert arrived a few minutes later, the Iceman put a number of questions to her, received the answers he needed, and then deactivated the radio. He waited a few minutes to make sure that no one had monitored his conversation and was coming to arrest him, then spent the next two hours working with the information he had received. Finally, physically and emotionally drained from the events of the day, he lay down on his bunk and was asleep almost instantly.

Praed Tropo contacted him via radio the next morning just after sunrise and demanded his presence. It was already hot outside, and getting hotter by the minute, and the Iceman took a broad-brimmed hat with him to shade his eyes from the sun.

"I have considered your proposition very carefully," said Praed Tropo as they walked toward a waiting vehicle, "and I have decided to let you attempt to stop the assassin."

"Thank you."

"There is nothing to thank me for, Mendoza," answered the Blue Devil. "We are confronting a dangerous situation. You are risking your life to resolve it."

"As I told you, I'm being well paid," responded the Iceman.

Praed Tropo's expression indicated what he thought of a race that would do anything for money, but it made no reply.

"Where are we going?" asked the Iceman as they reached the vehicle and Praed Tropo motioned him to climb into it. Four armed Blue Devils were waiting for him, and Praed Tropo joined them a moment later.

"Where you want to go," answered the Blue Devil. Suddenly the windows all darkened, and a light came on, illuminating the interior of the vehicle.

"The Oracle's headquarters?"

"That is correct," said Praed Tropo. "Since you have no need to know its location, I have made the windows opaque."

The vehicle began moving, and the Iceman leaned back on his seat, trying unsuccessfully to get comfortable. For the first time since arriving on Hades, he became aware of the unpleasant, almost bitter odor of the Blue Devils. The vehicle wasn't air-conditioned, for the Blue Devils had evolved to cope with the intense heat, and his mouth suddenly felt dry. After a few minutes he found himself sweating profusely, and shortly thereafter his clothes were drenched, and his foot squished uncomfortably in his boot.

"How much longer?" he asked hoarsely.

"Perhaps an hour," said Praed Tropo. "Perhaps two."

"Wonderful," he muttered.

"You are uncomfortable?"

"Very."

"Oh," said Praed Tropo with no show of concern.

The vehicle sped on, and the Iceman finally found that he was less uncomfortable if he leaned forward, resting his elbows on his knees and cupping his chin in his hands. After about ten minutes his back began to ache, and he straightened up again, aware that he was causing the Blue Devils untold satisfaction, if not outright amusement.

"Are we heading toward a city?" he asked, hoping that conversation would take his mind off his discomfort.

"Why should you think so?" answered Praed Tropo.

"Because her headquarters would be harder to pinpoint if they were surrounded by hundreds of other buildings."

"She has no reason to fear attack."

"Tell me about her."

"Why?"

"I'm risking my life to save her, so naturally I'm curious," answered the Iceman.

"She is in no danger. You are here only to prevent any members of my own race from being harmed."

"Why is she called the Oracle? Does she make mystic pronouncements?"

"*Oracle* is a Terran word," replied Praed Tropo. "She chose it herself. I do not know what it means."

"Why is she living among you?"

"It is not necessary for you to know that."

"What does she look like?" asked the Iceman.

"Like any other member of your race."

"Every other member of my race can be killed. What makes you so certain that she can't be?"

"You ask too many questions, Mendoza," said Praed Tropo.

"The Democracy is paying me a lot of money to save her," said the Iceman. "That implies someone else spent a lot of money to have her killed. I'd like to know what makes her so valuable. Your claim that she is invulnerable seems like a good place to start."

"Be quiet, Mendoza," said Praed Tropo. "I find your questions tiring."

"Then why not answer them and I'll shut up?"

"Because it has occurred to me, as it has doubtless occurred to you, that Chandler may have been paid more than ten million credits to assassinate the Oracle. Since you know who hired him, and since greed is the prime motivating force of all Men, I consider it quite likely that you yourself will attempt to kill the Oracle if you feel the opportunity has presented itself."

"But you've already told me it can't be done," the Iceman pointed out. "Were you lying to me?"

"No," said Praed Tropo. "But in the process, you could kill some members of my race, and since you landed here on my authority, I would be held responsible for your crimes." He paused. "Therefore, I will tell you nothing about the Oracle. You are here to apprehend Chandler, and nothing more."

You know, thought the Iceman, *when I was younger and stronger, I probably would have tried to cut Chandler out and kill the Oracle myself—if my story had been true. You're too smart again by half, Praed Tropo. If all the Blue Devils are like you, I wonder why your people think they need the Oracle.*

"Well, then," he said aloud, "perhaps you can tell me about her headquarters. What are its dimensions, how many Blue Devils are guarding it, what kind of security systems have been built into it?"

"You will see for yourself when we arrive," answered Praed Tropo.

"Fine," said the Iceman with a sigh.

"There is one thing I will tell you now, Mendoza."

"Good. What is it?"

"My race is called the Lorhn," said Praed Tropo. "We find the term *Blue Devils* offensive."

"I assure you no offense was intended. I've only heard you referred to as Blue Devils."

"We call you Men, as you prefer, rather than—" It uttered a word that was unpronounceable in Terran. "And we have learned to speak Terran, though it bears no relation to our own language and is painful to our throats." It paused. "And yet, although the Democracy knows we are the Lorhn, it persists in calling us Blue Devils and does not teach its diplomats or its operatives our language. Is it any wonder that we have no desire to be assimilated by you?"

"I'm no politician or operative," said the Iceman. "I'm just a businessman, and from this moment forward I'll be happy to refer to you as Lorhn. If you feel the Democracy has treated your race with disrespect, tell *them*."

"I have no intercourse with the Democracy, nor do I expect to have any unless they invade us," said Praed Tropo. "I am telling you, because if you survive I will expect you to relay my message to them."

"Consider it done," lied the Iceman.

The Blue Devil fell silent again, and the Iceman, totally out of questions, rode in mute discomfort.

After another hour he felt the vehicle turn to the left, and suddenly the sound of the wind was broken by large structures, either buildings or natural formations. Then it began slowing down, and in another mile it stopped.

"We have arrived," announced Praed Tropo as the windows became transparent once more.

The Iceman's eyes began watering at the broad expanse of sand that reflected the intense sunlight, and it took him almost a minute before he could begin focusing.

The first thing he saw was the building, beautifully camouflaged in a depression beneath a large outcropping of rock. It was a crazily irregular structure, but if a wall with right angles had been built around it, the Iceman estimated that it would be close to four hundred feet on a side.

The quartz roof, reflecting a dazzling array of reds, oranges, and golds, with blue metal girders supporting it, immediately caught his eye. It seemed much more intricate than necessary, even if it served as a solar energy collector.

He looked for windows and doors, found a few where they shouldn't have been and almost none where he expected them to be, and shrugged. He'd been on enough alien worlds not to try to make sense out of their structures. If they thought a roof should be fifty feet high at one point and ten feet at another, with no rhyme or reason to justify the sudden changes, that was fine by him; all he was concerned about was the woman who resided beneath that roof.

At the far end of the building was a huge triangular door, and after he, Praed Tropo, and the four armed Blue Devils climbed out of the vehicle, the driver started it up again and drove through the doorway into what the Iceman assumed was an enormous garage.

There were eleven Blue Devils pacing the grounds, walking in intricate patterns that seemed totally unrelated to one another. None of them were armed.

"Who are they?" asked the Iceman.

"They are members of the house's staff."

"What are they doing?"

"They are performing their religious rituals," answered Praed Tropo.

"They make awfully easy targets," noted the Iceman.

"Then they will join our God that much sooner," replied the Blue Devil with a shrug.

"And what are these?" asked the Iceman, indicating a number of stone structures scattered around the landscape. "They look rather like fountains."

"What is a fountain?"

The Iceman explained it, and Praed Tropo looked disapproving.

"We have no water to spare for such nonessential purposes."

"Then I repeat: what are they?"

"Monuments, denoting where various Lorhn have fallen in defense of the Oracle." It paused. "In every case, they were killed by agents of the Democracy."

"Then it would seem that the Democracy has hired me to make amends," said the Iceman.

"For Men to make amends is contrary to my experience," said Praed Tropo.

"You've been associating with the wrong Men," said the Iceman easily.

"I will give you every opportunity to prove me wrong, Mendoza," answered the Blue Devil. "But I expect that you will prove to be no different from the rest."

"You know, you object to my calling your race Blue Devils, and I'm making an attempt to abide by your wishes," said the Iceman. "But you keep making generalizations about *my* race that you know to be false."

"Nothing I have said is false."

"You have stated or implied that Men are not to be trusted and that we hold your race in contempt."

"That is true."

"You forget the Oracle," said the Iceman. "She's a member of my race, and yet you trust *her*."

Praed Tropo stared at the Iceman for a long moment and then spoke. "I repeat: nothing I have said is false."

26

The Iceman was still considering what Praed Tropo had said as they toured the grounds.

"Which way do you think Chandler will approach?" asked the Blue Devil when they had finished their inspection.

The Iceman placed his hands on his hips and surveyed the landscape.

"Difficult to say," he replied. "I assume the fence on the west side is electrified?"

"Our security system does not use electricity," answered Praed Tropo. "It is too easy to disable at the source. The fence has a self-generating field that will kill anything that touches it."

"How about that overhang?" asked the Iceman, indicating the huge rock that towered over the house.

"It cannot be scaled."

"Not by a Lorhn, perhaps—but it wouldn't be that difficult for a human."

"Could *you* scale it?" asked Praed Tropo skeptically.

The Iceman smiled and shook his head. "No . . . but I've got a prosthetic leg, and I've never really learned to use it properly; there's some nerve damage to my hip. Twenty years ago I could have climbed it with no trouble."

"I shall deploy forces to guard all approaches to the overhang," said Praed Tropo after some thought.

"I wouldn't, if I were you."

"Why not?" asked the Blue Devil suspiciously.

"You're not dealing with an amateur here," replied the Iceman. "He'll spot anyone you post there, and he won't try to come into the compound—and if he doesn't come in, then there's no way I can contact him."

"You are certain?"

"The only way he'll enter the compound under those circumstances is if he kills every Lorhn you post there—and it's my understanding that that's what you've brought me here to prevent."

"That is true," admitted Praed Tropo. "But if we follow this philosophy throughout our defenses, it is almost certain that Chandler will at least reach the spot where we are standing without being apprehended."

"That's the whole purpose of the exercise," answered the Iceman. "We've got to entice him to breach your defenses or I won't be able to identify him and warn him off."

"And what if you can't warn him off?" asked Praed Tropo. "What if, having come this far, he elects to kill you?"

"He has no reason to kill me."

"Men lie to each other all the time. Why should he believe what you tell him?"

"Because he knows me."

"That is an inadequate answer."

"I'm sorry, because it's the best answer you're going to get," replied the Iceman. "Besides, what difference does it make to you if he kills me or not? You insist that no one can kill the Oracle. At least this way you'll know where he is, and you can make sure he doesn't get out."

Praed Tropo was silent for a moment. "Logical," it said at last.

"I'm glad we agree on *something*," said the Iceman.

"What do you suggest for the rest of the perimeter?" asked the Blue Devil. "It is possible to deactivate the fences."

"Not a good idea," answered the Iceman. "We want to pick and choose his approaches. If you just let him come in at random, I might never see him."

Praed Tropo stared at him, a strange expression on its face.

"Is something wrong?" asked the Iceman.

"No," answered the Blue Devil. "You are acting out your part very well."

"I'm not acting any part," protested the Iceman irritably. "I'm trying to earn my commission."

"I still do not trust you, Mendoza," said Praed Tropo. "But you have been very careful not to make a mistake. If you had suggested that we deactivate the fence, I would know you were an agent for the assassin, and I would have immediately imprisoned you." It paused. "I will continue to work with you, but sooner or later I expect you to make an error, and I will be waiting for it."

"You are doomed to be disappointed," said the Iceman.

"I have always expected the worst from Men," answered Praed Tropo. "And I have never yet been disappointed."

"If you're going to continue telling me what a treacherous race I belong to, can we at least walk over to some shade?" asked the Iceman. "If I stand out here much longer, I may not live long enough to prove to you that I'm telling the truth."

Praed Tropo led him to a bizarrely shaped lean-to that seemed to have no purpose except to provide shade to anyone who was willing to bend over at the waist.

"Aren't you uncomfortable?" asked the Iceman, staring at the slightly taller Blue Devil.

"You asked for shade. I have provided it."

"This is getting ridiculous," said the Iceman. "Your furniture and vehicles are bad enough, but if I'm going to roast to death, I don't see why I have to do it while I'm bent in half."

"You should have considered that before accepting an assignment on Alpha Crepello III," replied Praed Tropo, stepping back out into the sunlight.

"Look," said the Iceman, also stepping out from under the lean-to and straightening up painfully, "I know that you enjoy my discomfort, but my race wasn't built for this kind of heat, and I'm a very old man. You're going to have to provide me with some comfortable shade—and I emphasize the word *comfortable*—if I'm to stay outside and wait for Chandler to show up."

"He will almost certainly arrive under cover of darkness," answered Praed Tropo. "Our nights are quite cool."

"I experienced one of your nights, thanks. They're only cool if you're a Lorhn." The Iceman paused. "Do you know what an umbrella is?"

"No."

"I'll draw one for you," said the Iceman. "I want one of your Lorhn to construct one for me. And I'll need plenty of water."

"Water is very rare on Alpha Crepello III."

"Not as rare as assassins," shot back the Iceman. "If you want me to stop him, you've got to keep me alive until he shows up."

Praed Tropo seemed to consider his request. "I will see wha can be done," it said at last.

"Good."

Praed Tropo stared at him for a moment. "You have not ye inspected the entrances to the property which are used by vehi cles," it said, indicating two driveways. "Do you feel stron enough to inspect them?"

"Let's get it over with," said the Iceman. They had checked the first of them and were walking to the second when the Icema suddenly stopped, overcome by dizziness.

"What is the matter, Mendoza?" asked Praed Tropo.

"Heat prostration, I think," mumbled the Iceman. "I've got t get out of the sun."

"How does one treat heat prostration in a human?"

"I don't know," said the Iceman, grabbing Praed Tropo's ar for support. "I've never had it before. Get me to someplace coo and if I pass out, find a way to get some fluids in me. Just water I don't think my system can take anything the Lorhn drink."

Praed Tropo summoned two other Blue Devils. The Iceman last memory was of being half carried and half dragged into th foyer of the huge building.

Then he lost consciousness.

27

When he awoke, he was lying on the floor of a small cubicle, next to an oddly-shaped cot. Even in his weakened, dehydrated condition, he had evidently decided that the floor was more comfortable.

He stood up, leaned against a stone wall for support, and surveyed his surroundings. The cubicle was perhaps eight feet on a side, just enough for the cot, a small, multi-leveled table, and an intercom holoscreen. There was a container of water on the table. He immediately picked it up, spent almost a minute figuring out how to open it, and then took two long swallows. It was warm, and there were small things floating in it, things that he didn't want to think about, but it tasted like heaven.

He wanted to drink more, to drain the container, but he seemed to remember reading or hearing somewhere that he should drink frequently but in moderation until he regained his strength. He took a tentative step, then another, and found that he wasn't as weak as he had anticipated. Obviously the Blue Devils had gotten him out of the sun before any serious damage had been done.

The door to his cubicle was closed. He had no idea if it was locked, and at the moment he didn't particularly care. It would be another hour or so before he could take advantage of being here, anyway—if indeed there was any advantage to be taken by being inside the building.

He walked from wall to wall a few more times, getting some of the stiffness out of his body, then sat delicately on the edge of the cot and just luxuriated in being out of Hades' sunlight. In fact, the room was still quite warm, perhaps thirty-six degrees

Celsius, but it felt cool and comfortable compared to being outside.

He waited another five minutes, then got up and began walking back and forth again, feeling stronger this time. It was as he approached the far wall that he heard the voice.

"I see you're finally awake, Iceman," said a cold, dispassionate, vaguely familiar voice.

He turned and found himself staring at the image of a slender young woman on the holoscreen. He studied the face: the cheekbones were more prominent, the chin a little sharper, the hair a bit darker, but they were definitely *hers*. Only the eyes had really changed; they seemed strange, distant, almost alien.

"It's been a long time," he said at last.

"Fourteen years," replied Penelope Bailey.

PART 5

The
Oracle's
Book

28

"I'm getting sick and tired of waiting," remarked the Injun as he and Broussard sat in his room at the embassy. "I think it's just about time to go to work."

"I thought you weren't going to make a move until the Whistler showed up," said Broussard.

"For all I know, the Blue Devils killed him on one of the moons and he won't be showing up at all."

The Injun got to his feet and started pacing the room restlessly, while Broussard stared at him and tried to understand the change that had come over him during the past few days. He had grown more irritable, more restless, and had been given to violent outbursts of temper. It just didn't jibe with the cool professional with whom Broussard had been working, and the young man was sincerely worried about the Injun's mental state.

"Where the hell *is* he?" muttered the Injun, slamming a fist into the wall. "I can't wait much longer!"

"There's no deadline on killing the Oracle, sir," said Broussard. 'Or if there is, you haven't told me about it."

"I've got a personal deadline," snapped the Injun. "And I've just about reached it."

"A personal deadline?" repeated Broussard, puzzled.

"Just shut up and let me think!"

"I can leave the room if you wish, sir."

"Leave, stay—what you do doesn't interest me."

He continued pacing the room, faster and faster, and after watching him for another few minutes, Broussard walked to the door and went to his own quarters, deeply troubled about the change that had occurred to his superior.

Finally the Injun came to a stop in front of his computer and stared at it, as if it was some alien machine he had never seen before. Finally his eyes, which had seemed wild and unfocused, cleared and he sat down next to it.

"Computer—activate," he commanded.

"Activated," replied the computer.

"Check all planetary data bases and tell me if Joshua Jeremiah Chandler, also known as the Whistler, has arrived on Hades yet."

"Checking . . . unknown."

"Damn!" muttered the Injun.

He was about to begin walking around the room again when it hit him.

"Computer!" he yelled.

"Yes?"

"Every other time I've asked you, you said *No*. This time you said *Unknown*. Why?"

"Because a human has landed at the Polid Kreba Military Base and I have been unable to ascertain his identity."

"That's got to be him!" said the Injun. "Has he been incarcerated?"

"Unknown."

"It doesn't matter," said the Injun. "If he's in jail, he'll rot there and there's no sense waiting any longer—and if he's not, then he's talked his way out of a military base and probably has freedom of movement, and I've got to move tonight."

The computer made no reply, as no question had been put to it.

"Deactivate," ordered the Injun.

The computer went dark, and the Injun walked out of his room, went down the hall, and entered Broussard's room.

"I'm going after her tonight," he announced.

"You're quite certain, sir?" asked Broussard, obviously concerned.

"Of course I'm certain!" said the Injun. "The Whistler has landed on Hades!"

"You're sure of that?"

"The computer confirms it."

"The computer says that the Whistler has landed?" repeated Broussard. "Then why didn't it show up on our immigration lists?"

"He landed at a Blue Devil military base."

"Why would he do that?"

"How the hell should I know?" snapped the Injun irritably. "He's here, and that's all that matters."

"What name is he using?" asked Broussard.

"I don't know."

Broussard frowned. "Then how do you know it's the Whistler?"

"Who else would land in this godforsaken hellhole without going through Customs and Immigration?" The Injun paused. "I'm going to need your help."

"Sir, I don't mean to offend or to be insubordinate, but I wish you'd undergo a psychological evaluation first," said Broussard.

The Injun glared at him. "What are you saying? Do you think I'm crazy?"

"No, sir," answered Broussard. "But you haven't been yourself lately."

"I will be soon," said the Injun.

"You're nervous and short-tempered and you've become forgetful," continued Broussard. "I don't think you're in any condition to confront the Oracle."

"I'll be fine," said the Injun, struggling to control the rage and hunger that surged through him. "Believe me."

"I still wish you'd present yourself to our staff psychologist."

"He won't tell me anything I don't already know," answered the Injun. "Look, I'm going to go out there tonight with or without you, but it would make my life a lot easier if you'll come. All I need you to do is drive me to the same spot we went to the other day. I'll take care of everything else." He paused and stared at the young man. "Now, are you in or out?"

Broussard uttered a sigh of resignation. "I can't let you go out there alone."

"Good," said the Injun. "We leave at twilight."

Broussard turned to leave.

"One more thing," said the Injun.

"Sir?"

"I appreciate your concern for me, and I realize that you have my best interests at heart." He paused. "But if you or anyone else tries to stop me, you'll find out just how good a killer I am."

Broussard drew himself up to his full height. "That was unnecessary, sir," he replied with dignity.

"Let's hope so."

They left at twilight and took the main road out of town, driving at a leisurely pace. Traffic thinned out within twenty minutes and vanished completely after half an hour.

"None of this looks familiar," said the Injun, squinting into the darkness. "Where are all the rocks?"

"We'll reach them in another forty minutes, sir," said Broussard.

The Injun leaned back and closed his eyes.

"You haven't told me your plan yet, sir," remarked Broussard.

"I know."

"You do have one, don't you?"

The Injun patted his tunic. "Right here in my pocket."

"A gun?" said Broussard.

The Injun smiled. "That, too."

29

Two armed Blue Devils entered the Iceman's cubicle and silently ushered him down a long darkened corridor, then up a ramp, down another corridor, and finally came to a halt at a large door, where Praed Tropo was waiting for him.

"She wants to see you, Mendoza," it said.

"So I gathered."

"Do not approach her."

"I don't understand," said the Iceman.

"You will."

He uttered a low command, and the door receded, revealing a large, luxurious room almost fifty feet on a side. There were beds, chairs, desks, tables, even a holoscreen, each of them designed for the comfort of a human occupant.

The occupant herself stood about thirty feet away, tall, slender, with dark blonde hair and pale blue eyes that seemed to be looking through the Iceman into some hidden place that only she could see.

"Welcome to my domain, Iceman," she said.

"Hello, Penelope."

"You have seen her before?" said Praed Tropo, surprised.

"A long time ago," answered the Iceman.

"I had thought we would never meet again," said the Oracle. "I thought you would die where I left you, but I was very young, and my abilities were immature."

"And now you're an adult," said the Iceman.

"Now I am an adult," she replied vacantly, as if her attention were directed elsewhere. "Now I see things more clearly, more vividly, and now I interpret them more accurately."

"What kind of things?"

"Things that would drive you mad if you were to see them, Iceman." She paused. "A million futures, all struggling to be born; a trillion events, all lining up to take place, all waiting for my approval."

"I felt sorry for you when you were a little girl," said the Iceman. "I feel sorry for you now."

"Save your sympathy, Iceman," she replied. "I would not trade places with you."

The Iceman stared at a thin line on the floor about ten feet ahead of him, and noted that it ran up the walls and across the ceiling.

"In point of fact, you couldn't trade places with me even if you wanted to," he said.

She smiled again. "You refer to the force field."

"If that's what it is."

"It keeps me in . . . but it also keeps you out," she replied. "You and the others."

"What others?" he asked.

"Don't be obtuse, Iceman," said the Oracle. "It's unbecoming."

"Do you refer to the assassin, Chandler?" asked Praed Tropo.

"Perhaps," said the Oracle. She turned to the Blue Devil. "You must leave us now."

Praed Tropo turned and joined his two Blue Devils on the far side of the door, which immediately slid shut.

"How long have you been a prisoner, Penelope?"

"What makes you think I am a prisoner?"

"Can you leave this room?"

"Eventually," she said.

"But not right now," he said.

"I am content not to leave right now."

He stared at her for a long moment. "You've changed."

"I've *grown*," said the Oracle.

He shook his head. "You're scarcely human anymore."

"Look at me," said the Oracle, turning around before him. "Do I not appear like any other young woman?"

"Other young women concentrate on what they are saying and hearing. You're hours and days ahead of where everyone else is, aren't you? Our present is your past. You're mouthing words that occurred to you before I arrived."

"You are very perceptive, Iceman. I am glad I brought you here."

"I came of my own volition," he replied. "If it happens to serve your purposes, it's just a coincidence."

"You are free to think so," she said. Suddenly she turned sharply to her left.

"What's *that* all about?" asked the Iceman.

"Your friend the Whistler is on his way here," she replied. "He arrived on Hades three days ago, hidden in the hold of a cargo ship, and made his way out of the spaceport under cover of night. It took him this long to find out where I am. If I had stood where I was, he would have been seen by one of my agents as he left Quichancha."

"And you think that just by turning your body, he'll get out of the city unobserved?" said the Iceman skeptically.

"There are an infinite number of futures, Iceman. My freedom of action is limited, but in every future in which I turned, he leaves the city unobserved."

"How can turning your body make a difference in what happens a hundred miles away?"

"I do not know the Why of it, only the Truth of it," the Oracle replied serenely. "In a universe of cause and effect, I am the Cause, and by my willpower and my actions, I select the effect."

He stared at her and made no reply.

"Why do you look at me with such an odd expression on your face?" she asked.

"Because I'm surprised."

"By me?"

He shook his head. "By me."

"Explain, please."

"Why bother? You know what I'm going to say."

"I know a million things you *might* say," she replied. "I cannot consider all of them."

"All right," said the Iceman. "I'm surprised by my reaction to you."

"In what way?"

"The last time we were together, you caused the death of someone I cared for very much," he answered. "You caused her death, and you crippled me, and I thought I hated you. I thought that if I ever met you again, all I would want to do would be to put my hands around your throat and squeeze until you died."

"But this is not the case?"

"No," he said. "I hated a little girl, who killed out of passion and jealousy—but you're not that girl. You have no passion left. For all I know you don't possess any other human emotions, either. You're a force of nature, nothing more." He paused and sighed. "You can't hate a hurricane or an ion storm for being what they are, and I find I can't hate you."

She stared at him curiously, but made no reply.

"That doesn't mean you shouldn't be stopped," he continued. "When winds build up to hurricane velocity, we dissipate them. When an ion storm approaches a habitable planet, we neutralize it."

"You cannot stop me, Iceman," she said with detached amusement. "Surely you know that by now."

"Someone has already stopped you," he replied. "Or have you the ability to walk over to where I am standing?"

"I have not wanted it until now," she said placidly. "And now that I want it, I shall have it soon."

"How did they ever confine you here in the first place?"

"I was very young and very naive," said the Oracle.

"I'll agree that you were young," replied the Iceman. "I find it difficult to believe that you were ever naive."

"But it is true, Iceman," she said. "I came here with the Mock Turtle. We stopped to refuel on the way to a planet where I was to grow up, shielded from all outside influence, and learn to use my powers to their fullest extent." She paused. "And then I made a mistake."

"What was it?"

"I could foresee that the ship would fail to function if a minor gasket was not replaced, and I let them overhear me telling that to the Mock Turtle. He practically worshipped me, if you'll recall, and he immediately insisted that their mechanics fix the flawed gasket. When they found that it indeed was cracked, they told us that because their ships worked on different principles, it would take them some weeks to import the part. And because my abilities were immature, I could not see far enough into the future to know that the part would never come, and I believed them."

"And they imprisoned you here?" asked the Iceman.

"They explained that it was a protective device, and indeed

it is," she replied. "For just as I cannot pass through the field, neither can you." She paused again, as if the past were much more difficult to summon than the future. "By the next morning I realized that we were prisoners, but since I had no interest in the Mock Turtle's world anyway, and all my needs were provided for, I decided that this was as good a place to mature and grow strong as any."

"Why did you help the Blue Devils stay out of the Democracy?" he asked. "They can't mean any more to you than the Mock Turtle did."

"They thought, and probably still think, that I am helping them in the hope that they will someday release me, but in fact it was a chance to test my growing powers," answered the Oracle. "And I have no love for the Democracy. It was the Democracy that took me away from my parents and tried to turn me into a laboratory animal that would perform on command, and it was the Democracy that sent scores of bounty hunters after me when I escaped. No, I have no love for the Democracy at all." She met the Iceman's gaze with her own, and she seemed once again to be looking not at him but months and years past him. "I have plans for the Democracy, Iceman. I have interesting plans, indeed."

"And now you think you're ready to put them into effect?" asked the Iceman.

"I am an adult woman now. I am no longer Penelope Bailey, nor am I the Mock Turtle's Soothsayer. I am the Oracle, and it is time for me to go abroad in the galaxy."

"What happened to the Mock Turtle?"

"He died," she said with an unconcerned shrug.

"How?"

"Why do you care?"

"I'm curious," he answered. "I can't believe you couldn't have kept him alive if you wanted to."

She smiled once more, a smile that should have been very attractive, but which instead seemed cold and distant. "You are very perceptive, Iceman."

"Did you just get tired of being worshipped?"

"What god tires of being worshipped?" she replied.

"How did he die?"

"He was only concerned with what I could do for his insignificant race. It was all he talked about, all he thought about, all he cared for. He kept urging me to escape and return to his home world with him. Eventually he grew very tiresome."

"And?"

"And one day his heart stopped," she concluded.

"You made it stop, of course."

"You still do not understand, Iceman," she said, shaking her head sadly. "I do not cause things to happen. I choose the future in which they have already happened."

He frowned. "That sounds like a contradiction."

"Why?"

"Because things can't have already happened if you're looking into the future."

She seemed amused. "Perhaps not in *your* future," she replied. "But then, you are just a Man."

She raised her left hand above her head, held it in place for perhaps five seconds, then lowered it.

"And what future did you choose just now?" he asked.

"I am bringing about a confluence of futures this night," she said. "Any explanation would be beyond your understanding."

"Try me."

"I prefer to *use* you, Iceman."

"How?"

"It is time for me to leave my confinement," she said. "You will play an essential part in that."

"Not if I can help it."

She chuckled in amusement. "But you can't help it, Iceman. That is why you are here, in this place, at this moment."

30

The Injun left the darkened vehicle about half a mile south of the Oracle's compound, then began silently approaching the rocky overhang that he had pinpointed as the most likely means of ingress.

Just before he reached the base of the rock, he sensed another presence. Drawing his laser pistol, the most silent of his weapons, he crouched down and remained motionless, peering into the darkness and listening intently.

He saw nothing, heard nothing, but couldn't shake the feeling that there was someone out here with him. It could have been a Blue Devil, of course, but no Blue Devil would feel the need to be so silent unless he had already been spotted and they were after him, and he knew that he was too good at his craft to have given himself away yet. It *had* to be the Whistler, who had finally made his way to Hades from one of the moons.

The Injun realized that he needed his peripheral vision in this situation, and so, for the first time in days, he removed his eyepatch. It took him a moment to adjust to having a broader field of vision and renewed depth perception, and so he remained where he was for another few minutes, until he was certain that he wouldn't be disoriented by what he saw.

Suddenly he felt that the mysterious presence was no longer in his immediate vicinity, and he climbed, catlike, to the top of the rocky overhang. This afforded him a view of the far end of the compound, where two armed Blue Devils guarded the driveway, waiting to inspect or turn back any approaching vehicles.

He flattened himself out on top of the rock and spent another few minutes observing the yard, and pinpointed the locations of three more guards. He peered into the shadows cast by outbuildings and monuments, trying to spot the Whistler, but couldn't find him.

Finally he crawled to the edge of the overhang. It was only eight or nine feet above one of the metal beams that supported the quartz roof, and he gently lowered himself down until his feet were only twenty inches above it. Then he released his grip and landed lightly on the beam.

He walked along the beam until the shadow of the overhang hid him from any Blue Devil who chanced to look up, then pulled a cloth out of his pocket and wiped off his hands and face, which had become covered by sweat from his efforts in the warm Hades night. When he was finished, he tucked the cloth back into his pocket.

He didn't want to walk across the quartz, because he didn't know how much weight it would hold, so he continued walking down the beam until he came to an acute angle that meant he had reached either the end of the roof or at least the end of this particular level of it. He lowered himself to his belly and leaned his head over the side, looking for a window . . . and saw one, far larger than a typical door, about five feet below him and twelve feet to his right. He pulled himself along the beam until he was directly above it.

He was now some thirty feet above the ground, and he carefully lowered himself until his feet could touch the window. It had looked hinged to him, and he tried putting some gentle pressure against it. It resisted for a moment, then swung inward.

He waited to see if anyone inside the darkened room would walk to the window to see what had happened. When no one appeared after twenty seconds, he released his grip on the beam, landed lightly on the window ledge, and jumped into the room, almost in one single motion, then closed the window behind him.

The room was shaped like an equilateral triangle, some fifteen feet on a side and perhaps ten feet high. It was totally devoid of furnishings and served no purpose that he could determine. There were two rough-hewn wooden posts in the middle of the room, perhaps six feet high and five feet apart. He inspected them briefly, but their purpose remained totally incomprehensible to him.

He then turned his attention to the door. It did not recede as he approached it, nor could he find a handle or a computer lock on it. Finally he reached out and tentatively pushed against it, and it slid up out of sight so quickly that he jumped back, startled.

He drew his laser pistol once again, prepared to incinerate anyone who happened to see the door open, but when he stepped out into a corridor that widened and narrowed as pointlessly as had the street in the Blue Devils' sector of Quichancha, he found that it was empty.

The door snapped shut behind him as he turned to his left and began walking, only to come to a dead end before he passed any doors, stairways, or airlifts. He turned back and retraced his steps, walked past the room through which he had entered, came to a corner, turned right, and finally came upon a ramp that led down to a lower level.

He walked down it cautiously, then heard low voices up ahead, and crouched down, weapon at the ready. The voices were speaking in one of the guttural Blue Devil dialects, and when they neither approached nor vanished after he had waited for a full minute, he began descending the ramp again.

He emerged in a large, many-windowed room that was filled with alien furnishings. There were holograms and paintings of scenes no sane mind could have imagined, and chairs built not only for Blue Devils but also some for multijointed Lodinites and elephantine beings whose physical attributes were beyond his ability to conceive. A holoscreen in one corner showed a disconcerting pattern of flashing lights, all in varying shades of gray, which he decided would have an almost hypnotic effect on anyone who concentrated on it.

He heard footsteps approaching and ducked behind one of the oversized chairs. A moment later a Blue Devil entered the room from the far side, walked through it, and left through a doorway off to the left.

The Injun stood up, looked at both doorways, and finally decided to follow the Blue Devil. At least it had some destination in mind, and if it ran into any of its companions, he would probably hear them exchanging greetings before he stumbled upon them.

He gave the Blue Devil a thirty-second head start, then passed through the doorway and entered a long, winding corridor. It passed a number of closed doors, then terminated in another large room, this one filled with computers and radios of alien design, and manned by four more Blue Devils.

The Injun knew he couldn't pass through it unobserved, and while he felt no compunction about killing every Blue Devil in the room, he doubted that he could do so before one of them got off an alarm or distress signal, so he retraced his steps until he came to the room where he had seen the Blue Devil and walked through the other doorway.

It looked like it was going to dead-end against a large yellow wall, but just as he was about to turn back, he saw an extremely narrow stairwell off to his right. On the assumption that anyone as valuable as the Oracle wouldn't be kept on the ground level, he opted for climbing up rather than down.

He ascended the stairs, found himself on a large, irregularly shaped landing, and was trying to figure out what to do next when the smell of food—*human* food—wafted down a corridor. He followed the odor and came to a small kitchen where a Blue Devil was preparing a steak of mutated beef and a small salad.

He crouched in the shadows of the adjacent room and waited. After a few minutes a Blue Devil entered the kitchen, passing within four feet of him, uttered a terse command, and left. The Blue Devil who was preparing the food walked to a glowing sphere hovering near the wall, said something into it, and shortly thereafter another Blue Devil, this one unarmed, entered the kitchen through another door, put the food on a tray, and left.

The Injun realized that he would have to pass through the kitchen if he was to follow the Blue Devil with the tray. He stood up, entered the kitchen, coughed once to get the chef's attention, and trained his laser pistol on it.

"Not a move, not a sound," said the Injun in a low voice.

The Blue Devil stared at him and remained motionless.

"Where is the Oracle?" asked the Injun.

The Blue Devil made no answer.

"You heard me—where do you keep her?"

The Blue Devil said something unintelligible.

"Oh, shit!" muttered the Injun. "Don't tell me you can't speak Terran?"

The Blue Devil spoke again, and again the Injun couldn't understand a word of it.

He looked around, saw what appeared to be a half-opened storage closet, and, still pointing his weapon at the Blue Devil, he walked over to it and opened it.

"In here," he said, gesturing the Blue Devil to enter the closet.

The Blue Devil looked at him uncomprehendingly.

"I haven't got any time to waste! Now, move!"

The Blue Devil remained motionless, and the Injun reached out and grabbed it by the arm. It immediately reached out for his throat with its other hand.

The Injun planted a kick against the Blue Devil's major leg joint, then brought his pistol crashing down on the creature's skull. It collapsed in a heap, and, not bothering to check whether it was alive or dead, he dragged it over to the storage closet and crammed it in, after which he closed the door. There was a computer lock on the door, and he turned his laser pistol on it, intending to burn out the lock's memory, but when he pulled the trigger, no beam came forth.

He examined the pistol, found that the blow he had struck the Blue Devil had broken the connection to the power pack, and placed it in a drawer. Then, realizing that he was almost a full minute behind the tray carrier, he raced out the far door after it.

The corridor in which he found himself was relatively straight, and it soon broadened out and became almost as wide as a room. Finally it turned sharply, and as he stuck his head around the corner, he saw five armed Blue Devils guarding a large door.

"That's got to be it," he muttered.

He waited a minute, then another, to see if the Blue Devil with the tray emerged from the room that was being guarded, but it didn't appear. Of course, he reasoned, it could simply have turned the tray over to one of the guards and left by another route. There were a number of corridors leading off to both the right and the left, and there was no way he could reconstruct what had happened. It was even possible that these Blue Devils were guarding something other than the Oracle, and that the one he had followed was still carrying her food to her, but he doubted it. Besides, if that was the case, he was going to have to take all five guards out before he could continue his quest . . . but they hadn't guarded anything else in this crazily constructed house, not even their communication center, and it seemed likely that nothing but the Oracle could command so much attention from armed guards.

The Injun realized, with an enormous surge of eagerness, that it was time to put his strategy to the test.

He withdrew his sonic pistol and deactivated the safety. Then, with his free hand, he reached into his pocket, pulled out the alphanella seeds that he had ordered Broussard to confiscate back in Quichancha, carefully placed them between his teeth, and bit down, hard.

31

"They are within the compound," announced the Oracle, peering sightlessly off into space.

"Both of them?" asked the Iceman.

"Yes." She turned to him and smiled. "Everything is coming to fruition."

"I take it that *I'm* part of the plan?"

"In some eventualities you are. In others you are not."

"What do you think I'm going to do?"

She looked amused. "In none of the futures I can see do I answer that question."

He pulled out a small cigar. "Do you mind if I smoke?"

"Yes, I do."

"Tough," he said, lighting it.

"There," she said, still amused. "You've stood up to me. Do you feel better now, Iceman?"

"Not especially."

"But you do not fear me?"

"Not especially."

"You should, you know."

The Iceman shrugged. "Perhaps."

"Do you know that in all my life, there is only one man I have ever been afraid of?"

"Oh? Who was that?"

"You."

"I'm flattered."

"That was a long time ago," said the Oracle. "I see you now and I feel no fear." She stared at him, her eyes finally focused in the present. "My only reaction to you is contempt."

"Not hatred?" he asked.

She shook her head. "One must feel some respect to feel hatred; if not respect for the person, then at least respect for the harm he can cause."

"And you consider me harmless?"

"Yes." She paused, then spoke again. "Even with the explosives you have hidden inside your artificial leg, I consider you harmless."

"You know about them?"

"I know everything," she replied. "Am I not the Oracle?"

"You're an Oracle imprisoned in a force field," said the Iceman. "How can you stop me if I decide to detonate the explosives right now?"

"You are an old man, Iceman, and your heart has undergone many strains during your life. If you try to detonate the explosives, you will feel a searing pain in your chest, your heart will burst, and you will die." She stared intently at him. "Already it beats more rapidly, already it pumps your blood at a dangerous rate. In a million times a million futures, you will not even be aware of it. But," she added, stepping two paces to her right, "if I move *here,* there exists a future in which you feel a warning pain, does there not?"

The Iceman felt a sharp pain in his chest. Breathing suddenly became difficult, and he experienced an overwhelming sensation of pressure. He tried to conceal his reaction, but was unable to.

"You see?" she said with a satisfied smile. "There is one future, among the billions in which you detonate the explosives successfully, in which your pain does not cease. It becomes unbearable, and in that future, just before you die, you realize that what I have told you is the truth."

The pain finally began subsiding, and the color returned to the Iceman's face. He took a deep breath and leaned against the door for support.

"Can I ask you a question?" he said after a moment.

"That is what the Oracle does: she answers questions."

"How the hell have they managed to keep you locked up here? Why hasn't your jailor suffered a heart attack or a stroke at the proper moment?"

"They have chosen my keepers very carefully," she answered. "In no future that I have been able to envision have any of them suffered from any pain or disease to the extent that it would allow me my freedom."

"How do they feed you?" asked the Iceman. "Surely they have to dampen at least a portion of the field for that."

"A tiny portion," she replied. "You shall see in just a moment." She raised her voice. "You may enter."

A Blue Devil bearing a tray of food walked through the doorway, set it down on the floor right next to the force field, and then exited. A moment later a musical note sounded on the intercom system, and Penelope backed up against a wall, as far from the tray as possible. There was a sound of static as a portion of the field, no more than a foot square, dampened at floor level, and she walked forward, knelt down, reached for the tray very gingerly, and carefully pulled it to her. The moment it was across the dividing line on the floor, there was more static and a prerecorded Blue Devil voice informed them that the field was once again impregnable.

She carried the tray to a table and set it down there.

"You see?" she asked.

"And you haven't had a living thing on your side of the field for how many years?"

"Since the Mock Turtle's unhappy demise."

"You've had no human contact in all that time?"

"I've had no contact of any kind." She paused. "Well, that's not entirely true. I had a doll once, but it fell apart four years ago."

The Iceman tried to picture an eighteen-year-old Oracle playing with a doll, and couldn't. But he had no difficulty envisioning a lonely eighteen-year-old Penelope Bailey hugging the doll to her for comfort.

"I still feel sorry for you, Penelope," he said. "It's not your fault you were blessed or cursed with this ability, and it's not your fault that the Democracy didn't know how to handle you, and it's probably not even your fault that the Blue Devils have confined you here for all these years—but you are what you are, and you can't be allowed out of here. If you can't be killed, you have to be contained."

"Dream your dreams of heroism, Iceman," she replied. "What harm can they do?"

Suddenly she turned and faced the wall behind her, and stood perfectly rigid for a moment. Then she turned back to him.

"Who were you helping that time?" asked the Iceman.

"No one you know," she replied. "Tonight is all but resolved. I have other concerns to look after."

Her placidity vanished, to be replaced by a contemptuous frown.

"Fool!" she said. "Does he think that will affect my ability to deal with him?"

"What are you talking about?" asked the Iceman.

"Jimmy Two Feathers."

"Where is he?"

"He approaches, and he thinks to befuddle me by befuddling himself." She turned to the Iceman. "His mind is gone—but I do not read minds. I see futures."

"He bit into a seed?" asked the Iceman.

"As if it matters."

"It matters," said the Iceman. "If he doesn't know what he's going to do next—"

"*I* will know!" snapped the Oracle.

"I thought you saw a myriad of futures, and manipulated things to achieve the one you wanted. How can you manipulate a man who currently has the intelligence of an insect?"

"That's why you are here, Iceman," she said.

"Me?"

"If I can't stop him, you will."

"You've got a healthy imagination, Penelope."

"I do not imagine things, Iceman," replied the Oracle. "I foresee them."

"Well, you've foreseen this one wrong," said the Iceman. "If he can kill you, I won't lift a finger to stop him."

"You will do what you are destined to do."

32

The Iceman was about to reply when the door opened and the Injun, wild-eyed and disheveled, burst into the room. He held a sonic pistol in one hand and a knife dripping with blood in the other.

"Who are you?" he demanded of the Iceman in a strained, hollow voice.

"I'm a friend," replied the Iceman.

The Injun stared at him, uncomprehending.

"We both work for 32," continued the Iceman.

"That bastard!" screamed the Injun. "First I kill *her,* then *him!*"

"Keep your voice down."

The Injun giggled. "Why? I killed all the Blue Devils out in the hall."

The Iceman glanced at the Oracle, who was looking at the Injun with an amused smile on her face.

You're not worried, he thought. *He's standing right in front of you, out of his goddamned mind and planning to kill you, and you think it's funny. He's not the one.*

The Injun turned to face the Oracle.

"What are you grinning about, lady?" he mumbled. "You think I'm kidding?"

"No, Jimmy Two Feathers," she replied serenely. "I know you're not kidding."

He raised his pistol and sighted it between her eyes, then lowered it. "I'm thirsty," he announced.

"There's water on the main level," said the Oracle.

"There's water on the table right next to you," said the Injun. He began approaching her.

"Don't!" shouted the Iceman, but it was too late.

The Injun hit the force field, shrieked once, and bounced back off of it like a rubber ball. He pounded into the wall, spun off it, and fell in a crumpled heap at the Iceman's feet.

The Iceman knelt down next to him and felt for a pulse. It was still racing at almost twice the normal rate.

"What was *that* all about?" asked the Iceman, looking up at the Oracle.

"I don't understand you," she replied.

"Why did you let him get all the way to this room and kill those Blue Devils, only to wind up like this?"

"They were just Blue Devils," she said with an unconcerned shrug.

"I thought you needed him to get you out of here," persisted the Iceman.

"I was mistaken."

Too easy, Penelope. You knew he'd come in here, and you knew he couldn't kill you. This is still going according to plan— but what the hell kind of a plan requires a madman to be lying unconscious at my feet?

"You look confused, Iceman," she said, and again he could see amusement, and something more—condescension—in her pale blue eyes.

"I am," he admitted. "But I'll figure it out."

"If you live long enough."

"The same might be said for you," he retorted.

She smiled. "I *like* living, Iceman. I just might live forever."

"I have no objection," said the Iceman. "As long as you stay on your side of the force field."

She stared at him, a puzzled expression on her face. "I wonder . . ."

"What do you wonder?"

"I was born in the Democracy, and you on the Inner Frontier. I am twenty-two years old, and you are in your sixties. I know nothing of your past, and you know nothing of my future. We have nothing in common except our enmity. The odds of two people like ourselves meeting even once during our lifetimes are almost incalculable." She paused. "Why should our lives have become so interconnected, I wonder?"

"I don't know," admitted the Iceman.

"It is curious, is it not?" she mused.

"I'd have been just as happy never to know you existed."

"Happiness is not for you and me, Iceman," she replied. "And as for knowing I exist, soon more people than you can imagine shall know it."

"Not if I can help it."

"Ah, but you can't," she said with another tranquil smile. "All you can do is stand here helplessly and await what must happen next."

He offered no reply, and they stared at each other in silence.

"Step aside, Iceman," she said at last. "You're blocking the door."

He turned and saw Praed Tropo, weaponless, standing in the doorway. Then the Blue Devil was pushed into the room, and Chandler walked in right behind him, a small pistol pressed against its back.

"Mendoza!" exclaimed Chandler, surprised. "What the hell are *you* doing here?"

"I'll explain in a minute," said the Iceman. "Are there any Blue Devils after you?"

Chandler shook his head. "There are corpses all over the place. Was that your doing?"

"His," said the Iceman, indicating the still-unconscious body of the Injun.

"Who's he?"

"Jimmy Two Feathers."

The Whistler frowned. "The Injun? What the hell is *he* doing on Hades?"

"He was hired to kill the Oracle."

"Well, it doesn't look like he's going to be much competition." He shoved Praed Tropo a few feet ahead of him, then commanded the door to close.

"What's *he* here for?" asked the Iceman, gesturing toward the Blue Devil.

"He was examining the bodies when I showed up on this level," answered Chandler. "I figured I might need a shield, so I suggested that he accompany me." He turned to the Oracle. "Is she who you thought she'd be?"

"She's Penelope Bailey, yes," answered the Iceman.

"What's that line on the floor—a force field?"

"Yes. How did you know?"

"I knew they were keeping her prisoner," answered Chandler. "I didn't know *how* until just now—from what they tell me, force fields are still beyond our technology—but nobody seems to want to cross that line." He paused. "Is that what happened to the Injun?"

The Iceman nodded. "He's hopped up on alphanella seeds, and he walked right into it."

"Well, he cleared a path for me right to the door," said Chandler.

"You'd have managed if you'd had to."

"I doubt it," said Chandler. "I don't know what direction he approached them from, but the way I came, I'd have been a sitting duck." He paused. "You still haven't told me why you're here."

"New orders," said the Iceman.

"Oh?"

"Can you kill her?"

"I don't see why not," answered Chandler. "But if you're worried about the force field, I saw one hell of a big generator two levels down from this one. If it's powering the field, I think I can deactivate it."

The Iceman looked at the Oracle, who was once again staring off into time and space. "You don't even know how it works," he said.

"I don't know how the force field works," answered Chandler, "but I know how the *generator* works. There was one very similar to it in a Kobolian ship I owned once."

Praed Tropo had carefully backed a few steps away from Chandler, and finally the Iceman turned to it.

"Stop right there," he said. "I don't want to kill you, but I will if I have to."

The Blue Devil halted, then slowly retreated until he was standing next to Chandler again.

"Let's do whatever it is we have to do," said Chandler. "Those bodies aren't going to stay undiscovered forever."

"Or even for very long," interjected the Oracle with no show of concern.

"Well?" said Chandler.

"I'm still piecing it together," said the Iceman. *I thought I had it—but why did you need Praed Tropo here?*

"Mendoza, we haven't got all night," said Chandler impatiently.

"Just give me a minute!" snapped the Iceman. He turned to stare at the Oracle. "All right. He's the only one who can release you, and you needed the Injun to pave the way for him. But why me? And why Praed Tropo?"

She smiled enigmatically at him, but made no reply.

"She couldn't have planned *all* of this," said Chandler. "Even if she planned for the Injun to chew his seeds, how could she plan what he'd do once he'd sizzled his brain?"

"She doesn't *plan* things," explained the Iceman. "She *selects* them. She selected a future in which the four of us were in this room at this time . . . but I still don't know why she—"

There was a sudden movement from Praed Tropo, and Chandler, who had been concentrating on the Oracle, cursed and clutched at his right arm, which was gushing blood from where his nearly severed hand was hanging uselessly.

"Kill that sonofabitch!" snarled Chandler as Praed Tropo turned to face the Iceman with a knife that he had somehow concealed beneath his tunic.

"Freeze!" said the Iceman, drawing his own weapon and training it on the Blue Devil.

Praed Tropo hesitated for an instant, then stood motionless.

"Drop it," continued the Iceman as Chandler knelt down and tried to staunch the flow of blood. He dared a quick glance at the Oracle, who was watching the proceedings with an almost unnatural calm.

You're not surprised in the least. You knew this was going to happen. He frowned as he turned his attention back to Praed Tropo. *But it doesn't make any sense. You got the two best killers in the galaxy here, and one of them's half dead and now the other's crippled. Why?*

Chandler had ripped part of his tunic off and was wrapping it around his hand, cursing under his breath all the while.

All right. He's not dead. You want him alive but ineffective. Why? What am I missing?

"Give me another minute and I'll kill him myself!" grated Chandler, working on his hand.

"Kill?" muttered a hollow voice behind the Iceman. "Kill?"

The Iceman took a step back, then another, and saw the Injun rise groggily to his knees.

"Kill," he repeated, as if the word had lost all meaning to him. His pupils were dilated, his expression wild.

"Stay where you are, Jimmy," said the Iceman.

"Kill," mumbled the Injun, rising unsteadily to his feet.

"We're your friends," said the Iceman, trying without success to make his voice soothing and reassuring.

"I have no friends," whispered the Injun. "I don't know you!" Suddenly his gaze fell on Chandler. "I know *him,* though. He wants to rob me of my commission." He reached for his sonic pistol. "Well, you can't do it, Chandler!" he yelled. "I was here first! She's mine!"

His fingers closed on the hilt of the pistol, and he began raising his hand to aim the weapon at Chandler.

"It isn't fair!" he growled, slurring the words. "I won't let you rob me!"

The Iceman pointed his gun at the Injun.

"Hold it right there or you're a dead man," he said ominously.

"She's mine, damn it!" said the Injun as tears began to stream down his face. "I found her, not you! I killed all those Blue Devils out in the hall, not you! You can't cheat me out of what's mine!"

The Injun, swaying dizzily, aimed his gun unsteadily at Chandler as the Iceman's finger began closing on his own trigger.

And then the final piece fell into place.

The Iceman couldn't stop from firing his weapon, but at the very last microsecond he jerked his hand and the beam went harmlessly into a wall as the Injun shot Chandler.

"No!" cried the Oracle as Chandler pitched forward, facedown, on the floor.

The Iceman then trained his pistol between the Injun's eyes and fired again. He then turned to Praed Tropo.

"Be quiet and don't do anything foolish," he said, "and you just might live through this." He paused. "I was right, wasn't I, Penelope?"

She nodded her head.

"You had a lot of futures to put together, didn't you?" continued the Iceman. "You needed the Whistler, because only he knew enough about the generator to deactivate it. But the Injun had to arrive first, because there weren't any futures in which the Whistler could approach this room unseen."

"Yes," she said.

"If I hadn't figured it out, what would have happened? I'd have killed the Injun to save Chandler—I assume that was my function—and then Praed Tropo would have killed me?"

She nodded, her eyes already distant, examining still more futures.

"But I'm a fat old man with a limp," continued the Iceman. "I could never have gotten away from here. That's what I couldn't understand—why Praed Tropo had to be in the room with us, why he or some other Lorhn couldn't just pick me up later."

"I do not comprehend," said the Blue Devil.

The Iceman turned to it. "You had to disable Chandler without killing him. He was the most dangerous of us all: even without the use of his hand, he'd have found a way to kill you. But he'd have known that he couldn't fight his way out, not against whole squadrons of you, so his only option would have been to release Penelope and have her pick and choose futures in which the two of them escaped." He looked at the Oracle again. "And once you were safely away from here, and he thought he was taking you to 32 to pick up the rest of his money, he'd have had a heart attack. Am I right?"

"A stroke," she replied placidly. "His heart was in superb condition."

"Praed Tropo," said the Iceman, "do you understand what happened now? All of this," he continued, gesturing to the bodies of Chandler and the Injun, "everything that happened here, came about because she wanted to escape. That's why I'm here, that's why you're here. We're not enemies, you and I—we're her pawns, nothing more."

The Blue Devil stared at him, but made no comment.

"We can't let her out—not now, not ever. It's a cruel twist of fate that made her what she is, and it's a dismal future she's facing, but she's too dangerous ever to turn loose on the galaxy. Look what she was able to accomplish while you kept her imprisoned."

"No," said Praed Tropo at last. "She can never be released."

"You're a reasonable being, Praed Tropo."

"But others will come after her. They will be sent to kill her, but she will manipulate them as she manipulated us, and next time she may succeed."

"I'll see to it that there won't be any next time," answered the Iceman.

"How can you do this?"

"I'll tell 32 that she's dead. If you keep her incommunicado, he'll have no reason to ever suspect that I lied to him."

"That presupposes that I will let you leave," noted Praed Tropo.

"You have no reason to keep me here," said the Iceman. "And if you try, I have an explosive device on my person that I won't hesitate to detonate. It will blow you and me and this whole damned compound to hell, but *she'll* find some way to survive." He paused. "I'd much rather live. Wouldn't you?"

Praed Tropo stared at him for a long moment. "You may go in peace," it said at last.

"Thank you."

"You cannot leave the grounds without being apprehended," it continued. "I will arrange for an escort." It walked to the door and then turned to him. "Do not leave the room until I return, or I cannot be responsible for your safety."

"I understand," said the Iceman as the Blue Devil began walking away.

"I was wrong," said the Oracle when the two of them were alone. "I thought I was ready to go out into the galaxy, but I was mistaken. I shall have to wait until my powers mature still more."

"You'll never leave this room, Penelope."

She smiled. "On the day that I'm ready, I will. You underestimated me when I was a little girl; tonight I underestimated you. I think neither of us will make that particular mistake again." She sighed and shook her head. "I should have seen it—but there were so many permutations: what the Injun would do and when, where Chandler would stand, when Praed Tropo would act, when the Injun would awaken." Suddenly she smiled. "Still, I came very close. Another half-second and I'd have had it."

"Yes, you would have," admitted the Iceman.

"Next time I'll be more accurate."

"There won't be any next time."

"Perhaps not for you," she said serenely. "You're a used-up old man, and your strength is gone." She paused. "But I'm still young. Every day I grow more powerful, and there is a whole galaxy out there."

"Leave it alone," said the Iceman.

She smiled at him. "I can't, you know. I look ahead and I see great things, things you can't even begin to imagine. One day I will have to walk out of here and accomplish them."

Praed Tropo returned with a squad of six Blue Devils.

"Are you ready, Mendoza?" it asked.

The Iceman nodded and turned to join them.

"Iceman," she called after him.

"Yes?"

"I want to thank you."

"For what?" he asked, puzzled.

"For surprising me," she said. "One should always seek out new experiences, and I have never been surprised before."

"I hope you enjoyed it," he said sardonically.

"No," she replied thoughtfully. "No, I didn't. I do not intend ever to be surprised again."

Her words seemed to hang in the air like an ominous cloud as the Iceman left the room.

**RETURN TO THE BESTSELLING WORLD
OF <u>SANTIAGO</u>**

SOOTHSAYER

Mike Resnick

"Resnick is thought-provoking, imaginative...
galactically grand"—<u>Los Angeles Times</u>

Heroes and villains, spacers and bounty hunters,
with legendary names like Cemetery Smith, the
Forever Kid, the Iceman, the Mock Turtle. But the
most dangerous—and wanted—being in the universe is a frightened little girl with the unearthly
power to foresee, control, or destroy. Her name is
Penelope Bailey. The future willl call her...

SOOTHSAYER

___0-441-77285-4/$4.50

For Visa, MasterCard and American Express orders ($15 minimum) call: 1-800-631-8571

FOR MAIL ORDERS: CHECK BOOK(S). FILL OUT COUPON. SEND TO:	POSTAGE AND HANDLING: $1.75 for one book, 75¢ for each additional. Do not exceed $5.50.
BERKLEY PUBLISHING GROUP 390 Murray Hill Pkwy., Dept. B East Rutherford, NJ 07073	**BOOK TOTAL** $ _____
NAME_____	**POSTAGE & HANDLING** $ _____
ADDRESS _____	**APPLICABLE SALES TAX** $ _____ (CA, NJ, NY, PA)
CITY_____	**TOTAL AMOUNT DUE** $ _____
STATE_____ZIP_____	**PAYABLE IN US FUNDS.** (No cash orders accepted.)
PLEASE ALLOW 6 WEEKS FOR DELIVERY. PRICES ARE SUBJECT TO CHANGE WITHOUT NOTICE.	423

"A reason for rejoicing!" —<u>WASHINGTON TIMES</u>

THE THRILLING
<u>NEW YORK TIMES</u> BESTSELLER!

THE ROWAN

ANNE McCAFFREY

As a little girl, the Rowan was one of the strongest Talents ever born. When her family's home was suddenly destroyed, Telepaths across the world had heard her mental distress calls. Years later, the Rowan became a Prime Talent, blessed with a special power which spanned the universe. Completely alone without family, friends—or love, her omnipotence could not bring her happiness...but things change when the Rowan hears strange telepathic messages from a distant world facing an alien threat—a message from an unknown Talent named Jeff Raven.

__THE ROWAN   0-441-73576-2/$4.95

For Visa, MasterCard and American Express orders ($15 minimum) call: 1-800-631-8571

FOR MAIL ORDERS: CHECK BOOK(S). FILL OUT COUPON. SEND TO:

BERKLEY PUBLISHING GROUP
390 Murray Hill Pkwy., Dept. B
East Rutherford, NJ 07073

NAME_____

ADDRESS_____

CITY_____

STATE_____ZIP_____

**PLEASE ALLOW 6 WEEKS FOR DELIVERY.
PRICES ARE SUBJECT TO CHANGE**

POSTAGE AND HANDLING:
$1.75 for one book, 75¢ for each additional. Do not exceed $5.50.

BOOK TOTAL $ _____

POSTAGE & HANDLING $ _____

APPLICABLE SALES TAX $ _____
(CA, NJ, NY, PA)

TOTAL AMOUNT DUE $ _____

PAYABLE IN US FUNDS.
(No cash orders accepted.)

**From the writer of Marvel Comics'
bestselling *X-Men* series.**

CHRIS
CLAREMONT

The explosive sequel to *FirstFlight*

GROUNDED!

Lt. Nicole Shea was a top space pilot—until a
Wolfpack attack left her badly battered. Air
Force brass say she's not ready to return to
space, so they reassign her to a "safe" post
on Earth. But when someone begins making
attempts on her life, she must travel back into
the stars, where memories and threats linger.
It's the only way Shea can conquer her
fears—and win back her wings.

___0-441-30416-8/$4.95

For Visa, MasterCard and American Express orders ($15 minimum) call: 1-800-631-8571

FOR MAIL ORDERS: CHECK BOOK(S). FILL OUT COUPON. SEND TO: BERKLEY PUBLISHING GROUP 390 Murray Hill Pkwy., Dept. B East Rutherford, NJ 07073	POSTAGE AND HANDLING: $1.75 for one book, 75¢ for each additional. Do not exceed $5.50.

POSTAGE AND HANDLING:
$1.75 for one book, 75¢ for each additional. Do not exceed $5.50.

BOOK TOTAL $ _____

NAME_____

ADDRESS_____

POSTAGE & HANDLING $ _____

APPLICABLE SALES TAX $ _____

CITY_____
(CA, NJ, NY, PA)

STATE_____ZIP_____

TOTAL AMOUNT DUE $ _____

PAYABLE IN US FUNDS.
(No cash orders accepted.)

PLEASE ALLOW 6 WEEKS FOR DELIVERY.
PRICES ARE SUBJECT TO CHANGE WITHOUT NOTICE.

383

"Fast-paced...realistic detail and subtle humor. It will be good news if Shatner decides to go on writing."—Chicago Sun-Times

—WILLIAM SHATNER—

TEKWAR

Ex-cop Jake Cardigan was framed for dealing the addictive brain stimulant Tek. But now he's been mysteriously released from his prison module and launched back to Los Angeles of 2120. There, a detective agency hires him to find the anti-Tek device carried off by a prominent scientist. But Jake's not the only one crazy enough to risk his life to possess it.

___0-441-80208-7/$4.50

TEKLORDS

Jake Cardigan is back when a synthetic plague is sweeping the city. A top drug-control agent is brutally murdered by a reprogrammed human "zombie," deadlier than an android assassin. For Jake, all roads lead to one fatal circle—the heart of a vast computerized drug ring.

___0-441-80010-6/$4.99

For Visa, MasterCard and American Express orders ($15 minimum) call: 1-800-631-8571

FOR MAIL ORDERS: CHECK BOOK(S). FILL OUT COUPON. SEND TO:

BERKLEY PUBLISHING GROUP
390 Murray Hill Pkwy., Dept. B
East Rutherford, NJ 07073

NAME_____

ADDRESS_____

CITY_____

STATE_____ZIP_____

PLEASE ALLOW 6 WEEKS FOR DELIVERY.
PRICES ARE SUBJECT TO CHANGE WITHOUT NOTICE.

POSTAGE AND HANDLING:
$1.75 for one book, 75¢ for each additional. Do not exceed $5.50.

BOOK TOTAL $ _____

POSTAGE & HANDLING $ _____

APPLICABLE SALES TAX $ _____
(CA, NJ, NY, PA)

TOTAL AMOUNT DUE $ _____

PAYABLE IN US FUNDS.
(No cash orders accepted.)

394